THE DEVIL'S DRAPER

DONNA MOORE

First published 1st May 2025
Published in the UK by
Fly on the Wall Press
56 High Lea Rd
New Mills
Derbyshire
SK22 3DP

www.flyonthewallpress.co.uk
ISBN PBK: 9781915789402
EBook: 9781915789419
Copyright Donna Moore © 2025

The right of Donna Moore to be identified as the author of this work has been asserted in accordance with the Copyright, Designs and Patents Act 1988. Typesetting and cover design by Isabelle Kenyon, imagery Shutterstock and Adobe.

All rights reserved. No part of this publication may be reproduced, stored in or introduced into a retrieval system, or transmitted in any form, or by any means (electronic, mechanical, photocopying, recording or otherwise) without prior written permissions of the publisher. Any person who does any unauthorised act in relation to this publication may be liable for criminal prosecution and civil claims for damages.

This is a work of fiction. Neither the author nor the publisher will be held liable or responsible for any actual or perceived loss or damage to any person or entity, caused or alleged to have been caused, directly or indirectly, by anything in this book.

A CIP Catalogue record for this book is available from the British Library.
EU GPSR Authorised Representative
LOGOS EUROPE, 9 rue Nicolas Poussin, 17000, LA ROCHELLE, France
E-mail: Contact@logoseurope.eu

To my Mum, Joyce, and my Dad, Patrick

THE DEVIL'S DRAPER

FRIDAY 16TH JULY 1920
MABEL

To say that I was rather peeved with my assignment would have been an understatement. I wanted to be out in all the hustle and bustle of one of the busiest days of the year, not shut away in the Ladies' Waiting Room at Glasgow Central Station, gazing at the glaringly white tiles. However, I was to stay here where I couldn't 'get into any more trouble' as Superintendent Orr had put it.

He needn't have worried. I wasn't getting into any trouble at all. In fact, I was bored out of my mind. It appeared that very few ladies were looking to avail themselves of the waiting room today and I had been more or less on my own for the last three hours, other than an over-dressed, middle-aged woman in bottle-green charmeuse silk and old lace. The tendrils of the hat perched on the very top of her head, an elaborate concoction in the same bottle-green, fluttered as she moved. The whole outfit made her look like an overstuffed bluebottle. She had wafted in about three-quarters of an hour before, enveloped in a cloud of Mitsouko, with its distinctive peach and rose and jasmine scents. She was followed by a porter, puffing and red-faced as he hauled in a large brown leather portmanteau and an overstuffed carpet bag.

The woman plonked herself down in the corner and waved a gloved hand at the porter, directing him to tuck her bags against the wall. He promised to be back in plenty of time to see her onto the London train and she pressed a coin into his hand, the denomination of which clearly disappointed him, as he slammed out of the waiting room with a scowl. The bluebottle had ignored my friendly smile, settled herself down as comfortably as she could, and closed her eyes. Within a few minutes, her rumbling snores set the antennae on her hat quivering. And there she had been ever since, clasping her crocodile handbag tightly to her chest as she slept.

I sighed and stood up. The waiting room's seats were not made for long stays and my body was beginning to ache. I moved over to the door and peered out. The station concourse was mobbed and people were streaming in from every entrance; hundreds of people excitedly setting off on their holidays, this first day of the Glasgow Fair. A sea of hats of all sorts, ebbed and flowed towards the trains. Parents with tin boxes and wicker hampers, accompanied by children with pails and spades, were clearly off down the Clyde Coast to Gourock, Wemyss Bay, Ardrossan or Largs. Laughing young people with golf bags and tennis rackets, and dapper men and smart women with suitcases full of finery and faces full of anticipation looked up at noticeboards pointing towards trains going to places that would take them south and west – to London, Blackpool, Torquay, Paignton, Belfast and Portrush. I spotted an elderly couple, both dressed in black, quietly wending their way towards the ticket office. Perhaps they were going to northern France, or to Flanders, to locate the grave of a loved one.

I took a glance back at the sleeping woman. I would nip out for a few minutes and walk around the concourse, to take in the atmosphere. As I stepped out of the waiting room, closing the door behind me, the train to Ayr was announced. It was calling at other seaside towns: Irvine, Barassie and Troon, and I was swept up in a tide of excited holidaymakers as they rushed towards platform three in the hope of getting a window seat. I hopped to one side, taking shelter at the counter of John Menzies to avoid being forced onto the train with them and took in the scene around me. It was one which was doubtless being repeated across Glasgow, at train and bus stations, tramcar stops and at the Broomielaw for the steamers. Advertisements had appeared in the paper the previous week, with firms all across Glasgow reminding their customers that they were closed for the Glasgow Fair holidays, and work at the shipyards and factories had ground to a halt yesterday. It seemed as though half of Glasgow had taken the hint and was leaving the city.

THE DEVIL'S DRAPER

Superintendent Orr had told us that over a million pounds, maybe even two million, had been withdrawn from the savings banks and that very fact, he had said, had attracted gangs of pickpockets from across Scotland and even south of the border. "Not that we don't have enough of our own, home-grown scoundrels," he'd added. And that was the reason I had been ordered to sit for the whole day in the Ladies' Waiting Room at Glasgow Central Station. My colleagues – all men, of course – had free rein to roam around, participate in all the excitement and actually arrest people. Maybe they would even give chase, hunt criminals down, act as heroes. I, on the other hand, had been told to sit tight, make sure the first-class travelling ladies weren't bothered by those pesky lower classes and to be sure to call for a railway employee if anything untoward happened.

Well, I was going to take a turn around the station. I would be back at my post in just a few minutes and nobody would be any the wiser.

FRIDAY 16ᵀᴴ JULY 1920
JOHNNIE

Johnnie stopped outside the main doors of the Grand Hotel at Charing Cross. She started to wipe her clammy palms on her hyacinth-blue georgette dress, before whipping them smartly away, Meg's warning ringing in her ears: "Don't you get this grubby, mind, or you'll be for it, lass."

The dress was so uncomfortable and the wide, bell sleeves annoyed her every time she moved her arms. She also didn't care for the admiring looks she had attracted as she'd walked along Sauchiehall Street. She felt much more comfortable dressed as a boy; invisible and free to roam at will all over Glasgow. But her usual attire wouldn't do for this little escapade.

"Can't Hetty do it?" she'd said, when Meg had first raised the idea.

"Hetty?" The snort spoke volumes already, but Meg followed it up. "She looks too rough."

The object of this insult looked over. "Oh, aye? Too rough, am I?"

"You ken what I mean." Meg waved a hand from Hetty to Johnnie. "Oor Johnnie's features are more delicate, more... refined."

And so here she was, walking into one of the smartest hotels in Glasgow, up the broad, marble steps and into a cool corridor. The ground was dappled with multi-coloured light from the stained-glass windows above. On a sunny day it must have been some sight. Three staircases led upwards and Johnnie hesitated a moment, before following a group of smartly-dressed people up the central of the three and over towards a set of double doors, where a number of people waited to be announced. She had timed it perfectly.

THE DEVIL'S DRAPER

Johnnie spotted a family who would serve her purposes very well. They stood quietly towards the front of the throng, not gaily chatting to anyone else in the way that most people were, and not as fancy-looking as many of the other guests. They looked even more uncomfortable than Johnnie felt. Poor relations, perhaps? The four of them stood closely together, a man and woman in their early forties, accompanied by a young girl of about eight, who looked thoroughly bored, and an older girl who must have been about fifteen, just a couple of years younger than Johnnie. It was now or never.

Johnnie tapped the older girl on the shoulder. "Hello! How marvellous to see you! How are you?" The girl looked confused, but Johnnie ploughed on. "I haven't seen you for an absolute age. How is school? Are these your parents? And your dear little sister, of course!" The woman turned round and smiled at Johnnie, nodding her head distractedly, as they moved up in the line, closer to the doors. The girl opened her mouth to speak, but Johnnie gushed on. "I say, isn't this just too, too gorgeous? Didn't Adela look lovely as she walked up the aisle in the Cathedral? I didn't see you there. Are you Adela's side, or Duncan's?" She had done her homework, memorising the announcement in the newspaper. If necessary, she could reel off the names of the entire wedding party, the bride's parents, groom's parents, groomsmen, all six bridesmaids, right down to the two tiny flower girls, but it looked as though that wouldn't be necessary.

The girl was still looking at Johnnie with a puzzled look on her face, as her father handed over a gilt-edged invitation to the white-gloved man announcing the guests. He looked down at the invitation and boomed to the crowd in the ballroom within, none of whom was listening, "Mr and Mrs MacArthur, and the Misses MacArthur." Good. As she had expected, he hadn't specified how many Misses MacArthur were in the party.

Johnnie beamed at him as she swanned in with her new family. "Too, too delicious." Once inside, she turned back to the older

THE DEVIL'S DRAPER

Miss MacArthur. "Well, dear heart. How lovely it was to see you. Now I must go and find my people." And off she went with a gay wave. Without missing a step, she reached out and plucked a glass of champagne from a tray held by a young woman in uniform and melted into the crowd.

FRIDAY 16TH JULY 1920
BEATRICE

Business was booming and Beatrice was glad of an excuse to be working over the Glasgow Fair holidays. Since the death of her husband in the Battle of the Selle, in those last gasp moments of the War, Beatrice had tried to keep busy. Holidays, in particular, were difficult. She still hadn't forgiven Ronald for signing up after the new Act came in, extending the recruitment age. The irony was not lost on Beatrice —her son had been one of the first casualties of the war at the Battle of Mons, and her husband one of the last. She unlocked the door of Price's Employment Agency for Ladies and closed it firmly behind her, turning the key to lock it once more. The building was quiet, with the other offices that shared the premises all closed for the fortnight.

The pride that came with stepping into her very own office had not left her, even after a whole year of being in business. Having moved up to Glasgow from a small village in Cambridgeshire to start a new life, Beatrice had discovered it rather more difficult than she had expected to find a job. As a woman of fifty, there were no opportunities left for her on the stage, which was really the only thing she knew, and she had no desire to work in service which, according to the employment agencies, was all she was suited for. Besides, she felt too tired for both of those occupations. Added to that, it appeared that Glasgow's employers found her too old, too educated and, possibly, too obstreperous, for jobs in shops, cafés, offices and factories. They could pay young women a pittance to do the same jobs. Men returning from the war were preferred to her for clerical jobs and, of course, she had neither the skills nor the strength for jobs in shipbuilding and engineering, nor the patience to be a teacher.

THE DEVIL'S DRAPER

So she had opened her own employment agency, catering specifically to women, and had discovered that she both enjoyed it and was suited to it. Advertising and then word of mouth had secured her clients of all ages and from all walks of life. She had discovered she had a talent for assessing her clients and placing them in suitable positions: from servant positions with demanding society ladies, to suitable staff for supercilious business owners; even nervous fifteen-year-olds looking for their first job could be placed.

Beatrice took off her hat, poured herself a cup of tea from a Thermos flask and sat herself at her desk. She would catch up on the correspondence which had piled up over the last few weeks. She picked up the first envelope on the pile and, with a flourish of her letter opener, sliced it neatly open. A reference for a young woman for whom she had recently secured a job at the telephone exchange. She opened the filing cabinet behind her and took out the young woman's file, placing the file and the letter on the left-hand side of her desk to be dealt with. The second letter was from a nurse at the Belvidere Fever Hospital. Having caught smallpox from a patient there during the outbreak in Glasgow earlier in the year, she had decided she wanted alternative employment where the risk of infection wasn't so high. Beatrice quickly scanned the rest of the letter. The Belvidere had a reputation for employing reliable nurses and the woman's letter indicated that she would be easy to place. Beatrice added the letter to the pile on her left.

The third envelope contained a thank you letter from a satisfied employer and Beatrice filed it away, opening the fourth. Reading through it, she frowned. A clerk at Hector Arrol and Sons, requesting a suitable young woman to work in the drapery department. This was the seventh such request in the space of as many months. Either Arrol's was doing a roaring trade in curtains and fabrics, or the girls she had sent previously were unsuitable. Beatrice doubted it was the latter, but the former also seemed unlikely. She prided herself on being a good judge of character and none of the girls she had placed at Arrol's seemed to her to be the flighty type and all had seemed very keen on the job. Arrol's was a large department store, but surely they didn't need seven girls in the drapery department? Perhaps the young women she had sent had been moved to other locations within the store. She opened the big ledger of regular employers that sat on her desk and flicked through its pages to Arrol's. Running her finger down the list of women she had placed there, she noted that three of them had telephone numbers recorded. The first one she knew was a private residence, a young woman from a relatively affluent family. She picked up the receiver of the phone on her desk and gave the number to the exchange. No answer. The family and servants were probably away for the Fair.

The second number was a boarding house. The breathless young woman who answered the phone there said she would go and look but she thought it unlikely that Agnes was in, but, after a few moments, there was a clattering as the receiver was picked up again. "Hello, this is Agnes?"

"Ah, hello Agnes, it's Beatrice Price, from the Employment Agency. How are you?"

There was silence on the other end of the line for a moment and Beatrice began to fear they had been cut off, but Agnes' guarded voice eventually responded. "Yes?"

"Are you still with Arrol's?"

A sharp intake of breath and another hesitation. "No, Mrs Price. I...I left."

"You left? Oh, I thought you were so suited to the job. May I ask why?"

"I'd rather...I have to go, Mrs Price. I'm sorry."

Beatrice stared at the dead receiver in her hand. Odd. She dialled the third number. Again, there was no response.

THE DEVIL'S DRAPER

FRIDAY 16ᵗʰ JULY 1920
MABEL

I was gone for ten minutes, that's all. It had taken me longer to make my way through the mass of travellers than I had thought, and I'd been distracted by the magazines at John Menzies, but it was still only ten minutes. My heart sank when I got back to the Ladies' Waiting Room. A crowd had gathered round the door and inside, two porters and a guard were trying to calm down the hysterical woman in green, who was sitting on the ground, propped up against the bench.

I pushed myself through a small gap in the crowd of nosy bystanders and stepped into the waiting room. "What's happened?"

The guard turned to me, flapping his hands. "Miss, I'm going to have to ask you to leave. You shouldn't be in here."

"I absolutely *should* be in here. I'm with the police." It was still a matter of annoyance to me that I couldn't announce myself as being *in* the police, rather than *with*. Superintendent Orr never tired of telling me that I wasn't a police officer, I was a statement taker.

He looked taken aback, but then said, "You got here quickly. It's only just happened."

"What, exactly, has happened?"

The guard gestured towards the bluebottle woman, who was still wailing incessantly. One of the porters was flapping a newspaper at her and the other was patting her hand and shushing her, as though she were a teething baby. It didn't look or sound as though either of these tactics was very effective. "The lady woke up just a couple of minutes ago, and discovered that she'd been robbed."

It dawned on me that the brown leather portmanteau, the fat carpet bag and the crocodile handbag were nowhere to be seen. Nor, indeed, was the rather handsome pearl and emerald brooch that had been attached to the front of her dress. I groaned. Superintendent Orr would have my guts for garters. He had insisted that my only job today had been to sit and watch and make sure women in the waiting room were safe from thieves. I had not sat, I had not watched, and now the only woman in the waiting room other than me for the last three hours had been robbed. I needed to try and salvage the situation. Perhaps I could find the miscreant. "Did she see who took her things?"

"No, she said there was a suspicious-looking woman in here with her, a woman who smiled at her evilly and when she woke up, both her belongings and the woman were gone."

I opened my mouth to speak but was cut off by an eldritch scream from the woman in green. "That's her!" A gloved finger pointed accusingly in my direction. "That's the thief! Arrest her!"

THE DEVIL'S DRAPER

FRIDAY 16TH JULY 1920
JOHNNIE

Johnnie wended her way through the well-dressed people chatting in small groups. She caught brief snatches of conversation as she passed: the happy couple were going to be honeymooning on the Riviera; the bride's father had a fine stable of horses; had anyone else noticed the ghastly hat worn by Mrs Ellice... She took in the lie of the land, noting entrances and exits and places where staff were positioned, and then followed the steady stream of people entering the anteroom, where the wedding gifts were on display.

The embarrassment of riches weighing down the tables and floor of the anteroom took her aback and she came to a sudden halt just inside the door.

"I say, m'dear, I'm terribly sorry." A red-faced gentleman had cannoned into her from behind. "You can't just stop dead like that, ya know. I could have knocked you over and then where would we have been, hmm?"

"I'm so sorry," Johnnie smiled at him and then turned her face quickly away, as if suddenly shy. She didn't want him to recall her face later.

Johnnie sauntered around the tables, affecting an interest in the cards attached to the gifts. And it was a fine array of wedding gifts: a tortoiseshell and silver dressing table set from Colonel and the Honourable Mrs Ferguson; two Rockingham china figurines from Mr and Mrs William Brody; a silver-plated inkstand and silver stamp box from the Misses Balfour; a rather ugly set of china jam pots from Mrs Ellice – presumably the same Mrs Ellice of the ghastly hat. Somebody had thoughtfully grouped the gifts into their different types, making Johnnie's job easier, and her eyes lingered only briefly on the furniture, the paintings, the linens, the kitchenware and the eight heavy volumes of *The War*, bound in red cloth. Really, what had the Major McPhee who had given *those* been thinking? What would a newly married couple want with books about a war they doubtless wouldn't want to be even reminded of, let alone read about it in eight volumes?

The books weren't the only dud gift. Eglantine Cameron-Head – clearly a sworn enemy of the bride – had given the gift of an umbrella; the bridegroom was getting the reel for a trout rod from a Mr Brand; and a Mrs Denholm had for some reason thought that an old steel trivet was a welcome gift for the happy couple.

One area of the table caught Johnnie's attention in particular. Pretending to inspect a Liberty blotting pad and calendar, Johnnie glanced at the display of items to its right: a solid silver etui case, a diamond and sapphire pendant and earrings, a pair of matching gold watches, amethyst earrings, a set of gold and ruby shoe buckles, a rather fine-looking string of pearls and what looked like an antique diamond bracelet. Those and some other small pieces would do very nicely.

She glanced around the room. As well as the door through which she and the other guests had come, was another, less obtrusive, door at the far end. Probably one for the staff. If she wasn't mistaken, this one would lead to one of the side staircases. At that moment, a bell tinkled and the wedding breakfast was announced. Johnnie, along with the other guests in the anteroom, joined the rest of the party in the main room as they made their way to their seats.

Johnnie fluttered around as if trying to find her place, managing instead to find her way back to the anteroom door. She glanced quickly around. The guests were greeting their seatmates and the staff were all busy. Johnnie slipped inside the now empty anteroom once again. Her dress had been especially fashioned with numerous, carefully sewn pockets everywhere. However, Johnnie had a better idea. She picked up Eglantine Cameron-Head's very thoughtful umbrella gift, unfurled it, swept all the jewellery from that end of the table into the folds of the umbrella, plucked two small, silver photo frames and a silver sugar shaker from their places, tucked them into two secure pockets in her wide sleeves, and exited the room via the small door at the far end.

She had been right. The corridor she was in led to a set of stairs and she tripped down them, smiling cheerfully at a young man on his way up, and left by the Woodside Crescent entrance. The weather had been overcast when she had entered the Grand Hotel and now it was raining. But the umbrella in Johnnie's hand would need to stay furled.

SATURDAY 17TH JULY 1920
MABEL

"Glasgow is such a delightful place to live in at this time of year," said Florence, pulling off her gloves as she entered the breakfasting room. She was closely followed by her constant companion, Josephine. "So quiet and peaceful. I swear I could have gone out in my nightdress and scarcely provoked a word of comment."

"Have you two been out already?" I was tucking into the delicious kedgeree that Mrs Dugan had made me for breakfast.

"*Already?*" Floss took a pointed look at her watch. "It's half past ten, Mabel, not the crack of dawn." She took off her hat and smoothed her hair, taking Jo's hat, too, and placed them both on a small, polished side table.

I took another spoonful of kedgeree from the warming plate. "You forget, dear Floss," (I always referred to my adoptive mother as such), "that I have been suspended – yet again – and have nothing to get up *for*."

Floss and Jo exchanged glances. "Well, my dear, then you may be interested to know that Jo and I have some news for you." I waved with my fork for them to sit down and they took their usual places at the breakfast table, Floss next to me and Jo opposite. "We've been having a chat with Professor Henderson."

"From Gartnavel?"

"Yes, but we didn't go to the hospital. We treated him to breakfast at The Eden."

I bit my lip to hide my smile. "And how did the good doctor feel about breakfast without sausage and bacon?" Floss and Jo had been vegetarians since before their Suffragette days: invitations to eat out were always at one of the vegetarian establishments in Glasgow.

"He seemed to enjoy it just fine," was Floss' response.

THE DEVIL'S DRAPER

I had no doubt that he hadn't dared to indicate otherwise. "Well, what did he say? Is there good news about my grandmother?"

Floss nodded. "We were right; the asylum she's in is definitely Beau Rivage, under the name Lillias Strang."

I tried the name out; up until now, she'd only been Lillias to me – it was all the information my birth mother had given Floss. "Lillias Strang." It sounded strange and unfamiliar in my ears.

"Her married name." Floss' face darkened. "That man had her committed to Beau Rivage over forty years ago. What sort of husband does that?"

The sadness I felt was overwhelming and the words came out as a hoarse whisper. "A very cruel one."

Floss reached out and grasped my hands tightly. "Perhaps, after all, it was her salvation, my dear. Who knows how she might have suffered otherwise?"

"Why was she even in there, anyway?"

A tear ran down my cheek and Floss wiped it away with her thumb. "The usual nonsense, apparently: hysteria." She snorted. "Henderson said that was the reason she was admitted – this Strang reported that she was often hysterical and the doctor who admitted her studiously made notes about her 'wandering womb'."

Jo gave a hollow laugh. "As though it roamed her body, a lonely organ seeking companionship."

There was a knock at the door and Ellen bustled in with a tray. "I saw you arrive back, Miss Adair. I thought you might all want some tea." She sniffed. "Lord knows what you and Miss Josephine were doing out at this hour on a Saturday morning."

"Thank you, Ellen. That's very kind of you."

"Going out without breakfast, too. Mrs Dugan was quite put out. She wants to know if you'd like some kedgeree."

"Oh, no, we're fine, Ellen. Do thank Mrs Dugan but tell her not to bother. We're not hungry."

I dipped my head and smiled. Floss had been very careful not to admit that she and Jo had eaten breakfast out. Ellen would be even more miffed, and Mrs Dugan would be positively apoplectic that her renowned kedgeree had been snubbed for the inferior fare at the Eden.

Ellen bustled out again, leaving a trail of reproach behind her.

Jo took charge of pouring the tea. "Tell Mabel what else Henderson said. The bit about Clemmie." Floss smiled. My birth mother, Clementina, had died just a few months after my birth, but she and my adoptive mother had become close during that time. "Well, Mabel dear. Your mother's birth is in Lillias' records and, as Clemmie told me, she spent the first eleven or twelve years of her life there. Henderson says there are occasional snippets of her life there." I gasped and she patted my hand. "He's going to try and get us access to them." Perhaps I would now be able to find out more about my mother, as well as my grandmother. I knew something of the final months of her short life – a home for wayward girls and death at the hands of an evil man – but I knew nothing of the child or the girl she had been, or what had brought her to Glasgow.

Jo reached across the table and placed a cup of tea in front of me; in my excitement, I almost knocked it over. "When can we see her? Surely, we can see her?" The authorities at Beau Rivage had been reluctant to speak to us, but surely, they couldn't stop us from seeing my grandmother?

Floss reached out and moved my cup slightly further away from me. "Ellen won't be happy if you break the best china. And don't worry, my dear, it's all in hand. Apparently, the asylum has changed hands many times since the 1890s, when some sort of quack, who wasn't even a real doctor, absconded with most of the funds. The fact that it's mostly run as an asylum for private patients has allowed it to survive, and it changed its focus somewhat from about halfway through the Great War. Now, most of its patients are men." Floss paused and sighed, leaning back in her chair. She and Jo had helped out in the hospitals during the War and we all knew men who had returned from the fighting with shell shock, and who had experienced shame and disgrace because of it. Many families considered hiding such men from view in an asylum an ideal solution.

Jo stirred her tea slowly. "Shell shock is such a dreadful, dreadful thing. I'm so glad Annabella didn't have to go into a place like that." Floss reached across the table and stroked Jo's arm.

Annabella was one of Jo's nieces, a bright and cheerful young woman, who had driven an ambulance on the Western Front. She'd come home changed after the War and had stayed with us for a while to give her parents a break. Like Lillias, she'd been diagnosed with hysteria, of course, not shell shock, but we knew what really ailed her. Jo, Floss, Ellen and I had all taken it in turns to sit with Annabella at night and soothe her when the nightmares came, as they did every night. She had recovered somewhat, but she was changed forever and would never be the gay young thing she had been before. I hated to think that my grandmother might be like that, too.

Floss carried on. "Anyway, Professor Henderson has spoken to the doctor who's recently taken over at Beau Rivage and he's happy to meet with us and, if he's satisfied, he'll let us visit your grandmother."

I jumped up, squealing, and flung my arms around Floss, and then around Jo. "That's wonderful! I never thought it would happen. When can we go?"

Floss beamed at me. "Well, I rather think Josephine here is looking for an excuse to give the new Hispano-Suiza a bit of a run. And, since you have a few days unexpected leisure, we thought we might go right now."

SATURDAY 17th JULY 1920
BEATRICE

Beatrice had not been able to reach any of the young women she had placed at Arrol's on the telephone, so she had written down a list of addresses to visit. There had been no response at the first two she had gone to that morning, but she wasn't giving up yet. She got off the subway at Merkland Street. Elsie McNiven had told her that she lived with her mother. Their close was just at the end of one of the streets off Dumbarton Road and Beatrice made her way up the neat, clean staircase with its green and cream tiles to the third floor. At the very least, she would get fit with all these stairs today.

She knocked and a middle-aged woman wearing an apron and rolled-up sleeves opened the door to her. She had a pair of wooden laundry tongs in her hand and her face was red and sweating. "Aye?"

"Mrs McNiven?"

"Aye?" the woman said again.

"I was looking for Elsie."

"Oh aye? And who might you be?"

"My name is Beatrice Price and I'm from Price's Employment Agency for Ladies. I placed your daughter in a position with Arrol's—"

"Oh, you did, did you?"

Beatrice was slightly taken aback by Mrs McNiven's tone.

"Yes, I did and I—"

"An' now I suppose you're here to apologise?" The word 'apologise' was spat through gritted teeth.

"Apologise? Why, no. I—"

"How dare you come here! You should be ashamed of yourself."

"I don't—" Beatrice found herself talking to a firmly closed door. She lifted her fist to knock once more, but thought better of it and turned away.

THE DEVIL'S DRAPER

SATURDAY 17TH JULY 1920
MABEL

Normally, Jo was a woman of few words, but today the Hispano-Suiza brought them all forth. As far as I was concerned, only half of them were comprehensible.

"The straight-six engine cuts out most of the vibrations and the suspension is superb." Jo's voice was raised as we sped along, the wind catching both our voices and our hair. She was, I had to admit, an excellent driver. But then, she had spent most of the war driving huge trucks all over Scotland.

I leaned forward so that my voice could be heard from the back seat. "Then why do I feel as though half my teeth are falling out?"

Floss, holding onto her hat in the front seat, laughed. "Embrace the excitement of a hundred fiery steeds obedient to the caress of a woman's touch, Mabel, dear. It's not often Jo gets to let rip like this. Besides, we're nearly there now." She looked down at the map in her hands, as it flapped in the wind.

"How can you tell? We've flown past every road sign since we left Glasgow and they've all passed in a blur." I decided to let the hundred fiery steeds comment pass unremarked.

"Don't worry, Mabel," a gleeful Jo shouted. "Going fast isn't a problem. This new Servobrake system is marvellous. I don't have to throw all my weight on the pedal like I did with the old Lanchester, as if our lives depended on it."

"Which, in fact, they probably did," shouted Floss and I couldn't disagree.

As if to prove the efficacy of the brakes, Jo brought the car to a smooth halt in front of a small gatehouse. To one side of the building was a set of wrought iron gates, with the letters B and R swooping and curling on each one. "There," she said, patting the steering wheel in a very satisfied manner. "Starts with a glide,

THE DEVIL'S DRAPER

travels with a glide, comes to rest with a glide. What more can one ask for?"

"Ooooh, I don't know," I said. "A return to thinking I'll survive the rest of the day?" I hopped out of the car and approached the gatehouse. Purple lupins and geraniums, vibrant blue delphiniums and bright gold and orange marigolds bloomed in the sheltered garden. I realised that I had been expecting a foreboding gothic mansion swathed in grey mists.

An elderly man popped his head out of the gatehouse, shrugging into a uniform jacket.

"We have an appointment to see Dr Baldwin," I said. "Florence Adair and party."

"Aye, Miss, they tell't me yis were coming. Ah'll open the gates for yis."

He took a big key from a hook just inside the door and at the turn of the key the gates opened smoothly. I got back into the car and we glided slowly up the driveway. (Yes, I had to admit, Jo was right about the gliding.)

As we rounded a curve, an imposing four storey building came into view, as well as various outbuildings, glasshouses and neatly kept lawns and beds. Some of the men working away at these glanced round as we approached, but soon lost interest, returning to their work. The building, with its battlemented towers and stone staircase, was surrounded by clusters of showy rhododendrons. As we got out of the car and climbed the steps, we paused to inhale their spiciness. With the engine of the car silenced, I could hear peaceful birdsong and the occasional answering whistle from the men working in the flowerbeds.

The big wooden doors at the top of the staircase were open and Floss and I went in, leaving Jo stroking the glistening dials of the car's dashboard. A nurse ushered us into the doctor's office. A tall, gaunt-looking man in his early sixties stood up and looked at each of us in turn, gesturing to two chairs in front of his desk. The room was spacious and bright and painted a calming shade of pale blue. Was that deliberate? "Good afternoon. I'm Dr Baldwin. Miss Adair?"

"Yes," we both said.

The doctor looked confused and Floss held out her hand, which he ignored. "I'm Florence Adair. Professor Henderson contacted you at my behest. This young woman is my adopted daughter, Mabel. The patient we've come to see you about is her grandmother."

"Lillias Strang."

It was a statement rather than a question, but Floss answered it anyway. "Yes. Her daughter Clementina was born here. In this asylum."

Dr Baldwin nodded slowly. He wiped a hand slowly across the pristine surface of his desk, as if he'd noticed an invisible speck of dust. "So I understand. And do you have proof that this young lady," he smiled towards me, "is Mrs Strang's granddaughter?"

I crossed my fingers in my lap — we had very little in the way of proof — but Floss breezed on. "When Clementina came to Glasgow she used a different surname — Watt. And, unfortunately, she didn't get Mabel's birth registered. I did that, later, and Clementina is noted on the certificate as her mother. I also have a letter..." she dug into her bag and took out an old and much folded letter, "... from Clementina, placing Mabel in my care."

Floss handed the certificate and letter to him and he took them from her, taking pains to touch as little of the documents as possible, and to touch Floss not at all. He read it carefully and then handed it back to Floss, wiping his fingers on a kerchief afterwards. It seemed a very odd gesture for a doctor. How did he manage to treat his patients if he found it difficult to touch *them*?

He was silent for a few moments. "We — the previous management of this institution and myself — have been trying to contact her husband, Mr Arthur Strang, for some time, several years, in fact. I am afraid that the inheritance monies left to pay for Mrs Strang's care ran out some years ago."

THE DEVIL'S DRAPER

Floss and I looked at each other. All we had been told when investigating my grandmother's whereabouts was that she had been committed to the asylum by Arthur Strang in the late 1870s. We had no idea of the circumstances surrounding her committal.

"Inheritance?" asked Floss.

"Yes. From an aunt, a Miss Gilfillan. From Bristol, I believe." How had a young girl from Bristol ended up in Scotland? Baldwin continued. "Mrs Strang – Lillias – came here with her maid, who then stayed on as a wardress, became head wardress, in fact. A troublesome woman, by all accounts."

Floss leaned forwards, placing her gloved hands on the doctor's desk. "Troublesome?"

The doctor looked down at Floss' hands, pointedly. She didn't move them. "Yes. Lillias had her own quarters, paid for by the inheritance but when the funds ran out, this wardress insisted that Lillias' health would suffer if we were to move her to the pauper wards. She is rather delicate."

"Ah, I see." I think both Floss and I understood the situation. The doctors who dealt with her might have seen the wardress as troublesome; the patients would have viewed her completely differently, I had no doubt. My mother had told Floss about my grandmother's maid, Mary Grace. She had loved and cared for my grandmother, and, indeed, for the other patients in her charge and her promotion to head wardress was no surprise, based on what we knew from my mother's stories of her.

Floss' tone was pleasant; only those who knew her well would have detected the layer of ice beneath it. "So you were looking for her husband to continue paying for her keep?"

"Exactly so."

Floss stood up. "May we be taken to Mrs Strang's rooms. Her granddaughter would like to meet her."

"To her...? Ah, no. This wardress, Mary Grace, died in the influenza epidemic." He shrugged his shoulders. "My predecessor removed Lillias to the pauper wards the following week. However,"

THE DEVIL'S DRAPER

he looked at his watch, "at this time of day, she will be at work in the laundry. If you would like to go outside and take a turn in the gardens, I will have her brought to you for a while. Please try and break the young lady's relationship to her gently. We have tried to lessen the shock by advising her that she is to have visitors. As far as I understand from her records, you are her first." He stood and gestured towards the door and we took our cue.

Floss frowned. "Her husband never visited?"

The doctor wiped his kerchief over the spot on the desk where Floss' hands had been. "Apparently not."

No visitors in forty years? My heart hurt for this woman and I could tell that Floss felt the same.

SATURDAY 17TH JULY 1920
BEATRICE

Nell Donald lived in a narrow, terraced house with a small, neat garden in Maryhill. Beatrice hesitated and dried her slightly damp palms on her skirt, before opening the gate and walking up the path to the front door. She was troubled by the reception she had received from Elsie's mother and was worried the same fate might await her here. Beatrice was at pains to do right by the young women who came to her looking for employment.

It was Nell herself who came to the door. As she opened it, the smell of boiled cabbage wafted out. "Mrs Price!"

"Hello, Nell, are you well?"

"Well? Why...yes. I'm..." She drifted off and glanced nervously behind her. "Why are you here?"

Beatrice wasn't quite sure herself. "I wanted to see how you were doing. I...Are you still at Arrol's?"

"Let's go out into the garden." Nell turned her head and called out. "Da, the lady from the employment agency has come to see me. We're going to sit outside and chat." She turned back to Beatrice. "There's a bench just round the side."

The side of the garden was just as neat as the front, with a handmade bench, painted the same navy blue as the front door, positioned to receive sun all through the day. When they had settled themselves, Nell answered the question. "No, I'm not still at Arrol's. I only stayed there a week. I couldn't bear it no more."

"Couldn't bear what?"

Nell shuddered. "The way he touched me. An' the other girls said it would get worse. So I left. I didnae even get ma week's wages."

Beatrice turned to face her, staring at the young woman's downcast face. "*Who* touched you? Did you report it?"

THE DEVIL'S DRAPER

Nell looked at her, her eyes wide. "Report it? Who to?"

"I don't know – the department manageress? Or Mr Arrol himself?"

Nell laughed, but it was a hollow sound. "An' what would I say? 'Mr Arrol, sir, I'd like to report that you touched me, an' I'd like you to stop'?"

"It was *Mr Arrol*? Mr *Hector* Arrol?"

Nell finally looked up and glared at Beatrice, her eyes flashing. "Aye, Mrs Price. Mr God-almighty himself, Mr Hector Arrol."

"I'm so sorry, Nell. If I'd known..." Beatrice stopped. What would she have done if she'd known? "What did he...?"

The fire went out of Nell's eyes and she looked down at her hands once more. "I'd rather not say, Mrs Price. But it were horrible. Horrible." She looked up. "Don't tell ma da."

"Didn't you say anything to him? Or to your mother?"

Nell was picking at a loose thread in her skirt. "My maw's dead. It's me and ma da and ma three little brothers an' ma da's not keeping well at the moment. I just tell't him there wasn't enough work for me and they had to let me go. I'll need to find another job soon, though."

"I'm so sorry." Beatrice dug into her purse. "Here. Take this." She held out a pound note and two half crowns. "Your wages for the week you worked."

It was clear that Nell was torn. "But...you shouldn't have to do that. It shouldn't come out of *your* pocket."

Beatrice pressed the money gently into Nell's hand, folding her fingers around it. "And *you* shouldn't suffer any more for what that man did to you. I promise you: I won't let this matter rest."

Nell shrugged. "I don't think you can stop it. Not at Arrol's and not anywhere else. Who's going to believe a shop girl over an important businessman like him?"

"*I* am," said Beatrice. She patted Nell's hand, which she was still holding in her own and then stood up. "Come and see me next week and I'll sort out another job for you."

THE DEVIL'S DRAPER

SATURDAY 17TH JULY 1920
MABEL

Jo gave us a wave as we went outside. She was polishing the Hispano-Suiza with a chamois leather cloth. We had decided on the way up that we didn't want to overcrowd my grandmother.

We waited in silence on a bench in a shaded part of the garden. I chewed my lip. What was actually wrong with my grandmother? Would we be able to communicate with her? Would she understand us?

I didn't have long to fret. After only a few minutes, we saw a woman dressed in a nurse's uniform slowly walking over to us, her hand under the elbow of a small, rather frail-looking woman dressed in a brown dress of rough material. Floss and I stood up and walked over to meet them.

The woman's head was bent and all we could see was the neat grey bun on top of her head. Here and there, wisps of shorter hair had escaped and curled around her lowered face. As the sun came out from behind a cloud, I drew in a sharp breath. The grey in her hair was mixed with the golden colour of the lock of hair I kept in my treasure box.

The woman looked up at my gasp and gazed at me, her eyes clear and blue. "Clementina?" It was almost a whisper but both Floss and I caught it. Floss had told me how much I resembled my mother. We had the same colour hair and eyes, although Floss said I was taller and more sturdily built. Tears pricked at my eyes upon hearing the name of my mother, and I let out a small whimper, which my grandmother didn't seem to notice. She stood there looking at me, her head tilted to one side and a puzzled smile on her face.

"Do come and sit down." Floss took my grandmother's hands and led her over to the bench. We sat next to her, one on each side.

THE DEVIL'S DRAPER

The nurse backed away, out of earshot, but never taking her eyes off her charge.

Once we were seated, my grandmother turned to look at me again. "You're not my Clemmie, are you?" Her voice was quiet, but strong. I shook my head, unable to trust my own voice. "But you look so very like her. As I imagined her, growing older. Into a fine young woman. Are you...?"

I could only nod, feeling tears pricking at my eyes. "This is Clemmie's daughter, Mabel," said Floss, gently.

"Mabel Jean Lillias," I said. "That's what my mother called me. She gave me your name."

My grandmother smiled. "I'm glad she didn't forget me." She didn't take her eyes off me. "And this other lady?" she said.

"Her name is Floss. Florence Adair. She adopted me after..." I didn't know what to say.

"I understand." She turned to Floss, clasping one of Floss' soft hands in her own, red and cracked. "Thank you." She turned back to me and cupped my face in her hands. "I'm very happy you've come."

Monday 19th July 1920
Mabel

It turned out that my suspension only lasted over the weekend. It seemed that Superintendent Orr had thought better of it. "We're too busy for you to be twiddling your thumbs," he said. "We need all hands on deck. Even almost useless ones."

I stood at the other side of his desk, chin down on my chest, eyes on the floor, as he chastised me. "Aye, you may well bow your head in shame, Adair. You should think yersel' lucky that the woman at the station didnae press charges against you for theft."

My head was only bowed so that he wouldn't see my big smile. Constable Ferguson had caught me on my way in and shared the interesting snippet of information that Orr had been given a dressing down by the Chief Constable for suspending me in the first place. "Yes, sir," was all I said.

His hands clenched and I heard the click of his jaw as he growled, "I'm doing you a favour by letting you come back at all."

I put my finger to my lips, as though contemplating my luck. "Yes, sir. Shall I go back to my office, sir?"

"No." His growl was even more fierce than normal. "I need to speak to you about something else." I racked my brains. What could my latest infringement have been? I'd got back to the station on Friday, only to be suspended immediately, so was struggling to come up with anything else I could possibly have done. In the past, I'd been hauled over the coals for things as wide-ranging as having a cake crumb on my cheek (insubordination, apparently) to finding a dead body. Since I hadn't found a dead body for a while, I raised a surreptitious hand to my cheek to check for cake crumbs.

But Orr didn't put me out of my misery, simply glared at me, until a knock at the door of his office broke the – on his part, anyway – resentful silence.

THE DEVIL'S DRAPER

Detective Inspectors Lorrimer and Channing entered the office. Lorrimer nodded at me. Channing ignored me as usual. Channing immediately took one of the seats opposite Orr and Lorrimer nodded me towards the other one. I shook my head and made a face towards Orr, who was scanning some papers on his desk. Lorrimer grinned and leaned up against the wall.

Orr picked up the papers, a serious look on his face. "You all heard about this burglary up by the Botanics last week, I assume?"

"Yes, sir." Lorrimer adjusted his empty sleeve, tucking the end of it more firmly into his pocket. "One of the big houses up that way, wasn't it?"

"Aye. There've been a number of burglaries in the area and there was a constable from Partick on patrol, but some wee chit of a girl inveigled him into conversation for a good twenty minutes, looking for advice on certain matters. His reward for his politeness was a burglary committed not two minutes' walk away. By the time the alarm was raised, there was no trace of the girl, or her gang."

Channing straightened in his chair. "How do we know she was part of the gang, sir?"

"Partick are pretty sure. There've been a number of burglaries and other crimes on their patch in recent months, involving what have been described as a gang of razor-wielding, Amazonian women." Lorrimer snorted and Orr glared at him and continued. "And they caught a suspected pickpocket last week. She let slip she was in an all-woman gang called the St Thenue's Avengers, before clamming up. We couldn't get another word out of her and had to let her go."

It was Channing's turn to snort. "St Thenue? Never heard of him. What sort of gang name is that?"

"She," I said. "St Thenue was a she."

Orr snapped his head in my direction. "What?"

"St Thenue. Said to be the mother of St Mungo, Glasgow's Patron—"

THE DEVIL'S DRAPER

"I know who St Mungo is, Adair. I'm no' stupid."

"No, sir."

"Well?"

"Well, what, sir?"

"Enough of the cheek, Adair. This Thenue. Who was she?"

"The story goes that she was a sixth-century Princess and Scotland's first official victim of sexual assault and rape, sir." They all looked at me, aghast, more, I think, because a lady wasn't supposed to talk about such things, rather than being shocked at St Thenue's fate. "Her father had her thrown off a cliff when he discovered she was pregnant out of wedlock. She survived the fall, so she was set adrift in a coracle." I shrugged. "I think he thought she was a witch, because she was still alive. She's also sometimes called St Enoch. Like the station," I said, helpfully.

"Thank you for the fairy story, Adair." Orr stabbed his finger at the papers in front of him. "Anyway, this gang has been causing mayhem across the city: burglaries, thefts, pickpocketing, shoplifting. All the major department stores are reporting losses – big losses in some cases, including some furs on Monday from Copland & Lye. We've advised all of them to increase their security. It's shoplifting on a grand scale like we've never seen before. And last week, a woman ordered a fur coat from Treron's to be delivered to an address in Scotstoun for her husband's approval. Worth over five hundred guineas it was. Well, the husband approved it and the man who delivered it was asked to send the bill on. He said he needed payment immediately and wasn't going to leave without it. Treron's are lucky he was on the ball. In his statement, he said that there was something funny about the so-called husband. Said he thought it was a woman in disguise."

Lorrimer leaned forward. "So, did they get the pair?"

"Naw." Orr's voice was sour. "The Treron's man took the fur coat back and went away to fetch a policeman when they refused to pay. When they got back to the house, the woman and her supposed husband had disappeared. The house was shut up, and it turned out that the real residents and all their servants were away on holiday." Orr waved one of his pieces of paper. "An' that very same day, four other members of the gang robbed a jewellers in Argyle Street. Two of the women went in and asked to see two trays of rings. They distracted the jeweller, while another woman came in, lifted the trays and took them out to where a Bentley was waiting."

"A Bentley?" Lorrimer was surprised.

"Aye, a Bentley. Stolen, of course."

"Of course."

"And you want us to investigate?" Channing was no longer lounging. His sharp chin jutted forward and his neck was straining like a terrier who'd spied a rat.

"Aye. Detective Inspector Channing, I want you to follow up these stolen rings. Speak to the usual fences. An' choose a couple of men to help you canvas all the jewellers in Glasgow. See if any of them have had any visits or noticed any suspicious activity."

Channing nodded and Orr turned to Lorrimer. "Lorrimer, you heard of Chez Antoine?" Orr had managed to mangle both words, but Chez Antoine was such a famous club in Glasgow that we all knew what he meant.

"Yes, sir, of course."

"Aye, well, there's been a couple of incidents there recently. In the first, a young woman of some means, who was up visiting Glasgow from London, fell into company with two others at Chez Antoine. She'd gone there – alone." Orr's sniff clearly showed what he thought of young ladies who visited nightclubs alone. "She was dressed up in all her finery, including a rather fine diamond necklace and matching bracelet and earrings. She described these women as 'very fine ladies'. They bought a bottle of champagne which they insisted she share, an' the next thing she knew, she was waking up in her hotel room minus her diamonds, a pair of pearl earrings, and all of her money."

"And the second incident? Was it of a similar nature?"

"Only in that it targeted a lady. In this one, several members

THE DEVIL'S DRAPER

of the smart set were approached at the same club by a couple who told the group they could supply a substantial amount of cocaine. A very reasonable price was agreed, and one of the young women in the party went off to the ladies' dressing room with the female of the couple. That's where the money and cocaine were to change hands."

"And that exchange didn't happen?" said Lorrimer.

"Oh no, it happened right enough. An' the couple shared a wee dram with the smart set. It was only after they parted on very friendly terms that the group discovered that their cocaine wasn't cocaine after all."

"And what was it?"

"Epsom salts." Lorrimer laughed. It struck me that it was a sound I didn't think I'd ever heard before. In fact, I'd seldom seen him smile.

Superintendent Orr continued. "An' they also said that, in hindsight, the young man of the couple might not have been a young man after all, but a woman dressed up as a man. Just like the Treron's fur case. That's what led us to suspect these St Thenue's Avengers."

Lorrimer nodded. "So you want me to visit Chez Antoine and ask questions?"

"Naw," Superintendent Orr picked at his teeth with a fat finger. "I want you to spend a few evenings there. Have dinner, dance, look like a man who's on the lookout for cocaine."

"Dance, sir?" Lorrimer looked utterly horrified.

"Aye. An' nothing too fancy for the dinners, mind. No picking the most expensive thing on the menu. No oysters, no rump steak, an' absolutely no cocktails."

"No, sir, of course, but…dance?"

Orr ignored him and turned to face me. "And me, sir?" I said eagerly. This would be my first proper task. I would prove my worth on the track of this all-woman gang and my days of sitting in broom cupboards and railway station waiting rooms would be over. "What's my assignment?"

"Your *assignment*, Miss Adair?" I didn't like his tone of voice and light began to dawn. "Your assignment, Miss Adair, is to dance with Detective Inspector Lorrimer."

MONDAY 19TH JULY 1920
JOHNNIE

Most of the St Thenue's Avengers lived up two closes in Merchant Lane just off the Briggait, at the back of the fish market. On the ground floor of the two buildings were a rope manufacturer and a warehouse. In the basement of one was the club run by Meg's brother and the basement of the other was the Avengers' war room.

Johnnie lived on her own in a single-end on the third floor; her most recent roommate was currently in jail, serving a six-month sentence for theft. Johnnie enjoyed the solitude, and the extra space, and particularly relished the freedom to spread herself out in the bed. The other two flats on the third floor were bigger than this one, each of them boasting a room and kitchen. Meg, as the gang's queen, had one to herself and the other was shared by Gracie and Big Annie, the two sisters who were Meg's joint second-in-command. The third floor was the best – further away from the smells of the fish market and the noise of the street and Johnnie was grateful for Meg's favour.

She checked the clock. Just before nine. Time to go down to the war room. Meg didn't like it if you were late. Johnnie looked at herself in the long mirror she had found on the street. She had to bend and sway to see herself properly, as large parts of the glass had foxed and tarnished. Her suit was baggy and shiny with age in places. The jacket hung off her shoulders and the trousers were slightly too long, but she felt invisible in it and that was the main thing. And the tan Oxfords had been a great find, sitting neatly outside a hotel room, waiting to be picked up by the staff for polishing. They were nearly her size and, tightly laced and worn with two pairs of socks, they were the most comfortable shoes she'd ever had.

THE DEVIL'S DRAPER

Johnnie checked that her hair was all hidden under her tweed cap and bounded down the stairs, taking them two at a time. She opened the door out into the back court and, checking that no-one was around, she rapped smartly on the door that led down to the basement. A bolt was drawn back and Big Annie let her in. Johnnie helped herself to a pastry from the table near the door. The two lumpy settees were already stuffed full of Avengers, so Johnnie pulled up a hard wooden chair and sat down and crossed her legs, in the free manner that men had, right foot casually resting on left knee.

Meg nodded at her. She was standing in front of the huge piece of slate that had been fixed to one wall of the basement. "So, assignments for today, lassies. Aggie is settling into yon big house in Dennistoun. Bette, I want you to go round there today and see if you can get a word with her. Ask her what the lie of the land is. She was thinkin' the owners might go away for Fair Fortnight an' that would give us a good opportunity." Bette, leaning against the wall in the corner of the room, gave a serious nod. "Wee Bunny has managed to get a place as a kitchen maid in a fancy house on Byres Road. Not an ideal position for our purposes, but it's a good house, so we'll see what happens."

She checked the slate and ticked off names with the chalk she was holding. "Annie, Hetty, Lena and Polly – train stations and the Broomilaw. I'll leave it to youse who goes where. Wee Annie and May, Copland & Lye for youse pair. Concentrate on gloves and scarves today, I think. Watch out for that bastard on the doors. He nearly got Polly last week. Polly, I want you at Arrol's. Their security's not so hot." Johnnie sneaked a glance at Polly, who looked a bit peeved at this veiled insult, but certainly wasn't going to say anything; they were all afraid of Meg. "Jenny, Pettigrew and Stephens, hen. Mousie, you're going fancy today, so dress up. Trerons for you." Mousie let out a squeal of delight.

"Johnnie, the shows at Vinegarhill for you, since you're dressed for it. Just dipping today, nothing fancy. You had a busy weekend."

THE DEVIL'S DRAPER

Meg smiled. It was a welcome but uncommon sight and softened the hardness of her features. "You did well on Saturday. There'll be a wee bonus for you once all the wedding gifts are fenced." Meg took a final look around the room. "Right youse lot. Away and about your business."

As the women filed out of the basement, Meg turned back to the slate and wiped off the names, carefully removing every trace.

THE DEVIL'S DRAPER

MONDAY 19TH JULY 1920
MABEL

Lorrimer and Channing had been allowed to go. I, on the other hand, had to endure another ten minutes of recriminations for my behaviour at Central Station: apparently, I was a disgrace and if it were up to him, women wouldn't be in the police force. "A liability! I told the Chief Constable as much, but I might as well have been talking to myself."

"Yes, sir."

He looked at me suspiciously. "Get to your office. I don't want to see your face for the rest of the day. If I find out you've moved from your desk, there'll be hell to pay. Understand?" He took a paper and pen from his desk and started writing. I had clearly been dismissed.

"Yes, sir." I counted to three in my head. "Sir?"

He slammed the pen down and glared at me. "What?"

"Detective Inspector Lorrimer wants me to interview a woman in the cells. If I don't leave my office, how can I do that?"

His face turned puce and he spoke through gritted teeth. "You know exactly what I mean, Adair. Now get out of here before I re-suspend you."

He wouldn't, of course, but I turned smartly on my heel and left as though I believed him. I headed down to the cells to interview a woman who had been arrested for stealing linens from the drying green on Glasgow Green, before returning back upstairs to get on with some paperwork and keep out of mischief.

What Superintendent Orr had called my 'office' was actually a former broom cupboard: I wasn't allowed to share a space with the men. The desk and two chairs that were crammed in at one end were an afterthought to the broom, mop and pail and cardboard boxes at the other. The size of the room, the lack of windows and the damp smell that never went away, even in the summer, made it an unpleasant place to be, but I was delighted to see that in the middle of my desk sat a huge piece of ginger cake and a steaming mug of tea. Using my expert powers of deduction (that Orr clearly underestimated), I guessed that the tea had been made by Sergeant Ferguson and the cake had been made by his wife

I had just sat down at my desk and taken a huge bite, when Ferguson himself came in. I waved a piece of ginger cake at him, before popping it into my mouth. "Thank you, Archie. And do thank Mrs Ferguson for me, as ever." Constable Ferguson and I had not had the best of starts, but now we were firm friends. "Come in and sit down, do."

"I can't, Miss. Just off out on patrol, but I wanted to let you know that there's a lady waiting at the front desk to speak to someone about a 'delicate matter', as she put it. A Mrs Beatrice Price. Runs an employment agency for ladies. Shall I bring her through?"

As he went to fetch her, I put the rest of the piece of ginger cake in a drawer and pulled over a pad and pen.

The woman Constable Ferguson showed in was a pleasant-looking woman of about the same age as Floss and Jo. She was tall and plump and wearing a smart navy-blue poplin suit and a plain felt hat in the same colour. She assessed me in the same way I was assessing her... I felt as though I had been found wanting. From her frown as she gazed around my office, she definitely found *that* wanting. "Do sit down, Mrs...Price?" She nodded. "Would you like a cup of tea?"

"No. Thank you." She had an English accent and her voice was strong and confident.

"How can I help you? Constable Ferguson mentioned that you wanted to speak to me about a delicate matter?"

She didn't immediately answer, instead looking me up and down once more. "Are you a policewoman?"

"Yes," I said. Her clear brown eyes fixed on me as though she

THE DEVIL'S DRAPER

found it difficult to believe. "Technically, my title is 'statement taker', but I *am* a policewoman."

Her lips twitched briefly, with amusement, I thought, but she launched into her tale. I listened carefully, taking copious notes. "And how many have you spoken to now?"

"I've been able to get hold of five in total – some in person, some on the phone. Three of them have been assaulted."

"And they all tell the same story?"

She shrugged. "To greater or lesser extents, yes. That Hector Arrol has insulted them, touched them and, in one case, rather seriously assaulted her. It was only the arrival of another shop girl in the stock room that stopped him from going further."

"And did anyone else see these assaults?"

She frowned. "No, apparently not. He appears to have been very careful."

I sighed. "That's a shame. Then it's their word against his."

"*I* believe them."

She sounded offended and I hurried to placate her. "Oh, so do I, Mrs Price. So do I. Unfortunately, I hear rather too much of this in my job."

Her frown deepened. "About Hector Arrol?"

"No, not about him, but about other employers: from shop girls, young women in service, in factories, on the trams. Sadly, it's a common complaint."

"Well," she pressed her hands on the edge of my desk and leaned forward. "Something needs to be done about him."

I tapped my pen against my notebook. "Do you think any of these young women would come and report these occurrences to the police?"

Mrs Price snorted. "I doubt that very much. It was as much as I could do to get them to tell *me*. And surely it's Hector Arrol you should be speaking to?"

"We can put in a request for someone to go and speak to him, certainly." I wasn't convinced that any request would be listened to, but I wasn't about to tell Mrs Price that.

"You?" The tone with which this was said sounded rather dubious.

"No," I said drily. "A male colleague." For some reason, I didn't want to admit to this woman that my job was less than ideal. "But I have to warn you, Mrs Price—"

"I know, Miss Adair. His word against theirs." I nodded. "And rich, well-respected businessman trumps shop girls, no matter how many of them there are." She sat back in her chair, her shoulders slumped.

It was a statement rather than a question, but I nodded. "I'm afraid so, yes."

She seemed to pull herself together – I'd never seen such a perfect embodiment of that phrase – then stood up abruptly. "Well, please do what you can. I'll call by again in a few days for the outcome." She took another look around my office. "They don't like you very much here, do they, Miss Adair?"

"No, they don't." Even to myself, my voice sounded glum.

She smiled briefly and took another look around. "Well, in such circumstances, I would normally say that I'm sure I could find you better employment elsewhere but...well, something tells me you're trying to make a difference here, and that's important." And, with that, she nodded curtly and left the room before I could thank her.

though
THE DEVIL'S DRAPER

MONDAY 19TH JULY 1920
JOHNNIE

Johnnie decided to take the long way to Vinegarhill, with a stroll along the Clyde and a visit to the fish market. She loved this imposing building with its round windows, curlicues and carvings in the stonework, which softened the façade. She stopped for a moment as she always did and looked up at the magnificent winged sea horses over the archways. It always paid to look up as you wandered around Glasgow and this building was no exception.

This place reminded her of her grandfather, who had worked here for many years, and Johnnie particularly loved it early in the morning, when it was at its busiest. She loved to take in the din of shouts, whistles and the shrieking of electric horns as sellers did their best to attract buyers to their fresh produce: halibut from Iceland, cod from Greenland, haddock and whiting from the North Sea, hake from the rocky shores of the Hebrides. Crowds gathered around huge crates of Loch Fyne kippers and herrings and, across from them the cured fish, Arbroath smokies and finnan haddies. Strange calls rang out in loud voices: words like 'dannies' and 'jumboes' that meant absolutely nothing to Johnnie, although her grandfather must have explained the terms to her at one time. And it wasn't just a place for fish; hampers of chickens, rabbits and venison were also on display. The salesmen shouted out their bids continuously, but for the customers, it was a quieter affair. A brief nod or the flicker of an eyelid sealed the deal.

At this time of day, it was quieter than the early morning. Instead of going inside, she took a circuitous route through the Briggait and towards Glasgow Green. It wasn't as busy today as it was on a Saturday, but there were barrows with hawkers selling their wares, women selling rags and second-hand clothes; barrows full of poor quality cups and plates and bowls; carts laden with

THE DEVIL'S DRAPER

fruit, vegetables and fish.

Johnnie walked to the foot of the Saltmarket where she could hear the familiar sounds of Cheap Jack as he harangued his potential customers at the Jocelyn Gate. "I say, I say! This is the place for bargains, ladies and gentlemen. The place for bargains!" He continued to extol the wonderful virtues and extreme cheapness of his various wares, which consisted of every imaginable thing under the weak sun – from needles to anchors, from lace to doorknockers. "Get your monies ready. Here's something you'll all buy. It's a purse, made after the same pattern as that worn by no less than Queen Mary herself, God bless her: all finest Morocco leather outside, all velvet inside and shut by a patent steel clasp."

A small crowd ebbed and flowed around him: some of them genuinely interested in the goods on offer, eagerly fingering the coins in their pockets and purses; others simply soaking in the atmosphere and Cheap Jack's patter. Others, like Johnnie, were more interested in the crowd around him and had more nefarious intent, gauging the distracted crowd for what it might offer her.

Cheap Jack continued to talk up the purse, showing it off with expansive gestures. "Here you are, ladies. There's a place here for the dab, a place for the silver, a place for the gold and a place for all those £5 notes." The crowd rippled with good-natured laughter. The weather might not be ideal but it was Glasgow Fair and everyone was ready and willing to have a good time and spend their hard-earned money. "And for this wonder of cheapness, which you could not buy in any shop in the city for less than twenty-five shillings; I'll not charge you twenty shillings, nor fifteen, nor even twelve and six." He paused, dramatically, as the crowd surged forward, all agog for a bargain. "Eleven shillings is all, ladies and gentlemen." The crowd seemed to draw in a collective breath, sensing that he would go still lower, that he was teasing them, and Johnnie smiled at his patter.

"What? Are there no buyers for that mere trifle? Just eleven shillings?" Cheap Jack made an exaggerated face of disgust. "Well, if you'll not buy it for such a paltry amount; here, just take it, take it as a present for ten shillings. Yes, ladies and gentlemen, you're a hard crowd. Steal it from me for ten shillings." Several hands were raised into the air, green and brown ten shilling notes held high, clamouring for attention. "Yes, here you are, sir...sold again." Notes were snatched and purses tossed out to their new owners. "Yes, hear what the gentleman says, it's worth double the money. Treble, sir!"

But Johnnie shouldn't linger. Meg had told her to go to Green's Carnival and, reluctantly, she left the crowd behind and made her way across Glasgow Green. In less than half an hour, she was paying her threepence to get into the carnival grounds. The poster boasted, 'If it's Green's it's good, and if it's good it's Green's' and promised her twenty-three free shows on the open-air stages every half an hour: hand balancers, acrobats, clowns, ventriloquists, highland dancers. Johnnie hoped she was in time to see the contortionists or the wire walkers or even a performing animal or two. She was here to work, but Meg hadn't said anything about her not having fun, had she? Besides, she was looking forward to trying the two new rides she'd heard so much about: The Whip and The Frolic.

Johnnie had been at the shows during Glasgow Fair every year since she could remember, so she was familiar with the Fairy Fountains and the Japanese Gardens, and she made a beeline for the Clachan of Aberfoyle, with its farm steading stocked with animals. She walked around it, breathing in the scents of wet straw and warm animals, visiting in turn the sheep, goats and pigs before her ultimate goal - Tina and Tim. They were billed as the world's tiniest horses and Johnnie had no doubt that was true. They looked like the rocking horses she had once seen in a toy shop in Argyle Street, but with sadder faces. She came away feeling sorry for them, crammed into a tiny pen with bare earth on the floor.

After leaving the Clachan, Johnnie walked slowly through the grounds, concentrating on men, particularly those wandering round on their own or in groups. She glanced at, and instantly dismissed, those whose clothes looked in even worse repair than her own. Not simply because the poorer the clothing, the more measly the pickings, but also because the loss of a watch or a coin or two would spoil their day. Instead, her keen eye sought out those who could afford it. Her gaze lingered on three drunken young men over at the Houp-La, talking to the young woman behind the low fence. Her arms were crossed and her face was set in disgust. And she wasn't only targeting those who could afford it, Johnnie thought, but also those who might well deserve it. If the young woman's face was anything to go by, that included these three.

She walked casually over to the young men and stood close behind them, as if trying to see over their shoulders. "Keep yer drawers on, hen," slurred one of them at the stallholder. "Just havin' a wee laugh, awright?"

The other two sniggered and one of them turned to Johnnie. "You come to try your luck, too, young man?" Stale beer fumes smacked Johnnie in the face. "Well, I hope you have more luck than us." They staggered off unsteadily, still braying and hee-hawing like drunken donkeys.

Johnnie watched them go and then turned back to the stall. The young woman looked at her warily. Johnnie took out of her pocket the battered wallet belonging to one of the three men. With their attentions distracted and their wits addled by drink, it had been easy as pie dipping each of their pockets in turn. She opened it and pulled out ten shillings. "Three hoops, please. An' keep the change."

Monday 19th July 1920
Mabel

I sat at my desk for some time after Mrs Price had left. I knew that sending someone to interview Hector Arrol would be a pointless exercise, but that didn't mean I wasn't going to suggest it. My only problem was how to go about it. Superintendent Orr would pooh-pooh the suggestion if it came from me and, quite frankly, my stock was so low around here that I didn't think many of the other officers at St Andrew's Square would be too willing to take it on, either.

Constable Ferguson was my only friend here, and he was too low down the pecking order for Orr to take any notice of him. Besides, Ferguson liked to keep his head down as much as possible and I didn't want to put him in an awkward situation. No, this was something which needed someone in a more senior position. I stood up from my desk and went to find Detective Inspector Lorrimer.

I wouldn't exactly consider Lorrimer a friend, more of a reluctant and cautious potential ally. He used my services as a statement taker more than all of the other officers put together and, on occasion, even asked for my opinion on the women whose statements I had taken. We had worked together quite closely on a case about eighteen months before, just after I had joined the police service and, although he was wary of me, and I of him, it felt to me as though he respected me a little, at least.

I found Lorrimer in the file room, speaking to Sergeant McGillivray, whose domain the file room was. "Could I have a word, Detective Inspector?" I ignored McGillivray's glower. It was his normal facial expression when he saw me.

"Certainly, Miss Adair. Shall we go to your...office?" He held the file room door open for me with his good arm. His other was just a pinned sleeve. "Is this about our forthcoming evening of forced gaiety at Chez Antoine, or our snowdropper?"

"Sir?" I had no idea what he meant.

He smiled for a fraction of a second, which told me he was in a good mood. Generally, his face was closed off and unfathomable. "Our laundry thief." The woman I had interviewed in the cells earlier.

"Ah, no, neither of those. It's about something else. But I've taken the woman's statement. She says it was mostly shawls and men's shirts and women's underwear. She was wearing some of the items and told me she planked several of the others in hedges. I sent one of the new constables out to round them up."

The tiny smile was back. "I'm sure he'll be grateful to you for making him walk through the Green with an armful of ladies' undergarments."

I had felt sorry for the woman. "She's a widow with five children. Two of them are ill and she told me she couldn't afford the medicine."

Lorrimer sighed. "Previous convictions?"

"No, Detective Inspector."

We had reached my office and he opened the door for me. "Well, perhaps the Sherriff will go easy on her then. Now, what was it that you wanted to speak to me about?" He sat himself down in the same chair Mrs Price had sat in earlier.

I told him about Mrs Price's visit and he sat back, nodding slowly. "And she's spoken to several of them now?"

"Yes, five of them and three young women who she placed there over the last few months tell the same story. All of them left in the space of a few weeks."

"Are any of the other young women she placed still there?"

"I believe that one is still in the same department; another has moved elsewhere in the store."

"And none of them have reported any untoward behaviour?"

I frowned at him. "I believe not. But that doesn't mean to say

THE DEVIL'S DRAPER

nothing happened, or that the others are lying. I'm sure they're keen to keep their jobs."

He held his hands up as if to placate me. "Not at all; it wasn't my intention to suggest that. She doesn't think any of these women will come to us, you say?"

"Unlikely, she thinks."

"And so she wants us to...do what, exactly?"

I crossed my fingers under the cover of my desk. "Could you go and interview him?"

He raised his eyebrows. "Interview Hector Arrol? About what? We don't have an official report, just some vague comments from a third party about some unspecified and, if I might say, from what you've told me, some very *tame* actions from a man who's considered a pillar of society and who treats his staff as if they're family."

His response was much milder than anything Orr would have said if I'd approached him, but I pushed him anyway. "Oh, and we know that nothing bad ever happens in families, don't we, Detective Inspector Lorrimer?"

"I promise you, Miss Adair, if you bring me something concrete, I will go and interview Hector Arrol myself."

And that, I knew, was the best that I could hope for.

THURSDAY 22ND JULY 1920
BEATRICE

As Beatrice climbed the stairs up to her office, a woman standing outside her door came into view. All she could see at first was a rather scuffed pair of brown shoes – not the latest fashion – and a dusty black skirt of similar vintage. Beatrice took the last few steps two at a time. "Hello! I'm so sorry to keep you waiting."

"Please don't worry about it." The woman sounded as though she expected to be kept waiting everywhere she went. Her face was careworn and her shoulders were rounded, as though trying to hide in her own skin.

Beatrice unlocked the door. "Come in and have a cup of tea." She ushered the woman in and gestured towards one of the chairs, before taking out her Thermos. The woman took the proffered cup eagerly and gulped the tea down. Beatrice reached into her desk and pulled out the biscuit tin, which she had filled to the brim with custard creams only the day before. She removed the lid, allowing a puff of vanilla to escape, pushed the tin across and topped up the woman's cup. "Now, how can I help you?"

Mrs McDonald leaned forward in her chair, perched on the edge of it. She'd been employed as a charwoman but had been let go after a period of illness. As a result, she had been unable to pay her rent and had been evicted from her room and kitchen. She was currently living with her sister who kept hinting that there was no room for her there. Her knuckles were white on the arms of the chair. "I need a job, Mrs Price. I can't stay there any longer with my sister, she just doesn't have the space. Besides, I don't like to be beholden to anyone."

Earlier that week, Beatrice had been contacted by an elderly woman who was looking for a live-in servant to act as housekeeper, cleaner, cook and all-round help. Mrs McDonald had excellent

THE DEVIL'S DRAPER

references and, with a quick phone call to the elderly woman, Beatrice was able to set up an interview for later that day.

"I can't thank you enough." Mrs McDonald's voice was lighter and easier than before. "I've been to one or two agencies and they didn't seem interested. I even put an advert in the Daily Record an' never got one response. I think people are wantin' someone younger."

Mrs McDonald was a good ten or twelve years younger than Beatrice. "Come, now, my dear, you're not on the scrap heap yet. You mustn't let things get on top of you, so."

"I know; it's just..." The woman seemed to sink into herself. "It's been hard since Malcolm died."

"Your husband?"

"Aye. The Marne. He was in the Cameron Highlanders."

Beatrice had read of the battle, of course. She'd read about all of them. "Ah, he was early then. My son, too. Mons."

They sat quietly for a few moments before Mrs McDonald spoke again. "I still can't abide going into Central."

"Central Station?" Beatrice was puzzled by the reference.

"Aye. In the early months of the War they had a temporary mortuary set up there. Down and down and down in the depths of the place." Mrs McDonald shuddered as if at the memory that it brought up to her. "I'll never forget the darkness, or the heat. Or the noise of the trains rumbling above as I walked along the rows and rows of bodies."

"I'm so sorry to hear that. Did you...was he there?"

"Aye." She was silent again. "I had to take him away there and then, they said. I asked them how I was to get him up the stairs." She laughed; a small, bitter laugh. "They told me there were men hanging around the station, men who were too old for the War, or men who'd already come back, injured. Just waiting there. Waiting for women who'd found their husbands and sons down in those depths. They brought Malcolm up for a few shillings."

Beatrice poured Mrs McDonald another cup of tea and shook

the biscuit tin once more. The only thing which had worked for her was keeping busy and feeling a sense of purpose and she had no doubt that Mrs McDonald felt the same. Hopefully she could give her that sense of purpose back. "This woman you're going to work for. You'll be alright there, I know it."

After Mrs McDonald had left, Beatrice took the Arrol's file out once more. Mrs McDonald's visit had made her aware more than ever of the responsibility she felt to the women she found employment for. Maybe not so much a responsibility, but it was something she felt driven to do. Women like Mrs McDonald, the young women she'd placed at Arrol's, some of the other women who came to her, desperate for work, they needed someone to look out for them. It was up to Beatrice to do her utmost to help them, for herself, as well as for them.

Beatrice sighed and opened the file. She had been disappointed that there was nothing to be done about her report at the police station, but not surprised. The young woman, Miss Adair, had shared her frustration at the situation and Beatrice had been impressed with her. She picked up the telephone receiver and put in a call to the police station. The switchboard operator was efficient and put her through quickly.

The voice that answered the phone at the other end sounded bored. "Central Police Office." Beatrice explained who she was and why she was calling. "Aye? So, ye want tae speak tae Miss Adair? 'Cos she's no' here."

"Not necessarily. I just want to see what's happening as regards the report I made."

"Aye? Well, ah'm no' sure."

Beatrice took the receiver away from her ear and glared at it for a moment. "Well, do you think you could find out for me?"

There was a short silence and she wondered if the man was still there. "Whit? The noo'?"

"Yes, now please, if that's at all possible. I simply want to know what's happening now that I've reported my concerns."

THE DEVIL'S DRAPER

"Concerns aboot the young lassies?"

"That's right."

"An' Hector Arrol?"

Was the man dim? "Yes, that's correct. Can you please find out for me?"

The policeman gave such a huge sigh that Beatrice wouldn't have been surprised to feel the strands of hair around her ears moving in the breeze. He said nothing, but the receiver clattered down and she heard muffled muttering. Beatrice waited, flicking through the pages of the Arrol's file and frowning as she made notes in her neat handwriting. Only the faint background noises of the police office signalled to her that he hadn't simply hung up the receiver.

Eventually, there was a grunting and heavy breathing at the other end of the line. "You still there?"

His voice hinted at an optimism that she wasn't there any longer. "Yes, I'm still here."

He sighed his heavy sigh again. "Aye, well, Superintendent Orr says he's aware of the report."

"And?"

"An' it's no' a police matter."

Beatrice stiffened. "Not a police matter? Then whose *matter* did he say it was?"

The policeman cleared his throat. "Aye, well, nobody's ma'am." He hesitated. "He said the wee lassies have probably been reading too many of them love stories."

Beatrice gripped the receiver. "Love stories?"

He cleared his throat again. "Aye, the Girls' Own an' that." Beatrice felt her cheeks burn but was incapable of speech. He added helpfully, "Or Picture Show. There's an awfy lot o' that in those films. It's nae wonder their imaginations are running riot."

Beatrice quietly put the receiver back on its stand.

Sunday 25th July 1920
Mabel

Since visiting my grandmother, things had moved quickly. I didn't dare ask how, but Floss had managed to arrange for my grandmother to be released to her care and the house was now a flurry of activity. I had moved out of my bedroom so that my grandmother could have it. The house had plenty of rooms, of course, but mine was the nicest, big and bright. It had a view over Blythswood Square and a large separate dressing room which we'd set up as a parlour with a comfortable sofa, a couple of easy chairs, a table and a washstand. I say 'we', but essentially, Ellen, Floss' maid, had ordered us around, instructing us on the best way to hang curtains, place furniture to its best advantage, and how to beat a carpet into submission. Ellen had been with Floss since before I was born. She treated us all as though we were sent to try her patience at every step.

The housemaids had been set to cleaning the house from top to bottom. I had no idea why and had told Ellen that my grandmother wasn't coming to inspect the place for specks of dust, but she'd simply mumbled something under her breath and swept past me with a feather duster hoist aloft, as though she was Britannia brandishing her trident. Floss and Jo had driven to Stirlingshire to pick my grandmother up – with Jo under strict instructions not to drive too fast on the way back. Ellen and I were putting the finishing touches to my grandmother's new rooms – books, vases of flowers, little trinkets and knicknacks to make the place feel like home - and Mrs Dugan, newly returned from her sister's in Ayr, was in the kitchen singing tunelessly as she cooked up a storm. I had heard mention of glazed ham, roasted duck, oysters Rockefeller, Waldorf salad, veal and ham pie and goodness only knew what else. Floss had laughed, saying it would only be the four of us for dinner, not forty. Mrs Dugan's response had been to put her hands on her hips and say firmly, "The poor lady has been eating asylum food for decades and she'll not eat it for a moment longer."

There was also some of Mrs Dugan's fabulous baking on the menu, I was pleased to discover, as the warm scents of ginger, nutmeg and cinnamon spread throughout the house, soon joined by the sweet nuttiness of almonds. My mother's favourite dessert had been an apricot pithivier and we had discovered her tastes came from my grandmother, so Mrs Dugan was making not only an apricot version, but also cherry and plum for good measure.

"They're here!" Ellen's sharp hearing had caught the sound of the car pulling up outside and we took the stairs two at a time. Ellen reached the door before me and stood for a moment, smoothing out her apron before flinging the door open wide.

Floss was helping Lillias out of the car and Jo came round and took her other arm. Flanked by the two of them, my grandmother looked thin and frail. Jo herself had some health problems as a result of being force-fed in Perth prison during her time as a Suffragette, but even she looked far more robust than the tiny woman, who was looking around her with a mixture of fear and awe. I tried to imagine what it must be like for her, not having seen anything outside the grounds of Beau Rivage for so many years. It was unimaginable.

I stepped forward nervously. "Welcome home, grandmother." The word sounded strange in my mouth, but she smiled up at me. I hadn't realised just how tiny she was the day we saw her at the asylum. "Come in. Did you have a good journey? Are you tired? Would you like some tea? Oh dear, I'm babbling, aren't I?"

"Yes, my dear," she said. "And I would love a cup of tea, thank you."

I led her upstairs, Floss, Jo and Ellen following closely, and unusually silently, behind. I opened the door to the rooms we had prepared for her and she gasped. "Oh! Primrose yellow! How beautiful. It's so pretty, just like the room I wanted when..." A

THE DEVIL'S DRAPER

troubled look crossed her face and I gestured for her to come with me to the window.

"We thought you might like the view. That's Blythswood Square. We can go for a stroll there later, once you've rested."

A knock on the door announced the arrival of Mrs Dugan, red in the face and puffing, carrying a huge tray. One of the maids was hovering behind her, looking annoyed at having her job taken away from her. Floss smiled. "Well, Mrs Dugan, it's not often we see you up here."

Mrs Dugan had the grace to look embarrassed. "I'm sorry, ma'am. I just wanted to welcome the lady."

"That's perfectly fine, Mrs Dugan. I'm sure we aren't ones to stand on ceremony, not on a special day like today."

Mrs Dugan looked relieved and put the tray down on the table we had carefully positioned for the purpose. She gave an unpractised curtsey. "Welcome, Mrs...Miss..." She looked at Ellen, horrified. This was something we hadn't discussed and she continued hurriedly. "I've made you something nice. I hope you like it."

My grandmother looked at the plates of glistening pithiviers and smiled. "My favourite," she said. "Thank you, Mrs Dugan."

Floss cut her a generous slice of each of the pies and handed her a cup of tea. "Well, Lillias, you've met most of the household now. This, as you've just gathered, is Mrs Dugan, our wonderful cook; this is Ellen, who has been with us for many years; and this is Minnie, one of our two housemaids. You'll meet young Jane very soon. And Mrs Dugan has revealed to us that we have neglected to ask you how you would like to be known. At Beau Rivage they referred to you as Mrs Strang. Is that...?"

My grandmother shook her head, firmly. "I'd prefer to be known as Miss Gilfillan if that's...if that's acceptable? And, of course, as Lillias to you and Josephine." She clutched my hand, surprisingly firmly. "And to Mabel...well, I loved it when you called me grandmother."

Floss folded her in her arms. "Of course, Lillias. Well, welcome to our household of women. Welcome *home*."

MONDAY 26TH JULY 1920
JOHNNIE

Today, Johnnie's assignment for the day was Copland & Lye. Although it meant she had to wear a dress, this was always an assignment that Johnnie relished. It didn't come round very often, as Meg made sure that none of them visited the same haunts on a regular basis, so that their faces wouldn't become known. But it was one of Johnnie's favourites amongst Glasgow's department stores. It wasn't as tall as its neighbour, Pettigrew and Stephens, but it was grand and imposing, with its spectacular stairwell flanked by parlour palms. Standing on the stairwell galleries gave a good view of all departments. And, more importantly, its exits front and back on Sauchiehall Street and Bath Street made it perfect for her purposes.

Johnnie strode confidently through the store. In her navy gabardine, tailor-made costume, she was smart enough to blend in, without drawing undue attention. Her hat, with its front brim and huge navy bow, helped to hide her face and the carpetbag she carried was large, but not outrageously so. Her first task was to check the number and whereabouts of the security guards. Copland & Lye was so large that there were never enough for every department. Given the Glasgow Fair holidays, it was likely that there wouldn't even be enough to have a man on every floor. Meg had particularly requested furs today, so Johnnie was hoping that floor would be security free.

The silk department was her favourite and she walked through it slowly, stroking the satins and silks, the cashmeres and crepes and the jewel-coloured stacks of French velour. To anyone watching, she would have seemed like a woman of means without a care in the world, passing time before a luncheon appointment. In actual fact, she was taking in everything and everybody, as she made her

THE DEVIL'S DRAPER

way to the fur department. There were always fine furs to be had at Copland & Lye, even in the summer months.

She wasn't to go for the big stuff, Meg had told her, instead, she was to concentrate on the collars, muffs and neck and shoulder capes. As she ran her fingers across several of the furs, she wondered about the animals who had once inhabited those warm, soft skins. Nobody was around and, in a matter of seconds, she had swept a blue wolf muff, an opossum collar, a mink stole, an ermine collar and two fox shoulder capes into her bag, slipping them under the shawl she had brought with her. From there, she made her way to the gentlemen's department where she had spotted a beautiful paisley silk dressing gown that she wanted for herself. This she paid for, waiting patiently for the young man behind the counter to wrap the parcel.

Finally, the treat she had been looking forward to: a cup of Earl Grey tea and a plate of dainty sandwiches in the tea room, along with the store's famous pineapple cakes, all with the sounds of the live orchestra playing in the background. Copland's tea room was special, since it was situated around the stairwell. Nobody would expect someone who had just stolen over a hundred guineas' worth of furs to hang around in the shop. From there, Johnnie could watch what was going on elsewhere in the store and it would give her the chance to see if any of the store detectives were watching *her*.

After a leisurely tea, Johnnie tossed a few pennies onto the table, picked up her bag, and walked casually to the Bath Street exit, stopping on the way to buy Meg a pair of llama wool stockings; she was always complaining about her feet being cold in the winter. Nobody put a hand on her shoulder, nobody followed her out, nobody shouted, "Stop, thief!" Nobody, in fact, had even noticed her. Of *that,* she was sure.

THURSDAY 29TH JULY 1920
BEATRICE

The files on Beatrice's desk were in three small, neat piles: young women she'd placed at Arrol's who had told her of assaults by Hector Arrol, those who hadn't, and those she hadn't been able to contact. The pile of those who'd told her of assaults was the biggest. She needed to get into Arrol's and find out for herself, so here she was, on the phone, waiting to speak to Hector Arrol himself.

"Mrs Price?" The voice was cheery and self-assured.

She leaned forward and put her elbows on the desk, twirling the cord with her free hand. "Yes. Mr Arrol?"

"Hector Arrol, yes. Grand to speak to you Mrs Price. We've been very impressed with the girls you've sent to us in the past. How can I help you?

"Well, that's exactly why I'm calling, Mr Arrol. I'd like to set up a meeting with you to ensure your satisfaction with our young ladies and to see how we can improve our service to you in the future." There was silence on the other end of the phone. "It's something I like to do for all my important clients." Nothing wrong with a little flattery to butter him up. The more important the man, the more they responded to being reminded of it.

"Ah, well, that's very commendable indeed, Mrs Price. If only more businesses took the same pride in their work these days, hmmm?"

"Yes, indeed, Mr Arrol."

"Call me Hector, my dear lady. I do detest ceremony."

"Thank you, Hector. So would it be possible to come to your office for a chat?"

There was no response for a moment, but Beatrice heard the sound of distant raised voices on the other end of the phone. Then

THE DEVIL'S DRAPER

came Hector Arrol's voice, slightly muffled, and not quite as cheery. "Again? Goddammit, man, can't you stop them? They're making a laughing stock of us." Beatrice strained to hear the response, but was unable to make out the words. Then Arrol spoke again. "Well, don't just stand there. Go and do something about it. Are they sleeping?" He mumbled to himself for a second before speaking more clearly into the telephone. "Sorry about that, Mrs Price. Here, I don't suppose you have any men on your books, do you, hmmmm?"

"Men?"

"Yes. Is it just ladies you place in employment?"

"Well, yes, I'm afraid it is. Why?"

Arrol sighed. "We've been experiencing a rather rampant spate of shoplifting recently. Very bold, they are, too, I must say. We just don't have enough security men and those that we do have seem to be letting these women simply walk past them dressed in three layers of our furs, without batting an eyelid. And it's not just us. It's affecting all the top department stores: Copland & Lye, Pettigrew and Stephens. And Treron's poached the only two of our security guards who apparently have eyes. As of now, I have openings for four strong men who won't fall asleep on the job and can start on Monday."

An idea came to Beatrice. "And does it have to be men?"

"Does it have to...? Well, I should say so, yes. How's a woman supposed to strong-arm a shoplifter, hmm?"

"Oh, I think I can supply a *very* suitable woman, Hector. Very suitable indeed. I'll see you on Monday."

FRIDAY 30TH JULY 1920
MABEL

"Well, what do you think?" I was in my dressing room, surveying the array of dresses hanging on display around the room. Floss and my grandmother were sitting watching, as I paced around the room picking up one and then another, holding them against me. Copper lace over copper ninon, jade silk tricotine, cherry silk net.

"I favour the blue crepe de chine. You always look delightful in that." It was Floss' favourite, I knew. But for this evening's festivities, I didn't think it would do.

"I need something with more impact, something which will get me noticed." I stood back and surveyed the dresses.

"The gold one is so pretty." Lillias' hands were clasped in front of her face.

She was referring to a gold silk charmeuse with an intricate champagne lace overlay, which I had never worn. The skirt was a two-tier effect and there was an accompanying bolero in gold taffeta, embroidered with silver. I had bought it on a whim, but it always felt too showy for me to feel comfortable in. I smiled at my grandmother. She was right; it was just what I was looking for tonight. "Perfect," I said.

Floss helped me to get into the dress and I added a pair of champagne dancing shoes with gold embroidery, a pearl necklace with turquoise pendants, matching earrings and a large diamond ring that belonged to Floss, but which was so ostentatious that she never wore it. She had suggested it for this evening's shenanigans on the basis that it was 'so gaudy that all the thieves in the place will be drawn to it like magpies'. I topped it all off with an unusually frivolous turban of gold tissue, adorned with parrot feathers. Tonight was all about flamboyance.

THE DEVIL'S DRAPER

My grandmother clapped her hands, delightedly. "Oh! This young man of yours will love it!" I'd tried to tell her that Lorrimer wasn't my young man, but she didn't really understand. Nor did she understand my job, or even why I had one in the first place. And why should she? She had been locked away from everything for the last forty-two years.

I felt a rush of affection for her and smiled, thinking that even the War had passed her by and left her untouched. Perhaps that, at least, was something positive to take from her experiences. She had found the journey here from the asylum overwhelming, and it wasn't all down to Jo's driving. Glasgow had been a revelation to her: the traffic, the noise, the bustle, the smoke, the cramped buildings...She hadn't been out since she arrived. We didn't want to swap one set of four walls for another, no matter how comfortable those walls were. We asked her daily if she wanted to take the air, but she seemed quite happy inside.

I looked at my watch. "I'd better go. Lorrimer will soon be here and I don't want to keep him waiting."

"Are you not going to introduce us, my dear?"

Floss had a wicked smile on her face. "Introduce Inspector Lorrimer? I think not, Floss. The poor man is already in high dudgeon at having to take me dining and dancing. And, what's worse, having Jo drive us. He was all for driving us himself in that scruffy old Ford automobile of his, or getting a taxi-cab, until I told him that we needed to arrive in style if we were to give the right impression. No, Jo's going to honk the horn when he arrives. And you are *not* to accompany me outside."

As if on cue, the horn honked. I kissed Floss on the tip of her nose and grandmother on the top of her head and dashed downstairs, plucking my black satin evening cloak out of Ellen's outstretched hand as I dashed past her. "Enjoy yourself, Miss Mabel!"

"Unlikely, Ellen, but thank you."

Lorrimer and Jo were standing by the Hispano-Suiza. Lorrimer's eyes opened wide when he saw me – I presumed it was

THE DEVIL'S DRAPER

the hat – and before he could step forward, Jo reached for the handle and opened the door for me with a mock bow. "Why, thank you," I said, as she handed me inside. Lorrimer climbed in stiffly beside me and nodded at me.

Jo climbed into the front seat. "What time do you want me to pick you up?"

"Oh heavens, no. We'll walk, Jo. We don't need to make an impression on the way out. But thank you."

"Well, you'll certainly make an impression in *that* hat, my dear, so I don't think you need to worry." I stuck my tongue out at her.

We drove the short way to Chez Antoine in silence. I could tell this was going to be a long evening. As we pulled up smoothly outside, Jo jumped out and opened the door for me. "Madam," she said, playing her part perfectly.

It was only then I noticed that she had dressed for the occasion, in a smart grey outfit that I didn't think I had ever seen before. I took her outstretched gloved hand. "Tell me you didn't buy that get-up just to drive us around the corner."

"Don't be ridiculous, Mabel," she muttered under her breath. "It's one I wore for driving during the War. I took it up and tweaked it here and there."

"Well, you look just the thing." Lorrimer came around the car and held out his arm, which I took, with a flourish. "See you later, Jo." She touched her hat, got back into the car and drove off.

"Well, Inspector Lorrimer, I suppose we should go in and meet our fate." He nodded glumly at me and we stepped towards the door. A doorman bowed low and opened the door for us. We swanned in as if we belonged. Lorrimer handed our outerwear to the young woman at the cloakroom and we were swiftly shown to our table. I was pleased to see that it was in a prominent position, where we could see everything and where, more importantly, *we* could be seen. If anyone was here for nefarious purposes, they couldn't help but notice my twinkling jewels, especially the ostentatious diamond ring, in competition with the glistening ceiling of gold

THE DEVIL'S DRAPER

mosaic, with its inlay of jade, mother of pearl and turquoise.

Lorrimer handed me to my seat, looking me up and down. "You look very nice, Miss Adair," he said, rather stiffly.

"Oh dear."

He looked puzzled. "Why do you say 'Oh dear'?"

"Well, 'very nice' wasn't exactly the look I was going for when I dressed this evening." I picked up the menu. "In fact, it's rather insulting."

He looked mortified. "I'm terribly sorry, Miss Adair. I meant that you look…"

I decided to put him out of his misery. "Really, I'm just joking. Now," I leaned forward and lowered my voice, "I think we ought to lose the 'Miss Adair' and 'Inspector Lorrimer' thing, oughtn't we? That will really give us away."

"Yes, you're right, Miss…Mabel."

"Excellent, James. And do try and look as though you're enjoying yourself in my scintillating company. Anyone would think this is to be your last meal before you head to the gallows." A small smile flitted across his lips and I laughed. "Well, that's a start, I suppose."

We sat for a moment considering the menu. "It would appear that we have a slight problem, Mabel."

"We do?"

"Yes," he gestured at the menu in his hand. "No prices. How are we to comply with Superintendent Orr's entirely reasonable command that we don't pick the most expensive items on the menu? Remember? 'No oysters, no rump steak, and absolutely no cocktails'?"

"Oh heavens, I have absolutely no idea. It's rather a conundrum, isn't it?" We sat in silence for a moment longer. "Well, I rather fancy the Royal Whitstable Oysters, followed by the Sole Mornay, since there appears to be no rump steak on the menu. What about you?"

Lorrimer laughed. "Excellent choices. I, too, will have the

THE DEVIL'S DRAPER

oysters, followed, I think, by the roast grouse with orange salad. Cocktail?"

"Oh, I should say so, James. A Clover Club, if you please."

He signalled for the waiter and ordered my cocktail and an Old-Fashioned for himself, before ordering the food for both of us and we sat back to survey the room. "Any likely-looking candidates, Mabel?"

The restaurant was almost full and everyone looked to be having a marvellous time. "I would say just about everyone looks quite roguish. It seems to be one of those places. Have you ever been here before?"

"Me?" He snorted. "I'm afraid I don't go dancing very often." He gestured to his empty sleeve. "This isn't conducive to showing a lady a good time on the dance floor."

This was the first time he had made an open reference to his injury. While many of the other police officers spoke quite frequently about their experiences in the Great War, in a way that seemed to bond them, I had never heard Lorrimer take part in these conversations. The visible evidence of his missing arm and the puckered skin on one side of his neck that he was always at pains to disguise was all I had to go on, and I certainly wasn't going to ask him. "Well, we shall see about that later," was all I said.

Instead, we talked of other things. Strictly speaking, *I* talked of other things and Lorrimer joined in cautiously from time to time, revealing nothing but, I realised, managing to elicit a great deal of personal information from me.

I finished up the delicious strawberry Melba with punch jelly I had plumped for as dessert and took a sip of the rather fine 1908 Chateau Margaux, which the sommelier had recommended. We had also taken his advice and ordered a bottle of Chablis, which he had said was the only possible wine to drink with the oysters, and I could feel that my cheeks were flushed. Doubtless that was another reason I had revealed so much about myself. "Well, James, it seems that you now know every little thing about me and I still know nothing about you."

He laughed. "I think not. I know that you like jazz, despise tennis, can play Maple Leaf Rag on the piano, think that Miss Swanson shouldn't have got married at all in *Don't Change Your Husband*, enjoyed John Barrymore in *Dr Jekyll and Mr Hyde* and highly recommend Susan Glaspell's *Trifles* and Charlotte Perkins Gilman's *The Yellow Wallpaper*. Do I have that all correctly?"

I was impressed that he remembered it all, but mostly that he had actually been listening in the first place. "Indeed you do."

"And does that constitute knowing everything about you?"

"Indeed it does not. In fact, it makes me sound quite shallow."

"I disagree. Your mention of Susan Glaspell intrigues me, but doesn't surprise me. I was down in London last year and saw the play in Covent Garden in a quartet of plays from the Pioneer Players. It was very much my favourite of the four plays, although I also enjoyed Miss Christopher St John's play, too." He smiled slightly. "Miss Adair, your eyebrows are almost to your hairline. Can I surmise from the height of them that you're surprised that I should be such a supporter of feminism?"

I could feel my cheeks going even redder. I was very shocked. I didn't have him down as a particular supporter of women's rights but didn't want to offend him, so I avoided the question. "My adoptive mother, Florence Adair and her friend Jo, know Edy Craig, the founder of the Pioneer Players, and Chris St John very well." It was my turn to shock *him*. "Edy and Chris visited them when Floss and Jo were released from prison." I couldn't resist. "Inspector Lorrimer, your eyebrows are almost to your hairline. Can I surmise from the height of them that you're surprised that my adoptive mother has languished in prison on several occasions?"

Before he could answer, the band, who had been playing softly throughout our dinner, burst into life with a pacy rendition of *Someday Sweetheart*. "Come along, James. Let's get ourselves seen on the dance floor." He looked hesitant. "Do come on. It's a one-step – it's basically just walking, and I know you can do that."

THE DEVIL'S DRAPER

He reluctantly stood and led me to the dance floor. He was a remarkably good dancer, despite having only one arm and we stayed up for another one-step, two Foxtrots and a Hesitation, only sitting back down for the Argentine Tango. "I draw the line there, Mabel," he said, actually laughing, as we sat back down.

"Enough of the enjoyment anyway, we need to get to work." I picked up my bag. "I'm going to the rest room. Let's hope someone follows me in to offer me cocaine."

The ladies' rest room, too, was very grand, although much calmer. Blue velvet couches, marble everywhere, floor to ceiling mirrors and what seemed like hundreds of vases of flowers drew you in and invited you to stay for a while. I was happy to accept the invitation, sitting on one of the comfortable couches and fanning myself.

However, the exercise was pointless. The only thing I was offered was a spray of perfume from the young woman stationed in the rest room. She had quite the array: La Reine d'Egypt, Phul-Nana, April Violets, Mitsouko. My own favourite, and the one I was wearing this evening – Narcisse Noir, with its rich scent of incense and orange blossom - was not amongst them, so I declined. I looked at my watch. I'd been in there fifteen minutes; James would be starting to worry I'd been kidnapped. As the door opened, I heard the strains of *I'll See you in C-U-B-A* starting. It was one of my favourites, so I hurried out and grabbed James for yet another Foxtrot.

As we made our way smartly around the beautifully-sprung dance floor, I sighed. "Well, this has been rather a wash-out, hasn't it?"

"Thank you, Mabel." His voice was dry.

"Oh, I didn't mean that!"

He laughed. "I know. And yes, it has. But it does mean one thing, you know."

"What's that?"

"Dinner's on Superintendent Orr again tomorrow."

Saturday 31st July 1920
Johnnie

Johnnie waited until everyone had left the war room. Meg didn't like anyone questioning her methods. "I thought we weren't having anything to do with drugs, Meg."

"We're not, hen. You ken how I feel about that."

Johnnie nodded. They had talked about this because of the similarities in their stories. Meg's father had been an opium fiend and Meg had had to drag him out of opium dens across the city from when she was ten years old, until he died six years later. Not only that, it didn't make sense from a business perspective either. Glasgow was too full of gangs not afraid to leave a chib mark on anyone muscling in on their territory.

"Then why are we selling drugs in restaurants and clubs?"

Meg smiled. "We're *no'* hen. It's jist Epsom salts or boric acid, that's aw'. They're good fur yiz."

Johnnie folded her arms. "Boric acid is poisonous."

"Aw, hen, not as poisonous as cocaine."

"And that young woman who was drugged so that we could steal her jewels; that wasn't Epsom salts."

"Naw, but it wasn't drugs. That was just…it was just a sleeping draught. She wasnae harmed."

Johnnie knew what Meg had been about to say. Veronal. It was just Veronal. "You said we wouldn't be involved with drugs."

"An' we're *no'*."

"I don't want anything to do with it."

Meg shrugged. "An' I promise I'll no' send ye tae the clubs. There's plenty for you tae do that isnae that. An' you should be getting' away to it the noo. Queen Street Station will be buzzin'. You don't want tae miss the rush."

THE DEVIL'S DRAPER

Johnnie left the building, an unaccustomed knot in the pit of her stomach. She'd never argued with Meg and she turned the conversation over and over in her mind. Meg knew about her maw and she'd promised. She drew a sleeve across her eyes, put her hands in the pockets of her suit, pulled her cap down over her ears and set off for Queen Street, her feet pounding angrily on the pavement. Her maw had died of an overdose of Veronal. Johnnie had been five at the time. She'd woken up and discovered that her maw was still asleep. Johnnie had never seen her maw asleep. She was always doing something. Johnnie had patted her maw's face. She had looked rosy-cheeked, which was funny, because her maw was always pale and drawn. Next to her were several little glass bottles with labels on which Johnnie couldn't read, but which she'd later been told by the landlady was Veronal. It was such a pretty word, magical and strange, Johnnie had thought back then. She breathed the name now, but now it was dark and evil, definitely not a pretty word.

Johnnie hadn't been able to rouse her maw and had gone to fetch the landlady, who'd screamed and rushed off, coming back with a doctor. Johnnie had watched him try and put a tube down into her maw's stomach, and inject her with something, but she still hadn't opened her eyes.

Once she was old enough to understand, Johnnie had forgiven her mother. She'd forgiven the father who had left them, tempted by an easier life in Canada. She'd forgiven the new baby in her mother's belly. And she'd even forgiven the man who put it there, in return for a few pennies. But she hadn't been able to forgive herself for being sound asleep while her mother died on the bed next to her. And she hated the drug which had done it to her.

She had lived with her grandfather for a while after that, but then he'd started to cough. That's what she remembered of him most, the cough. She'd looked after him until there was nothing of him left to look after and then she'd been on her own. The streets had been about to swallow her up, when Big Annie had found her and Meg had taken her in, still a wee lassie. And St Thenue's Avengers had been her family ever since. The drug trade had no place in that family. For the first time, Johnnie was dissatisfied with her career choice.

MONDAY 2ND AUGUST 1920
MABEL

I sat at my desk, yawning. Three nights in a row of dancing, drinking and fine food had taken it out of me. And we had nothing to show for it either. Well, nothing other than a flea in the ear from Superintendent Orr and some ribbing from the other police officers. Luckily, James had taken the brunt of both of those. Hardly any of the other policemen ever spoke to me, so that cloud, at least, had a silver lining.

As punishment – it was unspecified as to whether this was for not catching any criminals or eating too many oysters – Orr had set me to typing up statements. For today, as had happened on many other occasions, I was to act as secretary to the rest of the station, something which I knew Orr – and many of the other men – felt was a position more suited to me. Typing up the statements was doubly galling. Not only was it not my job, but it also served to remind me that almost everyone else here was trusted to do the actual policing. I say almost everyone. Emily Miller, the other woman employed as a 'Statement Taker' was allowed to do her job with minimal interference from Superintendent Orr. Miss Miller's father was a cabinetmaker, a good, honest craftsman; whereas I didn't have a father, just an unmarried adoptive mother who'd been a Suffragette. And Miss Miller kept her head down and was good at her job. I, on the other hand, stuck my nose in where it wasn't wanted. Orr had never forgiven me for what he termed 'Miss Adair's antics' the previous year, when I had found a dead body and was, as he saw it, the instigator of one of his best men being arrested. He conveniently forgot that that man was a murderer, an abuser of women – of *children*, in fact, and the cause of many, many more deaths than the one he went to prison for. He had been a rotten apple in a barrel that contained very few good ones, as far as I was concerned.

I wondered, not for the first time, if this job really was for me after all. I had done the job I had entered the police force to do – solving the murder of my mother – and could, if I wanted, sit and embroider all day, every day for the rest of my life. But I had too much fire in my belly for that. I'd only been here a few months, but I was desperate to make a difference to the lives of women, whether they were criminals, victims, or witnesses. None escaped from a police encounter unscathed. I led a privileged life and I wanted and needed to use that privilege for good, even if it made my own existence uncomfortable. It was the least I could do.

I sighed. It was nearly lunchtime. I would go and see Winnie. She always made me feel better and would listen to my moans and worries with kindness and humour, dispensing wise words, welcome practicality and hot food.

MONDAY 2ND AUGUST 1920
BEATRICE

Beatrice was killing time before her meeting with Hector Arrol by reading the Daily Record. A new bill had been introduced to deal with crime in Ireland; Scottish workers were to strike later in August to protest rent increases; a houseboat had overturned in Loch Lomond. She turned the page and gasped as a name caught her eye. She took her feet off her desk and spread out the newspaper on it so that she could study the article more closely.

'Young Woman's Desperate Act: "Hard to leave you".'

An inquest was held in Glasgow on Friday, concerning the death of Elsie McNiven, who on Thursday morning was found dead in the kitchen at an address in Maudslie Street, Partick, with her head in a gas oven. The first witness called was the girl's mother, Mary McNiven. She identified the body and stated that her daughter was 17 years of age. Mrs McNiven had left the house at 7 o'clock on Thursday evening to visit a sick friend and when she left, her daughter was in the kitchen giving the cat its supper. Mrs McNiven told the inquest that her daughter had been upset recently, due to an assault that had taken place at her most recent place of employment, and that as a result, she would not take her food and she felt there was nothing in life for her. She had, on several occasions, told her mother that she wished she could die, but that there was nothing sufficiently unusual about her daughter's manner to attract her attention on that particular night.

When the girl's mother returned at 9 o'clock, she smelt gas when she opened the door. She rushed into the kitchen, where she saw the deceased lying on the floor, her head resting on a pillow in the gas stove oven, with the gas turned on. She was wearing her nightgown, with her feet and legs bare. The witness pulled her out and laid her on her back near the door, which she opened to let air in.

Mrs McNiven went to a neighbour's for help. A doctor was at once sent for but when he arrived the girl was apparently already dead, with her face and limbs being quite cold, but with some warmth in the trunk. Dr Harries thought she must have committed the act shortly before he was called.

The police found a letter in the young woman's bedroom addressed to her mother. The letter read: "My dearest mother, I find it hard to leave you, but I must. I am scared and ashamed. I am going to have a baby and I don't want to. Please forgive me. Your, Elsie."

A postmortem examination was carried out. All the organs were healthy, but there was evidence of asphyxia in the lungs due to inhalation of coal gas. There were no marks of violence and nothing to indicate any struggle. There was no sign of corrosive or narcotic poisoning. The deceased was not pregnant, despite the contents of the note. The inquest concluded that the deceased took her own life while the state of her mind was unbalanced.'

Beatrice dabbed at her eyes with her handkerchief. She stood up and took her hat from the coat stand, pinning it in place on her head.

Beatrice took her frustrations out on the pavement. She could feel her cheeks turning pink from the exertion. Passers-by moved speedily out of her way and she was glad of it. Today, she moved out of the way for no-one. She lifted her chin and pulled her hat more firmly down on her head. She thought about Elsie, the nervous and shy young woman who had come to her a few months ago looking for a job, and what she must have suffered to do that to herself. Beatrice owed it to Elsie, and to her mother, and to all the other young girls she had placed at Arrol's, to find out what was happening and to do something about it. She was under no illusions that Hector Arrol would be punished for his actions – her trip to the police station and that horrible phone conversation had confirmed that for her – but she would do her level best to make sure that he would never be able to do it again.

Arrol's took up a whole block of Sauchiehall Street. Like several of the other department stores, it had two entrances – a grand one on Sauchiehall Street with marble pillars and gleaming brass handles on the doors, and one slightly less grand on Bath Street. An impressive double staircase in the centre of the

THE DEVIL'S DRAPER

entrance foyer swept up and down to various departments. The ground floor was toiletries, small goods and knick-knacks, as well as a constantly changing display, depending on the season. At the moment, these were of holiday goods – bathing costumes, suitcases, hosiery, summer hats, Windsor scarves. The basement was cutlery and china, table linens and towels and a whole array of modern labour-saving devices, as well as a well-appointed café that served a very good luncheon. The first floor was ladieswear, the second children's wear, gentlemen's outfits, and shoes, as well as a hairdressing department, and the third floor was drapery, haberdashery and the various offices of the department store.

It was to the offices that Beatrice was headed and she chose to take the stairs to expend some excess of energy. The offices were to the very back of the shop, a walnut-panelled wall with a discreet door marked 'Staff Only' being the only outward sign of what lay behind it. Beatrice rang the buzzer and a soberly, but smartly dressed, middle-aged woman opened the door and ushered her in.

The woman led Beatrice past several doors and into a large space, with a window looking out towards the rest of the offices. The furniture consisted of two large walnut desks and a settee upholstered in polished Morocco and brown velveteen. The smart woman went to sit down behind one of the desks. The other was empty. "Mr Arrol will be with you in a few moments".

She turned to her typewriter and typed something with impressive speed. A few minutes later, a telephone on her desk rang and she picked up the receiver and listened a moment. "Yes, Mr Arrol, of course." She stood up and gestured to Beatrice to follow her. She opened a double door in the back wall of the office and ushered Beatrice in.

Hector Arrol was sitting behind a huge, shiny desk. Other than an inkwell and blotter, it was entirely empty. The office was on the corner of the building and light streamed in from two sides of the room. Arrol stood and held out his hand. "Mrs Price, Beatrice. Delightful to meet you in person. Thank you for coming."

THE DEVIL'S DRAPER

He was a tall, handsome man with a fine head of silver hair, close-cropped and almost military in style. He appeared to be in his late fifties, but Beatrice knew he was a few years older than that. "Thank you for seeing me, Mr Arrol."

He waggled a finger at her. "Now, now, Beatrice. Hector, if you please. I have to admit, I was intrigued by your suggestion. Until now, all our security people have been men. Isn't your suggestion rather...unusual, hmmmm?" As he spoke, he gestured to her to sit.

Beatrice settled herself in the comfortable armchair and smoothed her skirt. "Not at all. Women have been employed by department stores like yours for many years. Selfridges in London had a very successful woman working for them before the War, for example. And if I may suggest, the fact that you have all your security guards wearing braided jackets and hats does you no favours."

He seemed taken aback. "It's our tradition. With the exception of myself and my sons, all our staff wear uniforms with the Arrol's braiding."

"Well, with what I'm suggesting, that would need to change. The best store detectives are those who go unnoticed. In a uniform, they're easy to spot and avoid."

Arrol nodded. "Perhaps, perhaps. We have been losing rather a lot of stock lately, thanks to these so-called Avengers." He picked up a letter opener and toyed with it, pursing his lips. "Avengers, indeed. Just a nasty gang of thieves. But tell me, why should I employ you? Why not just have my men wear their ordinary clothes, hmm?"

The sun was streaming in through the window behind him and Beatrice wondered if he had ushered her to this seat on purpose, so that she would be at a disadvantage with the sun in her eyes. "Well, sometimes it takes a woman to catch a woman. And besides, even the most unassuming of men is going to stick out like a sore thumb in the lingerie department, isn't he?"

THE DEVIL'S DRAPER

He let out a sharp bark of laughter. "You may be right about that, Beatrice. But I am at a loss to understand why you, yourself, would like the job. After all, you are the owner of what I understand is a very successful employment agency. Surely you have enough on your plate, hmm?"

Beatrice had been expecting this question. "Well, when it comes to one of our best clients, I do like to get the lie of the land. It helps me to be better able to place the most appropriate young ladies with you. And what better way to do that than to be actually on the ground, as it were."

Once again, Arrol nodded slowly. "Of course. That makes absolute sense, dear lady." He steepled his forefingers and tapped them against his lips, thinking. "Yes, I think that's a splendid idea." He looked at his watch. "Now, it's time for my daily perambulation around the store. In the mornings, I'm here in the office very early, seeing to urgent business matters. Then I visit all areas of the store. I like to keep the staff on their toes, you know." His smile was without humour. "And in the afternoons, I take charge of the drapery and haberdashery departments. It's how Arrol's started many years ago under my great-grandfather and I think it's important to lead by example. Besides, it's something I enjoy doing. Tradition, hmm?"

He stood up and opened the door for her. "I'll introduce you to my sons. They each have charge of a department." Again, he smiled. "I like to foster a little healthy competition between them. After all, they will take all this over one day."

He looked at Beatrice as if waiting for comment. She stood and looked him straight in the eyes, almost as tall as he was. "Well, they'll be inheriting a very fine establishment, Mr Arrol. Hector."

He looked pleased with her response and ushered her along the corridor in front of him. "Indeed, indeed. I inherited the store from my own father, and he from his. Of course, in my great-grandfather's day, it was a very small concern, simply a small draper's shop, hmm? My grandfather built it up and my father moved us to this magnificent building. And I, of course, have expanded and improved it still further. I rather think it is one of the best department stores in Glasgow, hmm?"

This habit of his was getting annoying. It clearly wasn't a question, more of an affectation, and he was gearing up to launch into yet another blustering statement of his own importance, but she decided to treat this one as if it required an answer. "Oh, I'm sure it is, Hector. It's rather a good thing that you have *three* sons to take it over; it's surely too big for only one person to manage."

Again, he looked pleased with her response. "Yes. My daughter works here too."

This was the first time he had mentioned a daughter and Beatrice was surprised. "Ah, and does she also manage a department?" She was almost certain of what the answer would be.

"Eliza? No. My oldest son, Alfred, is in charge of our clothing departments. We have two floors dedicated to fashion and I would say they are our most popular departments. Very popular, indeed. Eliza is the face of the Ladieswear section, but Alfred is in charge. Now, this floor is my domain, so we will come back here last of all, hmmmm?"

As they went down the stairs, Hector Arrol boasted about the stock, the layout, the high class of customers, and even the very staircase itself.

Beatrice formed a swift opinion of each of his children, after the very brief introduction to each: Alfred was a balding young man in his late thirties, and almost as pompous as his father. Gilbert, in his mid-thirties, was very polite and proper, but much more relaxed. He was very keen to show her around the basement, with its household goods and beautifully laid out café. The youngest son, Roderick, was full of nervous energy and his focus was very much on pleasing his father, rather than on showing Beatrice around. The ground floor displays were, Hector Arrol said, entirely Roderick's doing and Beatrice got the impression from the tone of his voice that Hector Arrol wasn't entirely happy with their extravagance.

THE DEVIL'S DRAPER

Finally, seemingly as an afterthought, Beatrice was introduced to Arrol's daughter, Eliza, who Arrol told her, was actually the oldest of his four children. She had a quiet confidence about her that made Beatrice determine to get to know her better.

When everything was signed and sealed back in Hector Arrol's office and Beatrice had a starting date of the very next day, Arrol himself walked her back down the flights of stairs to the exit. Beatrice threw out a casual question. "Do you recall Elsie McNiven?"

He pursed his lips and furrowed his brow. "McNiven...no, the name doesn't mean anything. Should it?

"Oh, perhaps not. After all, I'm sure you don't speak to every young woman who takes a job in your store. I placed her with you a few months ago." Beatrice placed a hand on the banister and turned to look at him.

"I see. Well, as you correctly state, I don't speak to all the staff we employ, hmmmm?" He waved a hand expansively towards the floors below them. "As you can see, we have an extremely large staff. Just over four hundred, in fact."

"Impressive." He looked suitably pleased, but Beatrice pressed on as they carried on making their way down the wide staircase. "I do believe I actually placed Elsie in your own department. Yes, drapery, that was it. Of course, she wasn't here for very long; she left quite abruptly, in fact."

Arrol seemed bored. "Really? Well, these young girls come and go, don't they? It's difficult to keep up with them all. I have found that since the War it's been more difficult to keep staff, but it's been more noticeable with young women in particular – all the fault of this female emancipation nonsense, hmmmm? Well, that and the bad influences from America: jazz, lipstick, face powder and the like. As a result, they seem to want to flit from one thing to the next. Have you found that, Mrs Price?"

"Actually, no. All the young women I've placed have been quite steady young women."

It was Arrol's turn to stop and he put his hand on her arm. "Oh, please, don't get me wrong, Beatrice. I didn't mean to insinuate that you're sending us flibbertigibbets. I simply meant that the War seems to have...well...rather *unsettled* people. And, of course, it can't be easy being a young woman today. All these surplus girls. Society seems very different to us from how it was before, do you not think, hmmmm?"

"Perhaps." Beatrice was determined not to let herself be sidetracked. She sighed. "Such an awful shame about Elsie."

"Elsie? Ah, yes, the young woman you say worked here." He carried on walking and it clearly wasn't a question, but Beatrice decided to treat his comment as if it were.

"Yes. Unfortunately, Elsie took her own life just last week. She thought she was going to have a baby and couldn't see any other way out."

They had reached the ground floor and Arrol ushered her over to the Sauchiehall Street entrance. "How dreadful. Another sign of declining morals and standards, I'm afraid. We need to get back to sound Victorian values, don't we, Beatrice?"

TUESDAY 3RD AUGUST 1920
MABEL

I had decided to take my grandmother with me to see Winnie, so it was after work the next day when we got into Jo's car. Although Wilson Street wasn't far to walk and my grandmother was fit and sprightly, she was still wary about going outside. I didn't blame her. She had spent so many years locked up in the quiet environs of Beau Rivage, with familiar faces and a life lived at the slow and familiar pace of the stream that passed through the grounds, that Glasgow's streets held immeasurable terrors. When she had been committed, people travelled by horse-drawn carriage. Now, the horsepower involved in travel was altogether more powerful. She had seen cars, of course. They had arrived at the Asylum every day, bringing staff and visitors, but a car pulling up slowly on the gravel outside the house was a very different thing to being in one.

She turned her head from the window and smiled at me, placing a small, dry hand on my lap. "Such a lot of people, my dear. All these unfamiliar faces, I like to look at them. I spent all those years looking at all the same faces, most of them women."

I laid my own hand on top of hers and squeezed it. "It must be very strange."

"Oh, it is, in lots of different ways, but I think this is the strangest. In Beau Rivage, I knew everyone. I knew their habits and their little eccentricities; I'd heard their stories, seen them laugh, cry, sleep, wake up, eat…everything. Even the staff: wardresses, nurses, kitchen maids… we got to know them, too."

"Were they kind?"

She shrugged. "Some of them."

"And the doctors?"

She laughed. "Oh, no, we didn't really know the doctors. We only saw them from a distance, aloof and impatient as they did their weekly rounds."

"They didn't examine the patients?"

Jo brought the car to a temporary halt at a corner and my grandmother gazed as if entranced at the hats in a shop window. "Only if they were troublesome, or ill, and even then they didn't really speak to them." She turned her head back to me. "After the first few years, I think they examined me once a year, twice at most."

I gazed at her open-mouthed as Jo set off again. "But that's terrible! If they didn't examine people, how could they know whether they were…"

"Sane?" I nodded and she gave a sad smile. "Well, if you'd have asked me, I would have told you that most of the women in there were sane. Sad, yes, or distraught or confused, but many of them shouldn't have been in there at all."

We had tried not to ask her too many question about her life at Beau Rivage. She would tell us when she was ready. But I couldn't stop myself from blurting out: "But why..?"

It was her turn to squeeze *my* hand. "Some of them had lost babies, some had been badly treated, others had simply shown a spirit that was frowned upon."

The conversation didn't appear to be causing her too much distress so I pressed on. "How do you mean?"

"Well," she thought for a moment. "There was one young woman whose people had her sent there because she took a steamer to Luss and went into a hotel there."

She stopped, as if at the end of the story. I shook my head. "And did what?"

"Not a thing. Well, nothing extraordinary, anyway. She ordered a cup of tea. She was a lovely young woman. She'd been a schoolteacher; and she was very bright and inquisitive, quite a breath of fresh air."

I felt a catch in my throat. "What…what happened to her?"

"You can rest easy, my dear. Her people came and fetched her

THE DEVIL'S DRAPER

the following year."

She sat back and continued to look curiously out of the car windows, turning her head at every new sight, gazing up at the tops of buildings.

"It must have been horrible. I'm so sorry, grandmother."

She patted my knee. "Oh, don't be sorry, Mabel, my dear. We had some very pleasant times, too. I had Henrietta and Mary Grace with me every day." Her face clouded slightly. I realised how much she must miss them. "And once every two or three months, everyone came together for a dance, all the patients, men and women. It was a jolly affair, with ginger beer, aerated water and Barr's Iron Brew, along with empire biscuits, shortbread, spicy tipperary biscuits and delicate sandwiches. We had such fun."

"Men *and* women, together?"

"Oh, yes. We were all *quite* excited. Of course, the warders and wardresses watched their charges carefully and, at the first hint of hysteria or mania, the offending patient would be whisked away. The dances were only those of a very quiet type – quadrilles and waltzes and strathspeys; with jigs and reels being reserved for Hogmanay. I didn't dance, of course, just listened to the music. Oh, it was delightful, hearing the music and watching the dancing." She spoke with such a wistfulness that made me determined to hold a dance for her at the house.

Avoiding the main din and hubbub of the streets, Jo parked almost right outside Winnie's domain, the public toilets on Wilson Street. I helped Lillias through the heavy door that led to the quiet haven which had become so much a part of my life. The familiar scents of carbolic soap, polish and something delicious cooking on Winnie's stove came out to meet us. It should have been an uncomfortable and eye-watering mix of scents, but somehow it wasn't and I could feel my grandmother's hand on my arm relax, as the door closed behind us and she took in the scene around her.

As always, the gleaming white tiles were sparkling, the brass was shining and the glazed brick on the far wall was glowing with

THE DEVIL'S DRAPER

rich colour. We couldn't see the legs of the T that made up the space from where we stood, but I knew that Winnie was likely to be pottering around her domain in the left hand one and, as we made our way past the mahogany doors of the cubicles, her head popped around the corner.

She looked delighted to see me. "Mabel, hen!" She came around the corner and pulled me into a firm hug, her wiry frame a mixture of strength and softness. She held me at arm's length and looked me up and down disapprovingly. "Look at you. Not a pick on you. Come and get some of my pea and ham soup."

I laughed. "Winnie, according to you, I always look as though I'm starving. But I will have some of your delicious soup, thank you."

Winnie nodded, satisfied with this response and turned to my companion, bestowing a beaming smile her way. "And is this...?"

I pushed my grandmother gently forward. "Yes. This is my grandmother, Lillias Gilfillan."

My grandmother politely put out her hand, but Winnie ignored it, pulling my shocked grandmother into another of her bear hugs. "Aw, lovely to meet you, hen. Ah'm Winnie." She led my grandmother round to her little room, with its steaming soup pot on the small stove, its bookshelves and its two comfortable armchairs and settled my grandmother into one of them. "Now, ah'll get ye a bowl of soup and you can tell me all about everything."

THURSDAY 5TH AUGUST 1920
JOHNNIE

It was Johnnie's least favourite job. Not because she didn't love the Argyll Arcade itself, with its glass and cast-iron roof and its shops selling goods as varied as children's outfits and guns, musical instruments and wigs, pottery and wine to Glasgow's gentry; but because she was going to be working with other people. She didn't like relying on others for her safety and security, nor her purse. Not that either Lena or Big Annie were careless, but Johnnie simply didn't really trust anyone other than herself, and Meg, of course. The Argyll Arcade was also not a favourite with Johnnie, as the passageway was quite narrow and there were only two ways in and out, one at each end.

Johnnie had arrived early to check out which security guards were working today, as well as to treat herself to a toasted muffin in Cranston's Tea Rooms and a visit to the Clyde Model Dockyard with its tinplate rails and engines, rolling stock and engine sheds. She sauntered along the Arcade, striving to look casual, stopping to glance in each of the jewellers' windows as she passed, as though her gaze was caught by a pretty pair of earrings, or a sparkling ring, when really, she was looking to see how busy they were and how many staff were working today. Meg had given them some freedom to choose which jeweller's to pick and the choice was wide: Macgregor's, Johnston and Mackie, Boston's, Russell's, Todd's; none of them looked particularly busy, but Johnnie was most drawn to Porter & Sons.

She gave a brief nod to Big Annie and Lena when she spotted them strolling through the Arcade, just as she was, and gently inclined her head towards Porters. Big Annie looked stately as a battleship in black georgette crepe, trimmed with shiny ribbon and a matching hat with a veil, ostensibly to hide the sadness of

THE DEVIL'S DRAPER

a war widow but, in reality, more to disguise her well-kennt face from the security guards and shopkeepers. Lena was very prettily but nervously playing the part of Annie's daughter in a satin beauté day gown, its skirt trimmed with wide tucks.

Johnnie let her colleagues go into the shop ahead of her and slowly counted to a hundred as she continued to meander, but never let the shop doorway out of her sight. Finally, she too entered the shop and took in the scene. There were only two shop assistants, the third having gone out for lunch just five minutes before, a routine of which they were aware, one of the Avengers having been set to finding out this information for the last two Thursdays. On both occasions, the man had left the shop at exactly the same time and returned half an hour later with sandwiches for the three of them. Plenty of time.

Johnnie's own outfit was a simple cream and royal blue voile dress, with a pale grey gabardine cape with a royal blue satin lining. Her hat fell low on her face to one side and Johnnie made sure that was the side that faced the counter. Of the two remaining shop assistants, one - the woman - was looking after Annie and Lena, who could be heard cooing over two trays of fine earrings. Meg had told Lena not to speak, as she found a suitable accent impossible, but Big Annie was holding forth in fine voice, proclaiming this diamond rather poor and that ruby barely acceptable. The young woman behind the counter rushed to pull out a further tray. "I'm certain these will be much more to madam's taste."

The young man, who had been watching the scene with amusement, turned to Johnnie as she entered. "May I help you, Miss?"

"Oh, I do hope so." Johnnie's voice was just the perfect mixture of eager and upset that she had been practising for the last two days. "You see, my young man is returning from London this weekend, and I've been awfully foolish. I've lost my engagement ring."

"Oh, I say, that's a terrible pity."

"Yes, isn't it?" Johnnie looked down at her fluttering hands and

THE DEVIL'S DRAPER

pulled her gloves off. "Daddy says he'll pay for a replacement. It was a gold circlet with two deep blue sapphires and a diamond in between. You have one in the window which looks remarkably like it."

"Ah, yes," the young man beamed. "A very fine ring."

"Yes, if I could just look at it more closely, I could..."

"Of course, of course." He unlocked the window display and brought out the tray, placing it on the counter in front of her.

"May I try it on?" Johnnie's voice was louder than it needed to have been, but she wanted to make sure Big Annie and Lena heard her. This was their cue.

"Please do. We can, of course adjust—"

A loud groan followed by a thud drew his attention. Big Annie shrieked dramatically. "Henrietta, oh, Henrietta! Please! Smelling salts! A doctor! Sal volatile!"

The young woman hurried out from behind the counter and placed her fingers on Lena's neck. Lena started to shake and gurgle. Johnnie was impressed. The girl might not be able to put on a fancy accent, but she could certainly act as if she were taking a fit.

"Please!" wailed Big Annie. "Help my daughter! She will die!"

The young man was standing open-mouthed in horror. "Oh dear," said Johnnie. "We must do something. Can you lift her, do you think? She is very small and you look strong and capable."

The young man's chest puffed out and he strode into the fray. "Here, let me, let me."

As the two shop assistants and Big Annie hovered around the twitching Lena, Johnnie casually picked up the tray of rings and the three trays of earrings, scooped them into the special pocket underneath her cape and walked out of the shop, making her way to the Argyle Street entrance, as if she didn't have a care in the world which, in fact, she didn't. She had no doubt that Big Annie and Lena wouldn't be far behind her.

FRIDAY 6TH AUGUST 1920
MABEL

I found that I was rather looking forward to another evening out with Lorrimer and the thought of another weekend of pleasure at the expense of Superintendent Orr... When I arrived at the station for my shift that morning, however, the desk sergeant informed me that I was to go directly to Orr's office.

"What have I done?"

"Nothing as far as I know, Miss," said the Desk Sergeant, a rather lugubrious individual called Findlay. "He just said as you're to go to his office when you come in."

"Did he seem unhappy?" A stupid question. Superintendent Orr *always* seemed unhappy and, indeed, seemed to relish his Presbyterian misery. Sergeant Findlay didn't even bother to look at me as he shrugged.

I knocked on Superintendent Orr's door. "Aye." It was a snarl more than an invitation, but I went in anyway.

"Sir, you wanted to see me?"

He looked pointedly at his watch. "Aye, I wanted to see you first thing. Thank you for bothering to grace us with your presence half way through the day." I didn't bother pointing out that it wasn't yet eight o'clock and that my shift hadn't yet started. I had learned that Orr didn't respond well to reason, preferring to exist under the constant misapprehension that the whole world – and me in particular - was out to conspire against him. "I expect her ladyship needed you to lace her stays, or butter her crumpets, did she?" If it were at all possible, he disliked Floss even more than he disliked me, on the grounds that Floss was related to the Chief Constable and it was her that he had to thank for my presence in the first place. I didn't bother telling him that Floss hadn't even worn stays when they were in fashion and settled for a non-committal, "Sir."

THE DEVIL'S DRAPER

"I want you up at Arrol's this morning, taking statements. Which *is* your job if I'm no' mistaken?" I nodded. "Aw this nonsense wi' they girls thieving is getting out o' hand. One o' the jewellers in the Argyll Arcade yesterday, an' another in Buchanan Street at the same time." He looked at me suspiciously. "Arrol's asked for you in particular. Hector Arrol was most specific on that, apparently."

This was as much of a surprise to me, as it seemed to be to him. "Me, sir?"

"Aye, you, lassie. He go to Miss Adair's *soor-ayes*, does he?" As always, he pronounced soirées as though it caused him physical pain. "Anyway, you're tae head up there and speak to a Mr Price, Arrol's head of security." He waved me off. "Well, go on then. Don't just stand there catchin' flies." I turned to head out of the door. "An' don't you be thinkin' you can float around lookin' at aw the fancy goods. You're there tae take statements. That's whit we pay ye for."

But not as much as you pay the men, I thought.

As I made my way up to Arrol's, I wondered why I was still putting myself through this. Would my time be better spent at home right now, with my grandmother? It was obvious to all of us that she was struggling with the transition to life outside the Asylum. She didn't even seem very happy to be free, and I could understand that – taken away from everything that had been familiar to her for decades. She had brightened up a little, chatting with Winnie. Perhaps I could work on that. But, really, what sort of a difference was I making to anything at all? I wasn't able to really help the women I came into contact with every day. Whether they were victims or villains, all I did was take down their words, sympathise with them, give them a cup of tea and send them back to the same lives, the same problems, the same grinding poverty and unfairness. I had thought things would change after the War. We'd gone into factories, driven lorries, defended our fellow citizens, proved ourselves to be just as capable as the men and yet, when the men had come back, we'd been expected to stand aside, and, for the most part we had.

Perhaps I was kidding myself on. All I was, was someone who was good with a notebook and pen. I was in a job where I wasn't wanted, where I could do no good and was possibly even doing harm. According to the Daily Mail, I was just a surplus girl, de-sexed and masculinised by having to do something I wasn't suited to during the Great War, a victim of female emancipation, unfit for marriage and motherhood, even if I had wanted them.

By the time I reached the Bath Street entrance of Arrol's, I was thoroughly sick and fed up of myself. I was determined to simply take this Mr Price's statement, go back to the police station and hand in my notice, before going home and spending my declining spinster years tatting lace and making wholesome meals for the poor.

I pushed open the door and entered the cool marble and tiled calmness of Arrol's. At least, that was what I expected. Instead, I was met with shrieks and crashes and scenes of utter chaos. As I stood trying to work out what was going on, a slim young man ran into a table in front of me, sending a display of tins of bath salts spinning to the floor in all directions. The tins, which only a moment before had been lined up in neat rows of pastel colours symbolising scents of verbena, rose, lavender, violet and lily of the valley, now spun and rolled in all directions across the marble floor. Several of them lost their lids as they fell, sending crystals of the same pastel colours flowing across the floor like fractured rainbows.

"Stop! Thief!" A cry from across the shop alerted me to what was happening and, as the young man barged into me, I grabbed out at his jacket, catching hold of one of the pockets, which ripped off in my hand, as he pulled himself away with a force that almost sent me tumbling amongst the tins. Several silk scarves and an antimony box came away with the pocket, joining the bath salts on the floor.

THE DEVIL'S DRAPER

I steadied myself and lunged for him, as he pushed open the door, this time grabbing onto the belt of his trousers and holding fast. For a few stuttering steps, he dragged me along with him. "Police!" I yelled. "I'm a police officer!"

With my free hand, I reached out wildly for the door handle, trying to stop myself from being pulled along. The young man had the advantage of me in that one of his hands was still free. The other was clutching a beautiful French enamel and brass powder bowl. I had one just like it on my dressing table at home. I knew it was the same one, because I could see it in great detail coming towards my face, as if slowed down to a snail's pace.

I let go of the young man's belt and held my hands up to shield my face. He wasn't expecting me to let go and it unbalanced him, sending him toppling towards me, spinning us both to the floor. One of my hands knocked his hat off and his hair tumbled out. It wasn't a young man after all, but a young woman. She tried to pull back the fist holding the powder bowl, but it was too late. It met my nose with a crunch and everything turned still and silent for a moment, as I screwed my eyes tightly shut.

When I opened them again, a pair of brown eyes was directly above mine and I saw concern in them. But only for a fleeting second. "Sorry, hen," she muttered, before placing a hand on my chest to hold me down as she bounded up, taking off at top speed down Bath Street and disappearing around the corner.

Before I had time to draw breath, two security guards had scooped me up off the pavement and carried me back inside Arrol's, where I discovered that the Mr Price I had been sent to see was, in fact, the Mrs Price who had come to see me about girls being mistreated at Arrol's. I was sure that this would all be explained to me at some point, but right now, I was more intent on freeing myself from the not so tender administrations of the security guards.

"Gentlemen, you can put her down now. I'm sure Miss Adair has had enough of being lugged about like a sack of coal."

THE DEVIL'S DRAPER

The two men did as they were ordered, rather too enthusiastically for my liking, putting me onto a chair that had been brought over by Mrs Price. "Thank you." I closed my eyes and waited for the nausea to subside.

She took my chin in her hand. "Let me see that nose." She turned my head from one side to the other and tutted. "Oh dear."

I looked down at my blouse, the front of which was covered in blood and, as I did so, another drop of it dripped from my nose. "Put your head back. I've asked someone to get some ice from the kitchens. You're going to have a belter of a black eye, I'm afraid, Miss Adair."

"Is my nose broken?" I felt as though I was snuffling like a pig, but she understood me.

"I don't think so, but we'll clean you up and have a look. Can you stand?"

"I think so."

She helped me out of the chair and over to the elevators at the back of the store. "We'll get you out of the way of all these people. I'm sure you don't want to bleed in front of an audience, do you?"

I shook my head and instantly regretted it. "Ouch." We went up in the elevator without saying a word. The elevator man looked at me curiously, as I patted at my nose with my handkerchief.

At the top, Mrs Price ushered me out. "Come along into my office."

Her office? "But I thought—"

"Yes, yes, I'll explain all that to you when we get there."

She must have seen the shocked look on my face underneath all the blood when we got to her office, because she grinned. "Nice, isn't it?"

"It is indeed."

She ushered me to a chair and poked her head out of the room, asking someone to get me a cup of tea, before coming back in and closing the door. "Well, we can't all be stuck in re-purposed broom cupboards, you know."

THE DEVIL'S DRAPER

"No, I suppose we can't. So..." I waved my hand at the splendour around me. "What have you done to deserve all this?"

She explained to me her plan for trying to discover what was happening at Arrol's, to try and get justice for the young women she had sent there. A knock at the door interrupted her and a young woman in a smart uniform came in with a cup of tea and a fancy biscuit.

"And what do you think?" I asked her, as the girl was leaving. When the door opened, I heard a gruff voice outside in the corridor. "What's he like, this Hector Arrol?"

"Oh, he's quite charming, but you don't need me to tell you that, Miss Adair."

"I don't?"

"No, I think you may just be about to make your own mind up on that."

A peremptory knock came at the door and, without waiting for a response, a tall man with a fine head of silver hair came into the room. "I'm so terribly sorry, young lady." He came over and grabbed me by the hand, looking with deep concern at my face. "That this happened here, that one of our esteemed customers was set upon by some ruffian in this dreadful fashion on my premises." He clasped my hand closer to his chest and closed his eyes with a look of pain, as though he could see the whole dreadful scene enacted behind his eyelids. "What, dear lady, what, I ask, can we do to apologise, hmmmm?"

I tried to extract my hand from his clutches. "I do assure you, sir, I am quite alright."

"But you don't look it, Miss...?"

"Adair," said Mrs Price. "Miss Mabel Adair."

"Miss Mabel Adair?" He looked even more aghast.

I waved my finally extricated hand. "Please, Mr Arrol, I'm perfectly fine. I'm a police officer. I'm used to such little indignities." I wasn't, of course, but he seemed absolutely devastated by the situation.

THE DEVIL'S DRAPER

He simply repeated my name. "Miss Mabel Adair? Daughter of Miss Florence Adair? Oh, this is just dreadful. Dreadful."

I groaned inwardly, my hopes of getting out of here without any further fuss all but disappearing. My adoptive mother's favourite Glasgow department stores, and the ones to which she gave most of her custom, were Copland & Lye and Treron's, but that didn't stop the others from trying to court her business.

"Your blouse, Miss Adair." At least he had moved on from my nose. "I shall send my secretary to fetch you a replacement."

"Oh, please don't, Mr Arrol. I assure you I'm perfectly fine, I only have to walk up to Blythswood Square. I can change when I get home."

"I insist, Miss Adair. We have a delightful new model of luncheon blouse just in from London. Finest crepe de chine, trimmed with guipure lace. With my compliments, and as a thank you for your bravery. I understand that you single-handedly tackled a fearsome ruffian intent on theft."

I opened my mouth to tell him that the fearsome ruffian was a girl who was slighter than me, but something made me keep quiet and he bustled out of the room, shouting orders to his secretary. Poor woman. I looked at Mrs Price. "He's quite…"

"Yes. Yes, I'm afraid he is. Look, he'll be back soon for more of the same, I'm afraid. But I want to talk to you about what's been happening here with these girls." I opened my mouth to speak, but she held up her hand. "I know the police won't…can't…do anything about it, but I thought you and I might be able to do something. What do you think? Will you meet me to discuss it at least?"

I only had time for a quick nod, before her prophecy was borne out and Hector Arrol came back into Mrs Price's office, brandishing a fine, lemon-coloured blouse, as though he were the proud standard-bearer for an extremely well-dressed regiment. "Here you are, Miss Adair, a new blouse, one of our finest. And with it, two special invitations to a formal presentation of the new

THE DEVIL'S DRAPER

Autumn styles direct from our buyers in Paris and Milan in two weeks' time. For yourself and your mother. With champagne and canapés, of course."

"Of course," I said, reaching out to take the blouse. He was right, it was very fine indeed. "Paris fashions and canapés. How delightful! I can't think of anything nicer."

THE DEVIL'S DRAPER

FRIDAY 6TH AUGUST 1920
JOHNNIE

Johnnie couldn't believe she had been so stupid. She'd run all the way back home, making sure she wasn't being followed, of course, and now she was sitting on the sofa in the war room, having told the whole tale to a grumpy Meg.

"This isnae like you, Johnnie." She poured boiling water from a pan into a cracked brown teapot.

"I know. I'm sorry. I just got careless."

"Aye. An' now we're a woman down for a few days. Ah tell't ye, just silk scarves."

Johnnie picked at a loose thread on the arm of the sofa. "I'm sorry. I don't know what—"

"We have procedures. Strict procedures. Ye cannae just go anywhere and grab whit ye want, you know that. This is whit happens when ye dae." Meg took her anger out on the slate, rubbing every remaining trace of chalk from it, sending chalk dust into the air.

"I know. I promise it won't happen again."

Meg sighed. "An' a woman polis, ye say?"

"Aye, so she said, anyway."

Meg wiped her hands absentmindedly with a cloth to get rid of the remaining chalk and perched on a stool at the bar they had set up in the corner, facing Johnnie. "Well, that's a turn up for the books."

"Some of the lassies have been interviewed by a woman before. At Central."

Meg nodded. "Aye, but actually chasin' ye an' that. Ah've never heard o' that before. Good on her. We'd better watch out for that, but good on her." She stood up and mashed the tea in the pot a bit more, before pouring Johnnie a mug full. "Anyway, you're staying

THE DEVIL'S DRAPER

out of the shops for a few days. They might have your description circulated, especially if this police officer got a good look at your face."

"Aye, she might have. An' she got the pocket of my favourite jacket."

Meg ladled a couple of spoonfuls of sugar into her own mug of tea and took a sip of the strong, sweet brew. "Well, we'll have to find something else for you for a wee while."

Johnnie was not best pleased, but she knew Meg was right. They seldom lost a girl to arrest, simply because Meg made sure of discipline. And now she'd gone and wasted it all. "What am I to do?" She hoped Meg wasn't going to send her into service. The lassies that did that played a long game and had to clean and cook for the gentry meantime.

Meg glanced around. They weren't on their own, but the three other Avengers who weren't out on jobs were playing a raucous game of cards in the far corner and drinking beer. "Wee Ruby's gone missing."

"Ruby?"

"Aye. Two nights ago." Meg frowned. "I'd sent her out pickpocketing. Easy stuff. The Kensington, when they're all rolling out drunk." Meg always sent the new lassies out to the Gentlemen's clubs to practise their skills. "She didnae come back."

"Do you think she got scared and just decided it wasn't for her?"

Meg screwed her face up and shook her head. "Naw. Ah think she would have tell't me. Ah let her know there were other options." Meg had a sharp tongue and ruled with a firm hand, but she was always gentle with the new ones. "Besides, Evvy said all her stuff's still up in her room. Her mother's locket an' that. She widnae have left that."

"Do you think she got herself arrested?"

Meg shook her head again. "We would have heard."

"So, what do you think has happened?"

THE DEVIL'S DRAPER

"Nothin' good, onyways." Meg was silent for a moment. Johnnie gulped down the rest of the tea in her mug and poured another one. "So what now?"

Meg looked over at the three card players. "Ah'm a bit worried about the others."

"The others? The other lassies?"

"Naw. The Norman Conks, the San Toi, the Ging-gong Boys. Who knows?"

Johnnie caught on immediately to what Meg was saying. Glasgow's gangs were a festering stew of violence and danger, constantly on the boil and threatening to erupt at any time. Some of them were simply in it for the fighting; others were out to take their chances when they saw the opportunity of a quick score; a few, like the Avengers, were well-organised and business-like, less interested in pitched battles to defend their territory and more focussed on the financial gains to be made. Some of those were the most dangerous of all. St Thenue's Avengers kept their heads down and tried to stay away from the notice of the other gangs. Their targets and tactics were different and, on the whole, the others let them be. Gangs like The Waverley and the Calton Tigers carried out housebreaking and factory raids and plied their trade at the horse and dog tracks but, sometimes, their paths crossed. The Avengers had discussed the dangers of the jewellery store heists and the fact that it wasn't only the police they had to worry about, but Johnnie didn't know what they might want with a fifteen-year-old lassie like Ruby. "You think they've taken her?"

Meg picked up her mug and gestured with it, tea slopping out onto the floor. "Who knows? A message, mibbee. We've picked up our game recently and we're making a fair bit these days; mibbee they're no' happy. All's I know is that Ruby's disappeared."

"And what do you want me to do?"

The answer, when it came, was not very helpful. "Find her."

SATURDAY 7TH AUGUST 1920
MABEL

The previous evening's plans with Lorrimer had fallen victim to the throbbing ache in my skull, a lingering reminder of my ill-fated encounter. As Saturday's pale light crept through my curtains, I roused myself from a fitful slumber, my head swimming in a sea of discomfort. My reflection in the mirror on my dressing table revealed an eye blooming with hues of twilight, while my nose had taken on the proportions of a prize-winning squash. Nevertheless, I steeled myself and descended to face the day, the scent of Mrs Dugan's breakfast a siren call I couldn't resist.

Floss and Jo had seen me the evening before, but my grandmother had already retired and taken dinner in her room, so my appearance was rather a shock to her, although Floss had warned her about it.

"Mabel! Oh, Mabel! You look dreadful."

"Thank you, Grandmother." I planted a kiss on the top of her head and one for Floss and Jo, too, while I was about it. I sat down and pulled over the plate of toast and the jar of Mrs Dugan's delicious plum jam, helping myself to a generous spoonful in the hope that it would ease my pain.

The door opened and Ellen appeared with my usual kippers. She gave a shriek when she saw my face. "In the name of the..."

I reached out and took the plate from her. "Now, now, Ellen. Give me that before those kippers slide into my tea."

"What have you *done*, Miss Mabel?" Because, of course, it was always my fault.

"I know, Ellen, dreadful, isn't it?" My grandmother seemed to be much more comfortable with Ellen and Mrs Dugan and the maids than she was with Floss, Jo and I, but I hoped that that would change as she got used to us.

THE DEVIL'S DRAPER

Ellen unceremoniously took my chin in her hand none too gently and inspected my face. I pulled away. "Ouch."

Her face loomed towards mine as she peered at my nose. "This looks very bad, Miss Mabel."

"It was alright until you started wrenching my face around." I patted her hand away, but she continued to scowl at me until I repeated the story of what had happened for the benefit of her and my grandmother. I may have embellished it slightly in the telling.

Floss plucked a piece of toast out of the rack. "Somehow, your bravery seems to have increased overnight, Mabel. Give it until Tuesday and I'm certain you'll have chased off a large gang of men single-handed."

"It's not funny, Miss Adair." Ellen had been with my mother long enough to take liberties. "I knew Miss Mabel would come to harm at that place. The police station is no place for a woman."

"I have no doubt that most of my colleagues would agree with you, Ellen. But I'm staying there until they throw me out." Given that every other day I had misgivings about my role, I rather surprised myself with my vehemence. I realised that I had quite enjoyed yesterday's little escapade.

Ellen sniffed and looked glumly at my face once more, before turning on her heel and heading to the door. As she left, she threw a final comment over her shoulder. "Well, that may be a good thing, Miss, it'll give you something to do in your old age, seein' as no-one will want to marry you with a face like *that*."

"Ouch," I said again. She shut the door behind her with more force than was absolutely required, and before I could respond with a smart comeback.

Floss laughed. "Well, Mabel, now that your future is settled, what are you doing today? Jo and I are going to take Lillias here for a drive to the coast. We thought Ayr or Troon. Do you want to come with us?"

I would have liked nothing more, but I'd promised to go and see Mrs Price. I looked at my watch. "What time are you setting

THE DEVIL'S DRAPER

off? I said I'd go and see Mrs Price first thing, before she goes to Arrol's."

I'd told Floss and Jo the night before about Mrs Price and the young women her employment agency had placed at Arrol's. Jo tutted. "I can't believe the poor woman is doing two jobs."

I reached out and took another piece of toast, spooning some more of the sweet, tangy jam on top. "She's going to her office early every morning, then back there after Arrol's closes and working all day Sunday in order to keep up with her own work, but she wants to do it. She feels a responsibility to the young women she finds jobs for."

"And that's admirable," said Floss. She looked at Jo. "I wonder if we could—."

"No." My voice was sharp.

"I was just—"

I held up my hand. "*No.*"

Floss sat back, exasperated. "Honestly, Mabel. We're not entirely useless, you know."

I immediately regretted my sharpness. "I know you're not, Floss, dear." They were far from useless. The proof of it was on the wall behind Floss, where their Suffragette hunger strike medals were hanging, beautifully framed, in pride of place. "I *do* know you're not, I really do. But..." I moved my eyes over towards Lillias, who had finished eating and was now gazing, unseeing, out of the window that looked out on Blythswood Square.

Floss nodded, understanding what I meant. "We're planning on setting off at midday. Mrs Dugan's going to make us a splendid picnic and we're going for a nice long walk along the beach. We may even go for a paddle, isn't that right, Lillias?"

My grandmother jolted out of her reverie. "A paddle? Oh, yes. A paddle. That will be lovely."

I shoved a final piece of toast in my mouth, licked the last of the jam off my fingers and jumped up from the table. "Then I'll go and see Mrs Price straight away and be back so that I can go with you."

THE DEVIL'S DRAPER

"Excellent." Floss beamed at all of us. "And tonight we've tickets for the Royal. A farce called *The Night of The Party*. And supper afterwards I think." I delivered another round of kisses and headed out to see Mrs Price.

Her office was on the third floor of a building on West Nile Street. On the ground floor was an auctioneers, and the other offices in the building included a Friendly Society, a Soldiers and Sailors Help Society, an adding machine company and a milliners. The close was neat and sparkling, a wally close with beautiful, scenic tiles depicting boats and lighthouses and coastal villages. I assumed this had been paid for by the headquarters of the steamship company on the first floor. By the time I got up to the third floor, I was slightly out of puff. I knocked and waited for her to shout me in.

As she bustled about making tea, I looked about me. The office, like the rest of the building, was clean and neat. The furnishings were sparse but homely – a big wooden desk, Mrs Price's chair, two chairs on the other side of the desk with what looked like home-made cushions, a filing cabinet and a colourful rug on the linoleum floor. A coat stand, a couple of large potted plants and a rather modern painting of a woman in shades of orange and blue hung on the wall behind the desk. The desk itself was almost empty, other than a notepad and pencil and a silver-framed photograph, pre-War, of a man with a large bristling moustache, his arm casually laid across the shoulders of a gangly teenage boy. She caught me peering at it. "My husband and son," she said, but offered no further information.

She pushed the cup of tea across the desk. "Miss Adair, I want your help."

"And I'd love to be able to offer it, but how?" She'd told me about her telephone conversation with one of my colleagues. She hadn't asked his name and "sneering and unhelpful" didn't rule very many of them out, quite frankly. "As you know, Superintendent Orr says there's nothing to investigate." She opened her mouth to

THE DEVIL'S DRAPER

speak and I held up my hand. "I know, I know. I agree with you. It's unfair, but that's the law."

She sat back in her chair and sighed. "I know. I've managed to persuade Hector Arrol that he should employ women as security staff. Me, to be specific. And he seems to be quite satisfied with how this is working out."

"This isn't new, though, is it? Women as security guards, I mean."

"Not at all. But he's very old-fashioned. And I can't do it all myself. The store *does* need security of this type. I've already stopped two shoplifters in the few days I've been there. So it's a necessary role, but I also want to watch how Mr Arrol behaves with the young ladies he employs and I don't have time for everything."

"So...?" I was still at a loss to see how I fitted into Mrs Price's plans.

"So I wanted to see if you and the others would be willing to help. Surveillance. On a non-official basis."

I looked at her, confused. "The others?"

"Yes, the other women who work for the police."

I started to laugh and kept laughing until a coughing fit made me stop. "Oh, Mrs Price, I'm so sorry. I'm afraid that Glasgow only has two women in its police force – myself and a Miss Miller. Well, there's the turnkey and the cleaner, of course, but she's the wife of one of the sergeants. And I would say that it's very unlikely that Superintendent Orr would let me do such a thing anyway."

"Oh. I see." She looked deflated.

"I really do understand, Mrs Price. And I *would* like to help. Really, I would. The idea of these young women being abused in this way..."

She stood up and I watched her pace the room, thinking. Finally, she came back to sit at her desk. "What if the request came from Hector Arrol himself?"

"Request?"

THE DEVIL'S DRAPER

"Yes." She came and sat at my side of the desk and grabbed my hands. "You've said that your Sergeant Orr, or whatever his name is, has a bee in his bonnet about these St Thenue's Avengers. What if Hector Arrol told him that there were arrests to be made at Arrol's; arrests that would reflect well on *him*?"

I was catching on. "And he needed someone on the ground, so to speak?"

She leaned back. "Exactly."

I sighed. "He doesn't like me."

"Well, he doesn't have much choice, does he? You've already said: there's only you and this Miss Miller. If Arrol asked for you - just for a week, mind - then that would at least give me another pair of ears and eyes for a little while."

And it would give *me* an actual, proper, policing job. I had no idea if Orr would go for it, but it was worth a try. "Maybe he'll be glad to see the back of me for a week."

MONDAY 9TH AUGUST 1920
JOHNNIE

Johnnie had spent the last two days asking around, trying to find Ruby, but the girl seemed to have disappeared without a trace. As far as she could tell, none of the local gangs even knew of her existence and none of the Avengers had seen her for nearly a week. Nobody appeared to be concerned about her absence either.

Ruby shared a single end with Christine and Evvy. Christine was an old hand and Meg often assigned new members to her care, if care was the right word. Christine was brusque and unsentimental, but she could be trusted to watch out for the new girls, while keeping them in line. Christine's view was that Ruby had gone back to her family, but Johnnie had been to their home in her search for Ruby and if she'd been Ruby, she would have wanted to stay as far away as possible. It was a grim slum in the Gorbals, shared by two brothers and their families – a pair of worn-out women and a total of eleven children. Johnnie had spoken to one of the older boys, a gormless-looking waif with a perpetually dripping nose. He was hard-pressed to even remember his sister and when Johnnie persuaded him with a penny, he stuttered out that they hadn't seen Ruby for nearly a year. No, Ruby hadn't gone back there.

Johnnie hadn't yet managed to speak to Evvy. Meg had sent her through to Motherwell with another of the younger girls to do some pickpocketing at the market there and they weren't expected back until the next day. Johnnie was bored just hanging around. She needed to keep a bit of a low profile, which meant that she should stay out of circulation, but not being allowed to work didn't mean that she had to stay cooped up indoors. She would go and see that woman Winnie at the public lavatories on Wilson Street. By all accounts, this Winnie seemed to have a lot of information

THE DEVIL'S DRAPER

at her fingertips and if there was news of Ruby of any importance, Johnnie had been told by a couple of Avengers that Winnie was sure to know it.

It meant, of course, that she would need to dress as a girl, but that was probably a good thing. The polis, if they were even looking for her, would likely be looking for a girl dressed as a boy. Johnnie climbed the stairs to her room and looked through her wardrobe. Several disguises were possible, but she selected a maid's uniform of a plain black dress, a white apron and a cap. She tucked her hair up underneath the cap and added a pair of black shoes. She checked herself in the mirror. Completely invisible – just what she wanted.

She ran down the stairs and out into the street, checking along it each way as she always did, since the police barracks were just around the corner, but today she checked with extra care. She kept her head bowed as she bustled along, just in case, heaving a sigh of relief when she reached the steps of the toilets without a heavy hand landing on her shoulder.

Johnnie didn't know the woman very well, having only been in once or twice – the toilets were too near to home to waste a penny - but a lot of the girls talked about her and said how kind she was to them, allowing them to use the toilets without paying and even feeding them from a pot of something that she always had on the go.

That pot was clearly full of something delicious today and Johnnie's mouth watered at the scent. Winnie was talking quietly to a pair of young shop girls at the top of the room and Winnie busied herself, as if she were looking for a penny. The shop girls left and Winnie went back to her stove, taking off the lid of the pot to stir the wonderful-smelling concoction inside. Johnnie's stomach rumbled and she realised how hungry she was.

Winnie turned and smiled at her, waving her over with the ladle. "Want some, hen? Mutton stew."

"Naw...aye, alright then. Aye, thanks."

THE DEVIL'S DRAPER

Winnie nodded and pulled a bowl off one of the shelves, ladling in a generous portion of the stew, with its big pieces of meat and carrot and turnip and glistening globs of fat. She held out the bowl to Johnnie. "Here y'are, hen. Brown stew, ma maw used tae call this. Ah tell't her all stew was brown." She laughed to herself and found Johnnie a spoon.

"That's lovely, that is." Johnnie hadn't tasted anything like it for a long time. Big Annie did most of the cooking for the Avengers, but that was only because no-one else wanted the job. Annie didn't want it either, but somehow it had fallen to her. This woman, on the other hand, was clearly born to the task.

Johnnie spooned up the stew hungrily. When she looked up, Winnie was watching her, her keen eyes kind and twinkling. "Ah've seen you before a couple of times, haven't I, hen?"

"Aye, probably." Johnnie's voice was noncommittal, as she scooped up spoonful after spoonful of the mutton stew.

"First time in that get up, though, is it no'. You got yersel' a new job?"

Johnnie shrugged.

"One o' they St Thenue's Avengers, aren't ye?" Johnnie looked at her without saying anything and Winnie scooped another ladleful of stew into her already empty bowl. "Don't you worry, hen. I'll no' say anything, but I like to make these things my business." She put the lid back on the pot and gazed at Johnnie with those knowing eyes of hers. "Means I can watch out for yis all, that's aw."

Johnnie wasn't good at trust, but somehow she trusted this woman. Enough, anyway. "Do you know a lassie called Ruby?"

Winnie surveyed her with steady eyes. "Aye, well, I know a couple of lassies called Ruby."

"This one's a wee skelf of a lassie, about fifteen, with dirty blonde hair that sticks off her head in all directions, like it's scared of her scalp."

Winnie laughed. "Aye, I know *that* Ruby right enough. She's one o' they Avengers an' aw', so she tell't me."

THE DEVIL'S DRAPER

"She did, did she?" Ruby prattled altogether too much. When Johnnie *did* find her, she would have words.

Winnie frowned. "Ah huvnae seen her for a good few days, though. Is she doin' alright?"

Johnnie ate the last of the stew and reluctantly handed the bowl back to Winnie. "We've no' seen her either."

"Ah, is that right? She has family in the Gorbals, doesn't she? You've tried there, huv yis?"

"Aye. They've not seen her for months."

"Naw, ah'm no' surprised. Not the most affectionate of families, by all accounts." Winnie wiped out the bowl and put it back on the shelf. "But Ruby disnae seem like a lassie who would just take off on her own. A bit feart of her own shadow, so she is. Ah wis surprised she'd taken up wi' youse Avengers, as a matter o' fact."

Johnnie wasn't sure if this was a slight. "We look after our own."

"Oh, aye, ah know yis dae, hen. She just disnae seem as gallus as the rest of yis, that's aw' ah meant."

Johnnie nodded. "Will you keep an ear out? See if there's any word of her?"

"Course, hen. An' who shall I ask for if I have news?"

Johnnie hesitated a moment. "Johnnie."

"Right then, Johnnie. Ah'll be in touch if I hear anything." Winnie turned back to her shelves and took a book down. "Here. Give this to Meg, will ye?" Johnnie looked down at the book in her hands. *Anne of the Island* by L M Montgomery. She frowned back up at Winnie, who smiled at her. "She's already read the first two. Tell her ah just got this one in."

MONDAY 9TH AUGUST 1920
MABEL

Not all the Max Factor foundation in the world was going to disguise the huge black eye or lumpy nose I was still sporting this morning, so I decided not to even bother trying and settled for scuttling, head down, into my broom cupboard. Sergeant Ferguson studiously and kindly, bless him, simply avoided looking at me when he brought me my morning tea and some of his wife's delicious baking, which had become a delightful habit. He was extra nice to me as he delivered them. Today's offering was a fat and pillowy Queen cake; a bun stuffed to bursting with currants and candied orange peel. As I unwrapped the brown paper it was wrapped in, the scent of it even masked the musty smell of the mop and bucket in the corner momentarily. I wondered if there was any chance of milking Ferguson's sympathy in order to get another one, but his next words put all thoughts of baking out of my head.

"Superintendent Orr wants us all in the big room in ten minutes."

It wasn't often I was included in such gatherings. Anything that was happening I usually found out after absolutely everyone else at the station, including the woman who did the cleaning. I wondered if Mrs Price had already made good on her promise to get Hector Arrol to request my services.

I put half of the Queen cake to one side to have later and headed for the main room, where most of the other police officers sat. Only Superintendent Orr, Detective Inspector Lorrimer and the new chap, Detective Inspector McInolty, had their own offices. I walked in and all heads turned. Clearly, news of my face had reached most of them already and they were keen to admire the damage. I wondered if this was why I'd been summoned – just the latest of the indignities Superintendent Orr piled upon me.

THE DEVIL'S DRAPER

I determined not to let it get to me and I lifted my head to stare them down. Lorrimer, however, looked shocked and made his way over to me. When I'd contacted him to cancel our appointment for the club at the weekend, I'd simply told him I was unwell.

"Miss Adair. What...*what* on earth has happened? Are you alright? Well, clearly you're not but..." I'd never heard him at a loss for words before.

Before I could answer him, Superintendent Orr breezed in. "All hands on deck this week." He looked around the room at each of us in turn, his lips twitching as his eyes stopped when they reached me. I'd never seen anything even remotely like a smile on his face before and it looked completely out of place. I knew why it was there. He was clearly delighted to witness the evidence shown on my face. "These so-called St Thenue's Avengers are getting out of hand; you'll all have heard about the jewellery robberies last week. We're becoming a laughing stock. Can't even find a wee gang of lassies."

He snapped out assignments left and right. "Lorrimer, since your dining and dancing companion looks like she's been slapped in the face by a lorry, I'd like you to concentrate on the jewellery thefts." There were a few snickers around the room and, with difficulty, I continued to hold my head high. "Take a couple of men and question all the known fences. Make it known that we'll be coming down hard on them."

Finally, he turned to me. "Miss Adair." He rolled my name around in his mouth as though it was a piece of rotting fish. "Or should I call you Sexton Blake?" I stared back at him, but said nothing. Orr turned to the rest of the room with a flourish. "Miss Adair has been up to wonderful and miraculous deeds of derring-do. Solving crime single-handedly, as though she's the plucky heroine of a penny dreadful. Almost halted a crime wave at Arrol's, if you'll believe it. Chased down a young thief in the street, ripping off his pocket and getting herself smashed in the face into the bargain."

THE DEVIL'S DRAPER

A murmur went around the room. This was my moment to mention that the thief had been a young woman, possibly one of the very St Thenue's Avengers we were looking for, but for some reason I didn't. By the time the security guards had come out to pick me off the pavement, she'd gone, and I was the only person who'd seen her face. I would keep that to myself for now.

Lorrimer raised an eyebrow at me and gave a slight bow in my direction. I bit my lip to keep from smiling. Orr continued. "While it has obviously marred Miss Adair's beauty and her career as a Hollywood star is now in some doubt," a low blow which set off sniggers around the room, "she has been specially requested by none other than Mr Hector Arrol himself to go...*undercover*." This was said in a tone of sarcastic awe. "Aye, that's what he asked for, right enough, if you can believe it. I think he's been at the penny dreadfuls, too. I'm no' sure exactly how undercover Miss Adair can actually be with a face like that, but who am I to naysay one of Glasgow's finest and most upstanding citizens?"

I was fuming and I could feel my cheeks blazing. I lowered my head, despite my determination to keep it raised. How dare he? I had to sit on my hands to try and stop myself from jumping up and punching him. I kept my head down, listening in mortification to the snickering that ran around the room.

Lorrimer cleared his throat. "Miss Adair is an integral part of many of my cases. How long are we to be without her?"

Orr grunted and the snickering died down. "With effect from this Thursday, and for a period of at least two weeks, we'll be without Miss Adair. Miss Miller will be back from holiday on Monday, so any statements as need taking can be done by her. Now, back to work."

We all filed out of the room. Constable Ferguson pressed my arm briefly as he passed me and Lorrimer was leaning on the wall outside my office. "Chin up, Mabel. He's a nasty piece of work with a chip on his shoulder the size of an oak tree."

"Thank you, James, for taking the focus off me in there."

He straightened up and gave me a lazy salute. "You are most welcome. Shall we get our own back by stinging him for expenses on Saturday evening at Chez Antoine?"

"Oh, let's. I feel I shall most definitely be in the mood for oysters and champagne by then. Lots of them."

WEDNESDAY 11TH AUGUST 1920
JOHNNIE

Meg had told Johnnie that Evvy was back from Motherwell. As she reached the door, Christine opened it. "You lookin' for Evvy? She's sleepin'. I'm away. Jus' go on in."

Evvy was curled up under a thin blanket and Johnnie shook her awake. The girl mumbled something and tried to pull the blanket over her head again, but Johnnie wouldn't let her. "I need to speak to you."

Evvy groaned. "Whit aboot?"

"Ruby."

"Whit aboot Ruby?"

"Do you know where she is?"

Evvy turned her back on Johnnie. "Naw."

"Evvy, wake up and look at me. This is important." Evvy grumbled but sat up, glaring at Johnnie with sleepy eyes. "When did you last see her?"

Evvy shrugged. "Dinnae ken. Few days before ah went tae Motherwell."

"Did she say anything?"

Evvy lowered her head and played with a strand of her messy hair. "Like whit?"

What was wrong with the girl? "About going away or anything?"

"Naw. Where wid she go?" Evvy rubbed the sleep out of her eyes.

Johnnie squatted on the floor, so that she could see Evvy's face more closely. "I don't know. That's what I'm askin' you for. Had she been talkin' to anyone she shouldn't have? Doin' anything she shouldn't?"

Evvy's eyes flickered away momentarily. "Naw."

"Evvy, you have to tell me if there's anything."

THE DEVIL'S DRAPER

"There isnae." But Johnnie could sense there was something that Evvy wasn't telling her. She stood up and looked about her. Clothing was strewn about the room: you could hardly see the threadbare rug that covered the worn floorboards. Johnnie recognised a shawl that belonged to Ruby, a pair of bloomers that were clearly Christine's and a thin shift all tangled up in a corner. *How could they live like this?* Johnnie thanked her lucky stars once again that she didn't have to share her space with anyone.

Christine had the only actual bed, which was tucked away in the recess. Ruby and Evvy apparently shared a thin and lumpy horsehair pad. The surfaces, such as they were – one rickety table and a small set of drawers with a leg missing – were covered with dirty mugs and plates. Days old remnants of food still clung to the plates. Amongst the mess, Johnnie spotted something that looked out of place. Idly, she picked it up. A small blonde tortoiseshell and gilt box with ivory edges. It looked brand new. She turned it around in her hands; she'd seen one just like it only a couple of days ago. She held it out so that Evvy could see it. "Whose is this?"

Evvy was watching her, warily. "Ruby's."

"Where did she get it from?" Evvy shrugged. "Where did she get it from? Come on, now. Tell me."

"Arrol's," Evvy muttered eventually.

Johnnie grabbed her shoulder and turned the girl to face her. "She got it from Arrol's?"

"Aye." Evvy sounded defiant. "Ow, you're hurtin'."

Johnnie loosened her grip, but still kept her hand on Evvy's shoulder. "She took it, you mean? Stole it?"

"Aye." Evvy looked at her, fearfully. "You'll no' tell Meg, will you? She said a man—" Evvy immediately clammed up.

"A man what?" Johnnie knew that Ruby had not been assigned Arrol's. She hadn't been assigned *any* of Glasgow's stores. Johnnie grabbed Evvy's arm. "A man *what*, Evvy? What was she doing there? She wasn't ready for that yet."

THE DEVIL'S DRAPER

"She thought she was ready; she was fed up of being sent out pickpocketing. Wanted to go for something bigger. But she was scared afterwards." Evvy pulled her arm away from Johnnie, rubbing her wrist.

"So she just started stealin' things on her own accord?" This was strictly forbidden. Meg was adamant about that.

"You'll no' tell Meg, will ye?"

"Aye, I'll have to. She'll be in trouble when she gets back."

THURSDAY 12TH AUGUST 1920
MABEL

I had dressed carefully for my first shift undercover – a summer frock in flowered lawn and a pair of box Gibson shoes. I was smart but unobtrusive and, above all, comfortable. I had put up with half an hour of Hector Arrol's toadying, before he left me alone with Mrs Price. We had agreed that today I would simply get the lie of the land: introduce myself to Hector Arrol's children and other senior members of staff, and speak to them about patterns of shoplifting and whether they had noticed any familiar faces. Once they had all got used to me, it would be much easier for me to blend in and observe the young female staff who came into contact with Hector Arrol.

Alfred Arrol turned out to be almost a mirror image of his father, personality-wise at least. He hadn't fared as well in the looks department, without the silvery head of hair that distinguished Hector. He showed me around the two floors of clothing that made up his domain, pointing out the latest fashions with a knowledgeable if pompous air and expounding at length on his trips to Paris, Milan and New York. He had brought in a policy of having both male and female models showing off the clothing for customers, by walking around the store, including down in the café, and his departments also possessed a fine array of mannequins. The clothes and the way in which they were displayed did look rather splendid and I reluctantly accepted that, while he might be pompous, he was good at what he did. Everyone, even his sister, Eliza, who ostensibly managed ladieswear, referred to him as Mr Arrol Junior, although it seemed to me that Eliza did it in a tongue-in-cheek way that made me warm to her immediately.

Alfred Arrol became practically apoplectic, as he told me about the furs they had lost recently. He was, however, quick to point out

THE DEVIL'S DRAPER

that there had been no major thefts of expensive items since Mrs Price had come on board and he seemed very impressed by her.

He reluctantly left me on the staircase, bowing over my hand as I descended to the ground floor, where the youngest son, Roderick Arrol, was waiting for me. He was slightly pudgy and self-satisfied about the jaw, but with the thick hair and handsome features of his father.

"Do, please, call me Roddy, Miss Mabel," was his first comment. "I may call you Mabel, mayn't I?" I took an instant dislike to the man, simply because he was so charming. He, at least, thought so, but he was trying far too hard and utterly missed the mark.

I asked Roddy to show me around his empire and he did so, most proudly. "It's the department that changes the most, and the most often, in the whole of the store. We are, of course, the very first department that the visitor sees and my father is always praising me for our innovative and elegant displays. He gives me free rein on fancy goods, you know."

He seemed to expect me to say something here, so I settled for an appreciative, "Mmmm, fancy," which seemed to satisfy him.

"And our seasonal displays are second to none. That's what my father says: 'Roderick,' he said to me, 'your summer display is second to none.'"

Again, a response seemed to be expected. "Goodness me, second to none. I see."

He beamed at me. "And we have goods in this department that you won't find in any other shop in Glasgow. I scour the world looking for treasures from its four corners." He waved a hand expansively. "The finest silk hosiery from Paris; leather handbags from Morocco; kidskin gloves from Bavaria; Vicuna scarves from the Andes; gossamer handkerchiefs from China; tortoiseshell combs from the East Indies; rosewood dressing table sets from Honduras; turquoise earrings from the Americas; antimony trinket boxes from Japan; ivory ink wells from—"

THE DEVIL'S DRAPER

"Oh how splendid indeed!" I had to stop him before he recited the other hundred and fifty or so countries in the world and the goods they produced. "I'm sure your father must be terribly impressed with such a fine array."

He puffed up his chest like a bantam surrounded by admiring hens. "Indeed he is, Mabel. Indeed he is."

"And what sort of goods do you find are the most attractive to shoplifters?"

"Mostly the smaller, finer items: silk scarves, trinket boxes, jade, turquoise... that sort of thing. Anything that can be easily popped into a pocket. Although a month or so ago, one of my staff members spotted that a small trunk was missing and along with it several fine Italian leather handbags and some Mexican silver photo frames."

Oh God, was he going to start again? But the memory of this brazen theft clearly caused him pain, if the dyspeptic look on his face was anything to go by, and he was silent for a moment.

"And do you, like your father and Alfred, think that most of these thieves are women?"

"Women? Oh no. Far be it from me to disagree with my esteemed father, but shoplifting on a scale like this is, quite clearly the purview of men. I don't believe that women are involved. The odd scarf here and there, of course, but the furs, the silver, the trunk full of fancy goods? No, no."

I wasn't quite sure whether he was saying that women weren't capable enough, or simply weren't venal enough, but I thought that discussion could wait for another time. "Well, Mr Arrol – Roddy – I've kept you far long enough from your marvellous displays. I'll head down to the basement and find your other brother."

"Ha, beard Gilbert in his lair, so to speak? Well, Mabel, it's been a delight chatting to you and I know that my father is of the same opinion as I am." He gave me a sly look. "I should very much like to continue our discussions." Oh, God forbid we should do such a thing. "Perhaps I could persuade you to take tea with me one day?"

"Perhaps you could, Roddy. Perhaps you could." And on that suitably vague note, I slipped downstairs to try and find Gilbert Arrol. I hoped he wasn't quite as awful as Roddy, but I didn't hold out much hope.

It turned out, however, that I was wrong. Gilbert was much more relaxed than Alfred and less frenzied than Roddy. Where Alfred had seemed rather scared of his father and Roddy sycophantically eager to please him, Gilbert was casually affectionate. "The old man can be rather a bore, Miss Adair, but he's a sound chap really, and quite concerned about these thefts."

"Has much been stolen from down here?"

"A couple of vases and a few pieces of bone china. We lost a full canteen of cutlery last month. I have no idea how, but it was a bit of a blow, I can tell you." He laughed a little tinkling laugh to himself. "But it's much more difficult to cart a chaise longue up the staircase."

"And do you think it's this gang of women thieves?"

He shrugged. "Perhaps. Although for my own department, I think it's more likely to be an inside job; you know, something disappearing from the stock room, that sort of thing. Father's very keen on this all-woman gang idea though. Who knows? Well, hopefully you and Mrs Price will find out."

"That's the idea, Mr Arrol."

"Oh, heavens, it's my father that's Mr Arrol. Do call me Gilbert. I'm not one to stand on ceremony."

I had gathered this from his office, which is where I had found him. Like mine, his was a windowless space; unlike mine, it was smart and contemporary and a riot of colour. The walls were covered with art of a very modern type and he saw me looking at the paintings.

"Do you like them?"

"I do. Yes, I do. I'm not sure I've seen anything like it before."

He beamed at me and stood up from behind his desk, gesturing

THE DEVIL'S DRAPER

for me to come closer. "Countess Colette von der Weid – a very fine artist from the Dada movement."

I'd heard of Dadaism, but didn't know very much about it. "They're very striking. Powerful."

"Indeed. A movement that came out of chaos after all the promises of utopia. The Dadaists reject rationalism and reason; for them the carnage of war is proof enough that all those promises were simply an illusion." He sighed. "A justification for the slaughter of millions. I was a conscientious objector, you know." He looked at me, as though expecting me to say something cruel. He must have been used to that during the War.

I didn't. "That must have been difficult for you."

His body relaxed. "Yes. Yes, it was, rather. I had to go up before a military tribunal, of course. They asked all sorts of questions. One of them was what would I do if my sister Eliza was raped by a German soldier; did I not think that I would want to fight on her behalf? Can you imagine being asked that?" He shook his head, sadly.

I hesitated. "And what did you say?"

He shrugged. "I told them that I didn't think it was right to fight evil with evil. I was put in the Non-Combatant Corps and sent to Dyce camp. I was a quarryman throughout the War. Anyway, that's why I feel an affinity with the Dadaists and Countess Coco in particular." He waved a hand at the works on the wall. "A clear critique of the systems of society and the apparatus of war."

I moved closer to one of the paintings and studied it carefully. "Are these works all hers?"

"Yes. Her favourite medium is photo-montage and collage, but, as you can see from these, she is a very fine painter, too. She lives in Switzerland, but she visits from time to time and we exchange letters. She has an exhibition here in Glasgow very soon. I suppose you could consider me a patron of hers." As quickly as his serious side had appeared, it was switched off again. "I say! Do you fancy a cup of tea? I can show you the café; I'm rather proud of it. We even

THE DEVIL'S DRAPER

have a ladies' rendezvous and reading room at the rear."

I always fancied a cup of tea, so I certainly wasn't going to say no to that. As he shepherded me towards the café, he laughed. "I expect Roddy invited you for tea, did he? 'Should you like to take tea with me, Miss Adair?'" His voice was a very fair imitation of Roderick Arrol's pompous tones. "I'll bet that's how he asked, didn't he? The old stuffed shirt."

I couldn't help but laugh back. "Almost exactly spot on, although *he* called me Mabel."

He gave a mock gasp. "Oh, I say, Miss Adair. That's quite stabbed a fellow in the chest."

"Well, you'd better call me Mabel, too then, Gilbert. I wouldn't like to be the cause of such pain." We entered the café and the hubbub of the shop faded away. The place was busy, but somehow it felt peaceful, decorated in Mediterranean hues and light rattan furniture.

He laughed and plucked an imaginary arrow out of his chest with a flourish. "Super! Now, let's sit over here by the palms. Then if Roddy comes down, he'll be able to see us laughing giddily as if we're old friends." I sat down at the table he pointed out and he handed me a menu. "A pot of Darjeeling? Orange Pekoe? Or are you a girl who prefers coffee? No, I'm sure you'll have tea. And I absolutely insist you have a slice of the blackcurrant tart – it's quite delicious."

He had clearly made up his mind on my behalf and was having far too much fun for me to spoil it for him. I gave him the menu back. "You choose, why don't you?"

"Orange Pekoe it is then. And a slice of the blackcurrant tart. And an almond Banbury. Yes. That'll do us." He waved over one of the waitresses. She was over like a shot, taking our order very efficiently, before scurrying off. "Now," he leaned in conspiratorially and perched his chin on his hand, "a lady detective – how very exciting! Tell me all about how you're going to catch these rapscallions."

FRIDAY 13TH AUGUST 1920
JOHNNIE

Winnie had asked one of the street girls to give Johnnie a message, so Johnnie was now on her way to see her. She hoped Winnie had some news, even if it was just that Ruby had gone back home after all.

Winnie was busy cleaning when she got there, but waved her to a seat and told her to get herself some tea from the pot. Johnnie did so, and poured one for Winnie, too. When Winnie came over, she lowered herself into her battered chair with a sigh. "Gettin' too old for this, now, but don't tell the council."

Her face was serious as she looked at Johnnie. "They fished a young lassie's body out of the Clyde last night. Just down from the Jamaica Street Bridge."

The cup rattled in Johnnie's hand. "An' they think it's Ruby?"

"Aye. Some papers in her pocket. They took her to Central Polis Station an' her da identified her first thing this morning."

"Ruby?"

"Aye, hen. I heard of it last night and spoke to George Geddes of the Humane Society this morning. He's the one that found the body. He's always the one that finds the bodies; it's his job. He says there's been a spate of suicides in the Clyde recently. A sad business, right enough." She leaned back in the chair and shook her head, sadly.

Johnnie was surprised. "She killed herself?"

Winnie looked at her. "That's what they're saying, hen, aye. Nobody saw her do it, but they're saying that she must have jumped off the Jamaica Street Bridge."

"But why?"

"Oh, they're not generally bothered wi' the why, hen. An' it usually comes down to one of two things wi' us women, men or

THE DEVIL'S DRAPER

money, so they'll jist put it down to one of those. It's no' easy bein' a poor woman, that's what it all comes down to in the end."

"She was *fifteen*. An' she was doing well with us. She had no reason to do...that."

Winnie reached over and put her hand on Johnnie's knee. "Ah'm just tellin' you what they're sayin' hen. Mr Geddes though, he disnae think that."

"He doesn't?"

"Naw. Says the body had too many wounds to be explained by a fall into the river. About the head."

"You mean...she'd been beaten?"

Winnie shrugged and took a sip of her tea. "George Geddes has fished a lot of bodies out of the Clyde. Some of them by accident, some of them suicides, an' some of them murdered."

Johnnie's cup tumbled to the floor but they both ignored it. "Is that what he's saying, that Ruby was murdered?"

"Not officially, hen. An' that's certainly not what the polis are sayin'." She sighed. "Too much on their hands to investigate the death of a daft wee lassie, who was no better than she should be."

"But she wasn't a daft wee lassie."

"I know. But who's gonnae stand up for her? Not her da, by all accounts. He didnae seem too upset by her death. One less mouth to feed."

Johnnie jumped out of the chair and feverishly paced about Winnie's small space, her arms crossed in front of herself. "Well, *somebody* should stand up for her. If she was murdered, somebody should stand up for her, shouldn't they?"

Winnie hauled herself upright and took both Johnnie's hands in hers, stilling her pacing. "Aye, they should, you're right, hen." She squeezed Johnnie's hands and sighed. "Look, hen, if you *do* want tae do something about it – an' I'm no' sayin' it'll do any good, mind – but I know a lady in the polis at Central Division." Johnnie drew her hands back, aghast at the very thought. "Ah know, ah know. Ah'm sure the last people in the world you want tae be speakin' to is the polis. But she's a good person. A kind person. She'll listen tae ye at least."

TUESDAY 24TH AUGUST 1920
MABEL

If nothing else, my work was going to keep me fit. I had spent my working days over the last couple of weeks walking up and down the staircases at Arrol's, keeping an eye out for shoplifters, and my weekend evenings dancing the night away with Lorrimer at Chez Antoine, on the trail of thieves and cocaine dealers. Of course, I had also been taking tea with Gilbert in the Arrol's café each afternoon, and he had been forcing me to work my way through the cake menu. It didn't take much forcing, I have to admit.

I thought it was unlikely that potential shoplifters had got wind of my presence or, more likely, Beatrice's presence in the store, but they seemed to have disappeared for some or other reason. I had now nearly come to the end of my allocated time at Arrol's and was due back at the station on Thursday, with very little to show for my efforts. If Beatrice and I were a deterrent, then that was all well and good, but it made for rather a boring day's work. I had had visions of chasing miscreants throughout the store, bringing down displays and mannequins, before rugby-tackling shoplifters to the marble floors as their ill-gotten gains spilled out of hidden pockets. The dull reality was that I had stopped the sum total of one girl in the process of stealing a handkerchief. I hadn't even told Beatrice about her, as I was too ashamed that I hadn't dragged her kicking and screaming to face the consequences of her actions. She was only about thirteen, a scrawny little thing with a perpetual sniff. I'd paid for the handkerchief and sent her on her way with it, with strict instructions never to come back.

However, at least my presence had given Beatrice the freedom to spend more time watching Hector Arrol and to speak to the young women who worked in his department, to ensure that he was behaving properly towards them. So far, all seemed to be in order and I think we both wondered if our time was being spent in worthwhile fashion.

I strolled through the menswear department, stopping to admire a faultlessly tailored, fawn herringbone tweed suit. "Ah, you have excellent taste, Miss Adair. Let me tell you where I bought this." My heart sank. I had studiously tried to avoid Alfred Arrol during my time here. His pretentiousness was almost as great as his father's and he was far more long-winded. It struck me that the higher up the building the Arrol men were, the more annoying they became. Gilbert, in the basement, was most excellent fun, although he tired me out after a while. It had become a habit for us to have tea together every afternoon and that was an enjoyable half an hour, but I didn't think I could cope with him for longer than that. Roddy was exceedingly annoying, but I enjoyed tormenting him – and having tea with Gilbert every day had turned out to be a fabulous way of doing that.

And Hector was the most infuriatingly imperious, self-satisfied and overbearing man I had ever come across. His constant solicitous questions about Floss and praise of my abilities were beginning to wear me down. I knew he was angling for an invitation to one of her dinner parties, but Floss' exact words when I told her this had been, "I couldn't spend five minutes with that tedious windy-wallets, let alone a whole evening," so I had studiously deflected any turns in the conversation that took Hector Arrol in that direction.

My mind always wandered when being talked at by Alfred and I reluctantly drew it back. He was now expounding the merits of tweed from the Isle of Harris and talking about the suit's designer, as though I should know who on earth he was rabbiting on about. "And if you would like to accompany me to the stock room, I can show you one or two more from the new collection that I think would excite you."

I made my excuses – the day I found myself excited by tweed, I would give everything up and escape to a convent. I took a wander through the ladieswear department. It was my favourite part of the

THE DEVIL'S DRAPER

store and Eliza Arrol kept it fresh and smart and neat as a pin. She was the only one of the Arrol clan that I actually liked. She was a few years older than me and determinedly single. I couldn't blame her with the fine examples of manhood she lived with. All of the Arrol children still lived at home, including Alfred, who was the only one who was married. He and his wife and their little girl lived in a separate wing in the Arrol mansion, out in Pollokshaws on the south side of Glasgow.

A newly-arrived evening gown in larkspur blue tulle, mounted over a pale lemon foundation and trimmed with enormous cabbage roses at the waist and bottom edge caught my eye. I had to admit that Alfred did have an eye for fashion and his taste in women's clothing was nowhere near as dull as his personality.

I was debating whether fifteen and a half guineas was a decent price, when one of the young assistants from Gilbert's department dashed over to me. "Miss, Miss! Come quick. Mr Roderick has caught a couple of thieves. Old women, very smartly dressed, they are. He says they're from that gang." She whispered the word 'gang', as though they were standing behind her. All the employees at Arrol's knew that I was with the police and their treatment of me tended into one of four camps. The young women, on the whole, scurried off when they saw me, or put their heads down nervously to avoid my eye, but looked at me with curiosity when they thought I wasn't looking; the older women watched me with a mixture of pity and disapproval; most of the male assistants ignored me completely and the security men universally looked down their noses at me. All the staff, however, had been told to send for me if and when a shoplifter was apprehended, and none of them, whatever they thought of me, would be likely to go against Hector Arrol's instructions, I was sure.

I followed the young woman as she scampered down the stairs and over to a display of suitcases and wicker hampers, where quite a crowd of interested shoppers and shop staff had gathered in a circle. I could hear Roddy's slightly nasal whine in the centre of

THE DEVIL'S DRAPER

the circle. "You two are in for it, I can tell you. My father's on his way, as is our very own lady policeman. Yes, indeed, you weren't expecting that, were you?"

I pushed my way through the circle. Two burly security guards hid the women from my view, their arms around the women's throats and upper bodies, but the women didn't appear to be struggling in any way. Roddy spotted me and beamed. "I got them, Miss Adair! These two elderly women were lurking suspiciously by the display of silver dressing table sets and I caught them at it. Goodness only knows what they were planning to steal. One of them has a capacious carpet bag with her; they could have been planning anything. Father will be delighted that I have foiled such a robbery. Delighted. Ah, here he is." Roddy looked like an eager basset hound, keen to perform tricks for its master.

Hector Arrol looked anything but delighted. "Roderick, clear all these bystanders away. This is not the impression we want people to have of Arrol's."

Roddy's face fell and he beckoned over two of his assistants to shepherd customers away from the area. I took pity on him and helped to direct people clear of the scene.

Hector Arrol let out a shocked gasp. "Oh! My dear lady! Let them go! Let them go!" As I turned around to see who he was 'dear lady-ing', he raised his voice, furiously. "Roderick, do you not know who this *is*?"

The security guards stepped away from the two women. Floss casually readjusted her hat, before brushing down both her and Jo's skirts and then turned to Roddy, one eyebrow raised in annoyance. "*Elderly* women?"

WEDNESDAY 25TH AUGUST 1920
JOHNNIE

Johnnie had spent the past week debating her next step. She'd told Meg that the likelihood was that Ruby had been murdered and Meg's response had been a shrug and a brief, "Poor lassie," and then she had rubbed Ruby's name off her board and allocated the day's duties, as if Ruby had never existed. It seemed that her concern over Ruby's disappearance was only that she might give the gang's secrets away. Johnnie had started to view Meg in a new light since their conversation about the drug trade, and this seemed another example of Meg's callousness. Perhaps it had been there all along, but she had chosen to ignore it, because of what she felt she owed to Meg and because it hadn't affected her before. Ruby had been a silly girl, but she had deserved more than this.

Having laid low for the previous couple of weeks, Meg was keen that everything should now be business as usual. They hadn't noticed any extra police activity following the jewellery shop thefts, and none of the other gangs seemed to be paying any particular interest to them, so Meg had decided they could now go back to their normal round of pickpocketing and shoplifting, although jewellery shops would be off the agenda for a little while.

Meg had allocated Johnnie to Queen Street station, but before she left, Johnnie went back up to Ruby's. Nobody had been allocated her bed yet and Ruby's things were still there in a pathetic little pile. Not much to show for her fifteen years, although Johnnie was certain that Christine and Evvy would have shared anything worth taking between them. There were no clothes, for a start. Evvy would have taken those, she guessed. The little blonde tortoiseshell and gilt box that Ruby had stolen from Arrol's just before she disappeared was also missing. Johnnie glanced around the room. It was lying next to Christine's bed and she crossed the room and picked up the box. She opened the lid; inside was the cheap locket that had belonged to Ruby's mother. Johnnie took the locket out and looked at it a moment, before putting it down where the box had been. She put the box itself into the pocket underneath her petticoat.

Ruby's death weighed heavily on her for a reason that she couldn't quite fathom and Winnie's words from the previous week rang in her ears. "You call yourselves the Avengers, don't you? Don't you think someone should avenge Ruby's death? God alone knows no-one looked out for her in life, by the sound of it."

Winnie had told her to go and see the woman at the police station, this Miss Adair. She didn't need to say anything about the St Thenue's Avengers, all she needed to do was say that Ruby had been murdered. This woman would take it from there, wouldn't she? Johnnie had no time for the police, but she didn't know what else she could do.

WEDNESDAY 25TH AUGUST 1920
MABEL

My grandmother seemed to be in a brighter mood this evening, as Floss and Jo regaled her over dinner with their tale of being arrested for shoplifting.

Floss speared a piece of asparagus. "We wanted to see Mabel at work, but we knew she wouldn't want us there."

"So we were hiding," Jo added.

"Behind the suitcases."

I groaned. The story became more and more embarrassing to me the more I heard it, but Floss and Jo weren't at all embarrassed by the experience. Roddy had come across them giggling like a pair of toddlers and had somehow come to the conclusion that they were there to shoplift.

"The only high point to all this," I said, fixing them both with a stern gaze, as if they were, in actual fact, a pair of recalcitrant toddlers, "is that the ghastly Roddy had to take a public dressing down from his revered father and slunk away nursing his wounds."

Floss raised her eyebrows. "Oh, he's not as bad as his father, surely? That man is the most sickening sycophant that it has ever been my displeasure to meet."

Jo made a retching sound and I sighed. "Honestly, you two are ridiculous. Grandmother, what do you think of this pair?"

She clapped her hands in glee. "I think they're delightful. I can just picture it."

Floss patted her arm. "You should have come with us, Lillias. Then we could *all* have embarrassed Mabel."

My grandmother's smile faded. "I wish I had the courage that you and Jo have. And the purpose."

"The purpose? We didn't have a purpose when we went, did we, Jo? Just fun."

THE DEVIL'S DRAPER

"But you always do everything with purpose. All of you." My grandmother looked at each of us in turn. "It doesn't matter what it is. I don't feel like that. I feel...lost. Aimless. I spent nearly fifty years at Beau Rivage knowing exactly what every day had in store for me. I had tasks to do. I breakfasted at nine, walked in the grounds at ten, sewed linens at eleven. I don't have that anymore."

"But you still do your sewing, grandmother."

"Yes. But at half past two, or three twenty-five or eight o'clock. I have no meaning."

Tears pricked at my eyelids and I blinked them away. "Oh, don't say that. You have meaning to us." I got up from the table to hug her from behind. "We love having you here."

She patted my hand and turned to kiss me on the cheek. "Oh my dear, I sound dreadfully ungrateful. And I'm not, I can assure you." She sighed and her face dropped still further. "And, with my money just about at an end, too; I would have ended up in the Poorhouse, and here I am in this beautiful home surrounded by beautiful people. At one point, I thought that Arthur..." This was the first time she had mentioned his name, her husband. My grandfather. A shudder went through her. "I just want to do something useful. It will just take me time, I'm sure. Just as with going outside; I simply need to practise."

This had been the thing we worried about most. Going out was overwhelming for her. "Where can we take you? Where would you like to go?"

She thought for a moment. "Well, my dear. I really enjoyed visiting your friend, Winnie. She reminded me of Henrietta. She smiled sadly. "I miss Henrietta."

She had told us about her friend in Beau Rivage, Henrietta – a patient, like her, who had looked after her, showed her the ropes and given her strength. Henrietta, along with my grandmother's maid, Mary Grace, had helped her when she found out that she was pregnant with my mother, Clementina. They'd looked after both of them when Clemmie was born.

THE DEVIL'S DRAPER

I got up from the table and went to get the glossy coromandel box out of its usual place. I brought it back and placed it in front of my grandmother. She opened it and took out the familiar items one at a time. "I made this shawl for Clemmie. Henrietta showed me how to knit." She laughed. "Look at all the holes. I can't believe she kept it. And Mary Grace made her this little doll from one of the laundry's clothes pegs." Her fingers lingered on the two locks of hair, nestled together in their little square of worn muslin, the blonde one that was her own and the chestnut one that was my mother's. "Your hair is just like hers, Mabel. Down to that stubborn little cowlick at the front." She reached up a hand and stroked my hair. "You are so very like her the day I last saw her. She was not quite fourteen." Finally, she pulled out the two letters again, one in her own neat handwriting, the other in the childish unformed scrawl of my mother and read them to herself, silently. We all four of us knew every word, every fold, every smudge on these pages.

I kissed the top of her head and went to sit back down in my place at the table. Mrs Dugan would not be pleased. We had quite neglected our fine dinners. "Tell us about Clemmie again," I said. "And Mary Grace and Henrietta. And you, grandmother. Tell us all about you."

THURSDAY 26TH AUGUST 1920
JOHNNIE

Johnnie took a deep breath, trying to summon up the courage to go into the police station in St Andrew's Square. Walking into a police station? Voluntarily? She glanced around her. She hadn't told Meg she was coming, of course, and it wouldn't do for any of the St Thenue's Avengers to see her walking into this place.

Nobody was around and it was now or never. She pushed open the heavy door; the inside smelled of wood polish and sweat. A portly policeman was standing behind the high wooden counter. He looked Johnnie up and down and seemingly found her wanting.

Johnnie had dressed very carefully for this visit in a navy serge skirt and cream poplin blouse. Something smart but forgettable. Her hat was of straw with a small veil and navy ribbon. She had tucked her hair fully underneath and had pulled the hat low to cover one side of her face. It was a completely different look from any of her usual ones. Even Big Annie had only just recognised her as she passed her on the stairs that morning.

"Aye, Miss. How can I help you?" She had never been spoken to so politely by a policeman.

She had practised a soft, precise voice for this. Nothing posh, just one which would suit a receptionist in a good hotel, or a ladies' maid, or a secretary. "I'm here to see Miss Adair."

"Miss Adair, is it?"

"Yes, to give my statement." Winnie had told her the best things to say.

"A statement about what, Miss?"

"I'd rather not say."

He nodded and smirked. "An' do you have an appointment with Miss Adair?"

THE DEVIL'S DRAPER

She hesitated a moment. Would this be something that was easy to check, or would he just not bother? "Yes."

"Name."

"She's expecting me." Johnnie looked pointedly at her watch. "At ten."

He shrugged and turned away, as if fed up of toying with her. "I'll get her for you, Miss."

But he didn't. He footered about behind the counter with some papers, before taking a huge bite out of a pasty and slowly chewing, like a cow chewing its cud. Johnnie shifted from one foot to the other and cleared her throat to remind him that she was still there. She felt exposed, standing here, right in the middle of a police station. Finally, he heaved a big sigh and walked heavily to the back of the office, exiting through one of the doors. He returned a few moments later and heaved himself back onto his stool without looking at Johnnie, or acknowledging her continued presence in any way. Johnnie sidled closer to the outside door. Should she just leave?

At that moment, however, a door in the far wall of the foyer opened and a young woman appeared. She looked puzzled. "Hello? You said you have an appointment, Miss...?"

Johnnie stared at her, her heart sinking. This was Miss Adair? The woman she had punched in the nose outside Arrol's? She debated making her escape while she still could. But this woman didn't seem to recognise her and this was Johnnie's only chance of finding out what had happened to Ruby. She hesitated. "MacBride," she said. "Mrs MacBride."

Miss Adair smiled and gestured her through the door. "Please, come this way, Mrs MacBride."

Johnnie hoped that this wasn't a trick and followed the policewoman through the door and along a long corridor, to a door halfway down. Miss Adair opened it and held the door for her. Johnnie went in and immediately tried to leave again. This *was* a trick. The room was dark and windowless, as small as a cell.

THE DEVIL'S DRAPER

It *was* a cell. But Miss Adair was standing directly behind her in the doorway and she couldn't leave. A flickering light came on overhead, as Miss Adair flicked a switch just inside the door.

Johnnie looked around her. Not a cell; cells didn't have desks. But still not pleasant.

"Yes, it's not very nice, I'm afraid. But it's my office and we won't be disturbed here. Do sit down, please. Can I get you a cup of tea?" Johnnie shook her head. She didn't want to be in here any longer than was absolutely necessary. Miss Adair sat down at the desk opposite her and pulled over a pad of paper and a pen. "I'm very sorry, Mrs MacBride, but I don't have you down in my diary. Did we have an appointment?"

"No. I just…I just said that."

Miss Adair smiled reassuringly. "Well, no matter. Now, how can I help you?" Johnnie hesitated. By now, she was sure this was a mistake. Miss Adair was looking at her, her head on one side, as if thinking. "I feel I know you – have we met before somewhere?"

"I…I don't think so, Miss Adair, no." Johnnie was making sure that she kept up her diffident secretary voice.

"Oh, well." Miss Adair sat, pen poised, waiting for Johnnie to start.

Johnnie was relieved that the other woman had let the matter drop. She hadn't recognised her, or she would have said. Johnnie knew she looked totally different to how she had that day, at Arrol's. Her hair was safely tucked under her hat and Miss Adair had only caught a fleeting glimpse of her face after all. No, she was safe. "It's about a friend of mine. Ruby. Ruby Fallon." Miss Adair nodded, as if trying to place the name. "She…she died recently. They fished her body out of the Clyde."

Miss Adair's face cleared. "Oh, yes, the unfortunate suicide. I know of it, as they brought her body here. I'm so sorry for the loss of your friend, Mrs MacBride. That must have come as a great shock; she was very young."

"Aye, aye, she was. It did."

THE DEVIL'S DRAPER

"Had you known her long?"

"Aye...well, no. Not long. I didn't really..." Johnnie was thoroughly regretting this. She hadn't thought it out well enough; how could she have been so stupid? She stood up. "Look, I...I'd better..."

"I'm sorry, Mrs MacBride. Please sit down. This must be very hard for you; are you sure you don't want a cup of tea?"

Johnnie sat back down and shook her head. "It's just...I don't think Ruby killed herself, Miss Adair. I heard she had wounds that made them think she was killed. Murdered."

Miss Adair nodded. "Well, they said that the injuries could have happened in the water, after she fell, but there was mention of possible foul play, yes. What makes you think it was murder?"

"She had no reason to kill herself. Things were going well for her, an' I just think something might have happened to her... that she might have done something..."

"Done something? Like what? What do you think your friend might have done? Was she in some sort of trouble?"

That was the problem – Johnnie didn't know; she just had a vague feeling and that wasn't going to be enough. She fingered the tortoiseshell box which was still in her pocket. She thought Evvy's mention of a man might be important, but she knew she couldn't bring up the fact that Ruby had been shoplifting in Arrol's the day before she disappeared. Not only could she not tell this policewoman that Ruby was a shoplifter, but the very mention of Arrol's would be likely to jog the woman's memory and she would remember where she'd seen Johnnie after all. And she certainly couldn't mention the connection with St Thenue's Avengers, of course. But she knew that her story was weak without all of that. How could she convince this woman to investigate Ruby's death, when all she could say was that Ruby wouldn't have killed herself? Coming here had been utterly pointless. "Are you investigating her death? The police, I mean?"

THE DEVIL'S DRAPER

"No. We have no cause to, unless you can give us one. *Can you?*" Johnnie shook her head and Miss Adair leaned forward, looking at her earnestly. "Mrs MacBride, please tell me if you know something; I can't do anything unless you do. Your friend's death has already been recorded as a suicide."

Johnnie thought back to what Winnie had told her about Miss Adair's kindness, about how she always stood up for those less fortunate, particularly poor and vulnerable women. But she couldn't trust her. Miss Adair was the police and she, for her part, was a thief; they weren't on the same side. She stood up. "I'm sorry to have wasted your time. Perhaps it was suicide after all."

"But you don't think so, do you?" Miss Adair didn't give her a chance to answer. "Does this have anything to do with your... employment?"

Johnnie was confused. "My employment?" As far as she could remember she hadn't said anything about working.

"Yes." Miss Adair put her hand to her cheek. "You gave me quite the black eye, you know, and for an awful moment I thought my nose was broken...Mrs MacBride."

THE DEVIL'S DRAPER

THURSDAY 26TH AUGUST 1920
BEATRICE

The girl in front of Beatrice was teary and red-eyed. Beatrice had come across her sobbing her eyes out in the stock room on the top floor, hidden behind a huge box of wool.

"What is it...Anna, isn't it?" She had placed Anna here a month or so ago and had seen her a few times since, but not to speak to.

"Yes, Mrs Price, Anna Nicholls."

Beatrice touched Anna's arm. "What's wrong, my dear?"

Anna shook her head, fearfully. "Nothing, ma'am."

"Now, I don't believe that for one moment. What is it?"

"It's nothing. Nothing at all." Anna stood up from her hiding place. "I need to get back out on the floor. Mr Arrol will be wondering where I am."

"Don't worry about him. Come along, we'll go to my office and have a cup of tea."

The girl looked horrified. "Oh, I couldn't Mrs Price. If he sees me with you, he'll think I'm...He told me not to... I cannae lose this job, my maw needs the money too much."

"He'll think you're what, Anna? Telling me something you shouldn't be telling me, is that it?" Anna looked at her and then wiped her eyes with the hem of her apron. "Has he been doing something to you that he shouldn't be doing? Is that it?" Anna was only fourteen. Beatrice would never forgive herself if she'd come to any harm. She looked down at her hands, which were trembling and clasped them together.

"It's no matter, Mrs Price. My maw says it's what all men do."

"You've told your mother?"

"Aye. She told me it was just what happened and that I should just put up with it. Oh!" she wailed and started to cry again. "I cannae get the sack."

THE DEVIL'S DRAPER

Beatrice took the girl's face in her hands. It was hot and damp and Beatrice wanted to take her in her arms and comfort her, but she needed to be business-like. "You won't get the sack, I promise you, Anna. And this *isn't* something you should just put up with; it's not something that just happens and it won't happen again, I promise you that, too, Anna." She gulped, shaken by the unwelcome thought that this wasn't something she *could* promise.

THURSDAY 26TH AUGUST 1920
MABEL

"Oh." The young woman on the other side of the desk flushed and had the grace to look embarrassed.

I crossed my arms and glared at her. "Yes, 'Oh'. Did you think I hadn't recognised you?"

She grinned. "I did, actually." Unlike me, she looked remarkably relaxed.

"Well, you clearly don't have a very good opinion of me, which makes me wonder why you came to see me in the first place." I sat back in my chair, trying to unclench my jaw.

She raised her hands. "Winnie."

My anger subsided somewhat. "Oh." My shoulders relaxed and I sat forward.

"Yes, 'Oh'," she repeated my words back to me, rather mockingly. "She had very good things to say about you and said that if anyone could help me, you could."

That made me feel all warm inside. To have Winnie's approval felt important. "So, can I take it that you're not Mrs MacBride?"

She hesitated a moment. "Johnnie."

"And are you one of the St Thenue's Avengers?"

"I'd rather not talk about that, if you don't mind. I'm here on my own account, not theirs."

"And why *are* you here?"

Again, she hesitated. "I'm not really sure. All I know is that Ruby didn't kill herself and I can't think of any reason anyone would want to murder her. But something happened before she died, I know it."

"What, exactly?"

She let out a big sigh. "That's the thing, I don't know. It's really just a feeling I have. One of the girls she shares a flat with mentioned a man."

"What man?" I picked up my pen and notepad.

"Again. I don't know. I've spoken to this girl a couple of times now and all I can get out of her is that Ruby stole something. Something..." she seemed to be carefully gauging her words. "She stole something that she had no right stealing."

"But isn't that what you do, you Avengers? Steal things that you have no right stealing?"

It was her turn to glare at me. "We have rules. We don't just do what we want. We have a strict..." she stopped, as though she'd said too much. "We need to be disciplined, professional, otherwise it will go badly for all of us. An' Ruby wasn't disciplined and I think that's why she's dead. She stole something and this man, whoever he was, caught her doing it and forced her to tell him stuff about...us." The words had come out in a rush and I could sense her distress. It was as though someone had let all of the air out of a balloon.

"About the St Thenue's Avengers?" She was going to have to admit that she was part of the gang at least, otherwise she would just tie herself in knots.

"Aye. That's what...what this other girl said. He threatened her, threatened *us*."

She was watching me carefully. "And now she's dead."

"Aye. An' not only do I want to find out who murdered her, because she was a wee lassie who didn't deserve it, but I need to make sure the rest of us aren't in danger." Her face was pinched and her eyes were full of tears that she was trying desperately not to shed.

I thought about all that she had said for a moment, and how insubstantial it was, tapping my pen on my notebook. I hadn't written any of this down; it seemed foolish to do so, somehow. "And does your... boss... queen... whatever you call her, know about all of this?"

THE DEVIL'S DRAPER

"No. I told her I thought Ruby had been murdered but...well, she didn't seem bothered. And that didn't seem right, either. We had a responsibility to Ruby — she was only a wee lassie and had only recently joined us. We let her down; we're supposed to stick together, an' look out for each other. That's what it was always like before, but now..." The words had come out in a rush, but now she stopped and shook her head. "Anyway, I never told M——; I never told my boss, as you call her, about this man. Not yet, anyways."

"And what was it that Ruby stole, do you think it important?"

"Naw." She hesitated and then fished into her pocket and pulled out a small, shiny box. "Just this. She stole it from -"

"Arrol's," I said, drily. I recognised it as one of the little treasures in Roddy's department.

She grinned, briefly. "Aye. Arrol's. I don't think the box itself is important, though. But this man must have seen her there, or followed her from there, or something."

"And is that why you were there when you...punched me on the nose? To find out about this man?"

She laughed, the memory of that giving her some relief, it seemed. "Naw. I'm sorry about that, by the way. It was more of an accident — your nose just got in the way. I wisnae there because of that, though. I was there because... well, it was my job to be there that day."

We were interrupted by a knock at the door. Before I had a chance to call out, Lorrimer opened the door and poked his head in. "Mabel, I just wanted to see if... Oh, I'm sorry, I didn't realise you had anyone with you."

I smiled at him, hoping I didn't look remotely guilty of anything. "No problem, Detective Inspector Lorrimer. I'll be along to see you shortly."

He looked curiously at Johnnie, who had lowered her head and raised her hand as if to scratch the side of her face that was closest to him. "Of course, Miss Adair. Apologies once more."

THE DEVIL'S DRAPER

Johnnie and I were both silent for a moment after he had shut the door behind him. "What do you want me to do?" I asked.

"Well, I thought maybe you could…investigate? Find out how she really died. Can you say that you've had a tip that she was murdered, rather than jumped? Won't someone listen to that?"

I laughed, hollowly. "I'm not sure what you think my role here is, Johnnie, but I can assure you that if I were to tell anyone what you've told me, they would just laugh at me and tell me I was imagining things and that I should just keep my nose out of things that aren't my business."

She frowned, obviously confused, and I couldn't say that I blamed her. "But you're a police officer, surely this *is* your business?"

I sighed heavily. This again. "I'm a statement taker. I take statements from women and children. Statements which the men around here then generally interpret in any way they want to and simply carry on as normal, as though those statements had never happened. Unless it suits them, of course." My tone was more bitter than I had meant it to be. There was something about this young woman that made me want to be honest.

"Oh." She looked crestfallen. "So Winnie was wrong and you can't do anything, so there was no point in me coming to see you?" She sounded like a little girl now, not the confident, gallus young woman she had been only a few moments ago.

I sat back in my seat and folded my arms. "I wouldn't say that, no. In my time here, I've learned that there's more than one way to skin a cat; I just don't want you to think it's going to be easy." She looked unconvinced. "And you have to accept that nothing may ever come of it."

"Aye, well, thank you for your time, anyway." She stood up and headed towards the door.

"How can I find you?" She turned and looked at me, suspicion on her face. "If I have any news, or I need to talk to you again?"

"Oh, aye." She shrugged. "Well, I'm no' giving you my address. I'll call in and speak to Winnie regularly. You can let her know if you need me."

"Rightie-ho," I said, brightly. I got up from my desk. "I'll see you out."

"No need." She pulled the door open. "I'll find my own way."

I'd hoped she would say that. I waited a few moments to give her time to reach the end of the corridor, then opened my door. I glanced to the left and the door at the end was swinging gently. I turned to the right and sped down to the other end of the corridor and turned into another passageway. My goal was one of the side entrances to the building. I peered out cautiously, just in time to see the young woman turning into Steel Street.

I closed the side door behind me and ran to the corner, where I watched her as she crossed Saltmarket and turned into the Briggait.

The Briggait was busy with hawkers and barrows and a stream of people going in both directions, so it was easy for me to follow her, unnoticed. I kept carefully back. She turned around once, and I quickly hopped into one of the spirit merchants that dotted the street. When I put my head back outside again, she was heading into Merchant Lane.

I reached the corner just in time to see her stop outside a close and, once again, she looked up and down the street, before heading inside.

I waited for about ten minutes, but she didn't come back out. By then, a man with a fruit barrow was beginning to look at me with suspicion. I checked my watch and shook my head, cultivating a look of disappointment, as though I'd been stood up and strolled off back the way I had come.

FRIDAY 27TH AUGUST 1920
MABEL

I had succumbed to the temptations of the larkspur and lemon dress at Arrol's, with the intention of wearing it to dinner at Chez Antoine's and I was very pleased with my choice. As he pulled out my chair for me, Lorrimer nodded approvingly. "Mabel, you look—"

I held up my hand. "James, if you say 'nice', I promise I won't ever speak to you again."

He laughed. "I was going to say 'delightful'. Does that meet with your approval?"

"It will do," I said, airily, as though gentlemen pronounced me delightful every day.

As we ate our meal, I sounded Lorrimer out on the subject of Ruby. "That young woman who was pulled out of the Clyde; I understand it may not have been suicide."

"Really? Where did you hear that?"

I popped an oyster into my mouth and waved a hand, nonchalantly. "Oh, just something someone said. That the coroner thought that her injuries were more likely to have been caused by someone hitting her over the head."

Lorrimer paused as he raised his soup spoon to his mouth. "I thought she'd hit her head on the rocks. Are you saying it was murder?" The cheery music tonight's band was playing lent a surreal feeling to our conversation, but at least it meant we wouldn't be overheard by any of the other diners.

"Mmmmm, well, I think it's a possibility, don't you? Perhaps Superintendent Orr might think it's worth investigating?"

He laughed. "You mean if *I* raise it? Is that what you're angling for?"

THE DEVIL'S DRAPER

I stabbed at another oyster with my fork, as though it were one of Orr's eyeballs. "Well, he's unlikely to listen to me, is he?"

Lorrimer looked at me, his eyes narrowed. "Mabel, do you know something about this?"

I feigned an expression of total innocence and tapped my foot in time to the music, as though I had not a care in the world. "Me? Of course not. I just wondered, that's all. It's not important."

We lapsed into silence and I went back to looking around me at the other diners. I was rather taken by the smart couple at the table behind Lorrimer. I'd been attracted to them first of all by the flamboyant feather the woman was wearing in her hair and the shimmering dress of oyster satin, which showed off her lithe figure. She sat directly under a chandelier of beaten copper, which cast a mellow golden light on her that set off the creamy blonde of her hair and I'd spent a good five minutes admiring her, before I'd turned my attention to her companion. He had his back to me and I could see very little, other than the back of a well-cut evening suit and his glistening, slicked-back hair.

One of the waiters had been paying particular attention to the couple and I had seen nods pass between him and the gentleman. This waiter was hovering by their table, intercepting any food, so that he would be the one to serve it. I was amused by this. Perhaps the gentleman had proved to be a good tipper in the past and the waiter was trying to take advantage of this fact.

We'd finished our main course, a rather fine fillet of sole Parisienne for me and roast lamb for Lorrimer, and the waiter had taken our dessert order. Superintendent Orr had told us that this was the last time we would be dining and dancing at his expense – although he had put it much more rudely than that, according to Lorrimer – so we were pushing the boat out with a bottle of 1906 Vintage Ayala. When Lorrimer got up to go to the gentlemen's room, I concentrated on the couple, inventing a story for them. She was a very striking woman, not exactly pretty, but with a face that you couldn't stop looking at, and a magnetic presence. She was

THE DEVIL'S DRAPER

a famous stage actress, I decided. Yolanda, yes, that was it, and he was a Duke or an Earl, who was besotted by her adventurous spirit and the sense of danger that came from being in her presence. They had just come back from a wild few days in Paris...no, Marrakech, where they had fled a Russian Tsar with evil designs on...

I was brought out of my reverie as the band struck up the Tiger Rag and the couple got up to dance. As he stood up, the man folded a five-pound note and tucked it into the plant pot on the table. As they moved onto the dance floor, the attentive waiter came over and started to clear the table. He piled the dishes up but, instead of carrying them off, he left them on the table, looked around him and then pulled a small package wrapped in blue paper from his trouser pocket. He took the five-pound note from the plant pot and replaced it with the blue package. Then he picked up the plates and disappeared towards the kitchen.

I was debating whether to go and see what the package was, when Lorrimer came back to the table. I told him what I'd seen. "Do you think it's drugs?"

He nodded. "Almost certainly. Are they still dancing?"

"Yes. You can see the feather in her hair." I pointed the couple out to him. The band had started on another tune, a foxtrot this time, and the couple had remained on the dance floor.

Lorrimer stood. "Wait here. I'm going to step out into the street. We always have patrols in this area to deter pickpockets."

I grabbed at his arm. "Wait! What should I do if they come back to their table?"

He glanced over at the couple again. They were still dancing gaily. "Watch them. And if they should take the package and leave, follow them. I won't be far away."

I nervously awaited his return, hoping against hope that the couple would keep dancing until he came back. As the last notes of the foxtrot died away and the band started to play something more mellow which I didn't recognise, the couple began to wend their way back to the table. I could see the man now. He had a weak

THE DEVIL'S DRAPER

chin and a narrow moustache, which he kept raising his hand to, smoothing it out in a rather affected gesture. As they arrived back at the table, the woman sank back into her seat with a high-pitched laugh, fanning herself, and the man reached over and plucked the little blue package from the plant pot, tucking it into his jacket pocket in one seamless gesture.

I breathed a sigh of relief, as I saw Lorrimer approaching. He raised his eyebrows at me and I nodded, gesturing towards my right-hand side, and patting the place where my jacket pocket would have been if I'd been a man. Lorrimer gave a faint smile and sat down. "Don't look, but there are two uniformed policemen over by the door. I want you to go over to the couple's table and distract their attention."

"How?"

"I'm sure you'll think of something. Praise that feather of hers or some such nonsense. I just need long enough to stop him from getting rid of the package."

I stood up and walked towards the couple's table. As I did, I pretended to trip, bumping into the woman and knocking her cocktail glass from her hand, onto her oyster satin dress. She stood up and shrieked. I pretended to be mortified. "Oh, I'm so sorry. Please forgive me." I picked up a napkin from the table and started dabbing at her dress, as she pushed my hands away. "No, no, I insist, let me do it. I shall pay for dry cleaning, of course. Oh, I'm so terribly clumsy. I'm so very sorry." I was quite enjoying myself.

When I turned round, Lorrimer had the man in an impressive arm lock with his one good arm. Two policemen dashed over and each took one of the man's arms. Lorrimer reached into the man's pocket. The band continued to play, not quite drowning out the shrieking of the woman and the blustering of her companion, but only a few tables seemed to have noticed what was going on. The policemen led the man away and the woman followed, still continuing to shriek incoherently. Lorrimer followed them. "I'll be back in a moment," he called over his shoulder. "Order us another

THE DEVIL'S DRAPER

bottle of that champagne. This calls for a celebration."

Two waiters appeared and removed the debris from the neighbouring table. Within a minute, it had been reset, another couple had been ushered in and seated there, and I had a bottle of champagne and two fresh glasses poured in front of me. I took out a handkerchief and dabbed away a bead of sweat from my forehead, then lifted the cold glass of champagne to my mouth with a trembling hand.

Lorrimer arrived back at the table, sat down and toasted me with his champagne glass. "Well done, Mabel; your acting skills are magnificent."

I toasted him back. "Where are they?"

"On their way to Central Division. Superintendent Orr will be delighted."

"And the waiter?"

"On his way there, too. A third policeman caught him as he tried to escape through the kitchen."

I sat back and gestured around the room. "And look at this. You'd never know that anything had happened."

He laughed. "I think they're used to this sort of thing at Chez Antoine. Although...I think there's someone headed our way. He keeps waving at you."

I turned around. "Oh, good grief."

A beaming Gilbert Arrol was making a beeline towards us. He lifted a hand in greeting. "I say, Mabel, how exciting! We saw it all happen, every bit of it."

Gilbert was accompanied by a very striking woman of about forty. Her hair was clipped close to her skull on one side, and ear length on the other and set in sharp waves. She wore a filmy outfit made up of multiple multi-coloured layers of silk, the uppermost of which was patterned with what looked like hand-painted eyes at intervals. On her right cheek was painted a further eye, and her own eyes were ringed and smudged dark with kohl pencil. Her lips were a bright orange-red.

THE DEVIL'S DRAPER

"Mabel, may I introduce my friend, Countess Colette von der Weid."

I was thrilled. "Oh, how marvellous to meet you, Countess. Gilbert has shown me some of your work and I found it fascinating."

She waved an airy hand in dismissal, before pressing it on my arm. "Please, ma chère, call me Coco. Gilbert has told me all about you, too." She looked at me and raised an eyebrow. "What he neglected to mention was how *brave* you are."

I laughed. "Oh dear, I'm sure you don't approve. I'm an authority figure after all, even if not a very good example of one."

"Au contraire, ma chère. You are...what is the word... subverting authority by your very presence. I am impressed."

I smiled and gestured towards Lorrimer. "Well, here's another example for you, and a much better one than me. Coco, Gilbert, this is one of my colleagues, Detective Inspector James Lorrimer."

He smiled and held out his hand to each of them in turn. "James, please. Delighted to meet you both."

"I say, can we join you?" Gilbert didn't wait for an answer and, instead, pulled over two chairs from an empty table nearby. "I'm absolutely dying to find out what that was all about. All that police business there. What had they done, that pair? Dope fiends? Jewel thieves? Human traffickers? Or just crimes against the bird population? That feather was rather de trop, was it not?"

I laughed and looked at Lorrimer. I wasn't sure how much we should say, but he seemed quite comfortable answering truthfully. "The former, I'm afraid. Or, at least, so we can only assume."

Gilbert turned back to me, reproachfully. "I say, Mabel, why don't you tell me exciting stories like this over tea? All I get to hear about is how dull your job is and how everyone hates you."

Lorrimer raised an eyebrow at me and I could feel my face reddening. "Don't exaggerate, Gilbert. It's only almost everyone."

He waved a hand to the waiter, gesturing him over. "When are you coming back to Arrol's, anyway? I miss our little tea parties. It's nowhere near as much fun annoying Roddy without your help."

THE DEVIL'S DRAPER

"Sadly, I don't think I'll be back in a working capacity, but I promise I'll come in and see you one afternoon. How about that?"

"More than *one* afternoon, if you please." A waiter appeared at his elbow. "Now, shall we order another bottle of champagne in celebration of your tireless police work?" Without waiting for an answer, he did so and the waiter dashed off. "By the way, that dress looks rather stunning on you, doesn't it, James?"

"It is rather nice, yes."

Nice. That annoying word again.

MONDAY 30TH AUGUST 1920
JOHNNIE

It had only been three days. The policewoman had warned her that nothing might ever be uncovered about Ruby's death, but Johnnie was impatient. She had no reason to distrust Miss Adair and was sure that she would do her best, but would the policewoman's best lead to anything worthwhile? She might have to accept the fact that Ruby's death would remain an unfair mystery.

As the Avengers gathered in the war room for their day's assignments, she looked over at Evvy. The girl was sitting on the floor, chewing her nails. She glanced up as though she could feel Johnnie's eyes on her and then looked away. Johnnie was struck once again by the suspicion that Evvy knew something more than she was telling.

Johnnie stepped towards her and crouched down. "Evvy, you have to tell me."

Without taking her fingers out of her mouth, Evvy mumbled, "Nowt to tell."

"Aye there is and you know it." Johnnie was trying to keep her voice low, but when she looked round, Meg was scowling at her.

"Johnnie, come and sit down. We've no' got all day." Johnnie reluctantly moved away from Evvy and took her usual place.

Meg called them all to order, standing in front of the big slate board, chalk poised. She allocated jobs efficiently and the women whose names had been called quietly disappeared. Meg didn't like them all to leave at once, so everyone had got into the habit of leaving immediately they knew what job they were to do, unless they had a specific reason to stay behind. Soon, only five or so were left, including both Johnnie and Evvy.

Eventually, Meg turned her way. "Johnnie, I want you in Treron's today and then Arrol's."

"Arrol's?"

"Aye, but don't worry. I don't want you stealin' anythin', so there's no risk. An' if you go in dressed as a girl, you can see if anyone takes special notice of you, if they remember you from before wi' the lady polis. I just want you to take young Evvy and show her the ropes. Best ways in and out, point out the security staff and the assistants who take notice."

"But—"

Meg held up a chalk-covered finger to her. "Aye, I know, you prefer workin' on your own. But you're one o' ma best. I want Evvy to learn from the best, right?"

Johnnie sighed. "Aye, fair enough, Meg." At least it would give her a chance to talk to Evvy. "And Treron's?"

"Evvy's to watch you. That's all. From a distance. I want you to just go for a couple of wee bits an' bobs. Whichever departments take your fancy. Show her how it's done. Evvy, you're only there to watch, is that clear?"

"Aye, Meg." Evvy's voice was subdued and she looked as though this assignment was the last thing in the world she wanted.

Meg fixed Evvy with a stare that made her shrink back. "An' don't make it obvious that you're watchin' Johnnie. Don't go in on her heels. Don't follow her around like Mary's little lamb. Do ye understand?"

"Aye, Meg." The girl's voice was even quieter, if that were possible.

The official name for Treron's was Treron et Cie, Les Magasins des Tuileries, and it definitely thought itself the smartest of Glasgow's department stores. It had forty departments, all of them richly carpeted and with plenty of windows to display the store's high-class goods. Johnnie watched Evvy as she entered one door and then strolled in through the next, acting as though she hadn't a care in the world.

Johnnie wandered through several of the departments, pocketing a trinket here and there. Evvy had taken Meg's words to

THE DEVIL'S DRAPER

heart and trailed her at a distance, almost managing to look casual and innocent most of the time. As Johnnie left the store, Evvy sensibly hung back and Johnnie dawdled and looked in one of the windows until the younger girl came out. Johnnie nodded briefly at her and then set off walking up Rose Street towards Phoenix Park, where she sat on one of the benches to wait for Evvy.

"What did you see me take?"

"A silk scarf." Her response was quick and sure.

What did it look like?

"It was rose-coloured." Again, her voice was sure.

"Anything else?"

"A sugar bowl, a silver one. Fancy." Evvy smiled, apparently enjoying the quiz.

Johnnie nodded. "Aye. Anything else?"

Evvy hesitated and then shook her head.

Johnnie took out the rose-coloured scarf and the silver sugar bowl and gave them to Evvy. "You can have those, for noticing." Evvy looked delighted as she put them away in her pockets, but her face fell as Johnnie pulled out the rest of her treasures: a man's silk scarf striped in mauve and fawn; a hand-embroidered tea tablecloth; an etui case in silver and leather; a brown suede purse; and a folding travelling clock.

Johnnie put them all back in her hidden pockets and stood up. "Come on. Let's go to Arrol's. This time I'm not going to take anything, remember, so we can go in together, like sisters out to window shop. I'll point out anything and anyone you should be aware of. Keep your hands out of your pockets and try not to look suspicious. You did well at Treron's, just keep it up."

They walked the short distance to Arrol's. Evvy kept looking at Johnnie, expecting her to say something, but Johnnie was biding her time. They reached the doors of Arrol's. "We'll start in the basement."

They went downstairs and walked through the household items. From time to time, Johnnie picked up small items. "This

THE DEVIL'S DRAPER

sort of thing is good." She always made sure to put the item back in an obvious way.

As they walked past the café, Evvy paused. "Can we have some cake?"

"No, we can't." Johnnie had decided she would treat the younger girl after they'd finished, but it wouldn't do to tell her that now. "Come on, ground floor."

They walked around the fancy goods on the ground floor and Johnnie stopped several times, pointing out small, valuable goods. She picked up a silver photo frame. "These are always good; and look at the price of them. But only ever take one of the same item."

Evvy nodded. "Look, there's the wee box that Ruby had."

"Aye," said Johnnie. "This is where she got it from."

Evvy picked up one of the tortoiseshell boxes and turned it over and over in her hand. "It's gone now. I don't know where it is. Maybe Chrissie's got it." She sounded regretful, but whether for the loss of Ruby or the box, Johnnie couldn't tell.

"I've got it. You can have it when we get home. Put that back now."

Evvy placed the box carefully back down and then Johnnie led them over to the stairs in the middle of the store. They climbed halfway up and then Johnnie held out a hand to stop Evvy on the step below hers. "Tell me, can you spot the store detectives on the ground floor from here? Don't make it obvious, just look around as though you're people watching."

Evvy glanced down. "Aye. They make it easy, don't they, having them in those fancy braided uniforms. He's standing by that stand of parasols."

Johnnie glanced casually around, as though she was taking everything in. "What about the other one?"

Evvy frowned and looked up at her. "There isnae another one."

Johnnie adjusted the neck of Evvy's dress in big-sisterly fashion. "That's where you're wrong. See that woman over where the dressing table sets are?"

THE DEVIL'S DRAPER

"The one in the blue hat?"

"Aye, that's her. She's a store detective, too. Watch out for her. She takes more notice than the ones in uniform."

"Is she the only..." Evvy trailed off and her face paled.

"What is it?"

Evvy looked at her. "Nothin'."

Johnnie frowned. "Come on, Evvy. What is it, what have you seen?"

"Nothin'."

A trio of women tutted as they went past Johnnie and Evvy. Johnnie pulled Evvy by the arm. "Come on, let's go up. We shouldn't stay too long on the stairs. We don't want to make ourselves too obvious."

They continued up the stairs and Johnnie led Evvy over to a quieter spot near the ladies' nightwear. "Tell me what you saw. Was it something to do with Ruby?"

Evvy hesitated and then nodded. "That man."

"*What* man?" Johnnie walked back over to the staircase and peered down to the floor below. The uniformed security man was now standing over by a display of suitcases. She scanned the rest of the floor. Most of the shoppers were women, but there were four men amongst them. Two of them were accompanying women, one was looking at a table piled high with straw boaters and the fourth was wandering over to the exit. "Evvy, what man?"

There was no response. Johnnie turned round, but Evvy hadn't accompanied her back to the staircase. Johnnie swore under her breath. She went back to the nightwear section, but Evvy wasn't there. Johnnie quickly made her way through the rest of the floor. Evvy was nowhere to be seen.

THE DEVIL'S DRAPER

TUESDAY 31ST AUGUST 1920
BEATRICE

Beatrice bit her lip: for the second day in a row, Anna Nicholls hadn't turned up for work. The girl's family had no phone at home, so Beatrice decided she would go and visit on her lunchbreak. She would get the number 11 tram to Battlefield.

She got off at the octagonal clock tower of Battlefield Rest, with its lustrous green and cream tiles. Anna and her mother and younger brother lived on the second floor of a well-kept tenement building. Beatrice knew that Anna's mother didn't keep well and that her father had been killed in the Great War.

She knocked on the door. For a short time, there was no noise from the other side, but then she heard a shuffling sound and the door was opened a fraction by a small, careworn woman, who looked to be in her late thirties. The woman looked at her suspiciously. "Aye?"

"Mrs Nicholls?"

The woman answered her question with another. "An' who might you be?"

"My name's Beatrice Price. I'm here to see Anna."

"Oh, are ye, indeed? Fillin' her head wi' more nonsense, I'll bet."

"I'm sorry?" Beatrice had no idea what the woman meant.

"She's refusin' to go to work. Told me as you said she shouldnae put up wi' it. Well, that's alright for those as have the luxury of no' workin', but it's no' alright for the likes of Anna."

Beatrice gritted her teeth. "Can I see her?"

Mrs Nicholls shrugged, but opened the door wider to let Beatrice in. "She's in the kitchen. Tell her to bring me a bowl of soup." The woman shuffled off down the hallway, opening a door on the right-hand side and closing it behind her with some force.

THE DEVIL'S DRAPER

She hadn't told Beatrice where the kitchen was, but there was only one other door at the end of the corridor.

She opened it. Anna was sitting at the table with her back to the door. "Who was that, maw?"

"It's me, Anna."

Anna swung round. "Mrs Price!" She stood up.

Beatrice was shocked. "Anna! Your face! what happened?"

Anna looked at her. "Mr Arrol; that's what happened."

THE DEVIL'S DRAPER

TUESDAY 31ST AUGUST 1920
MABEL

I stomped back up the road to Blythswood Square, hands clenched in my pockets. Superintendent Orr had spent most of our regular meeting that afternoon praising Lorrimer to the skies for breaking up a drug ring that had been operating out of Chez Antoine. The waiter who had been arrested had caved under interrogation and had given up several of his colleagues working at clubs and dance halls across Glasgow. To listen to Orr go on, you would think that I hadn't been anywhere in the vicinity.

"It was Miss Adair who spotted the exchange of money and drugs." I gave a small nod of thanks in Lorrimer's direction.

"Aye, well, Miss Adair has a habit of being in the right place at the right time. Shame she didn't use that skill to catch any of that gang of thieves while she was flouncing about like a ninny at Arrol's. Waste o' time that was. An' she lets hersel' get punched in the face by some wee boy."

I still hadn't told him the plain unvarnished truth about all that and he relished every opportunity to cast it up to me. I wasn't quite sure if I'd done the right thing in keeping quiet about Johnnie, but for some reason, I wanted to protect her. And I still needed to find a way to do something about Ruby.

I reached home and went looking for my grandmother. I had decided to take her again to see Winnie. It was a way to get her out of the house. "We'll walk today, shall we? It's a delightful afternoon. And Jo can come and pick us up in about an hour, to save us walking back up the hill."

As we strolled down towards Wilson Street, I pointed out some of the buildings as we passed, particularly the Stock Exchange building on St George's Place, with its grand Venetian and Gothic styles, and the City Chambers. Grandmother seemed less overwhelmed by people than she had previously been and I was happy to see that.

Winnie greeted us with her usual enthusiasm and a steaming pot of Scotch broth, which she ladled into bowls. We tucked in greedily. After she'd settled us and fussed over us, making sure we were comfortable and had everything we needed, Winnie settled herself into one of the chairs with a groan. "Ah, that's good."

"Winnie, you're doing too much." I knew that Winnie shared her duties with her daughter ordinarily, but she had recently been busy with her other job as a seamstress.

"No' much choice, hen. Daisy cannae do it at the moment and you know the council would have me retire if there was any sign that I couldnae do my job. It's way past time, so they say."

"Can't you find anyone to help in the meantime?"

"Daisy'll be back in a couple of weeks, it's no' long."

"I could help." My grandmother's voice was excited. Winnie and I both looked at her. "Let me help. I'd love to. It would make me feel useful for once."

I looked at Winnie. "What do you think?"

My grandmother stood up. "I can do it. I worked in the laundry at the Asylum, I cleaned the floors, even worked out in the kitchen garden. I'm strong and it is only for a couple of weeks."

Winnie held out a hand to stop her. "This isnae an interview, hen. I know you can do it, but are you sure you want to?"

My grandmother nodded her head, vigorously. "Yes, I want to, very much."

Winnie turned to me, looking dubious. "Mabel... would it no' be... strange?"

I smiled at her. "In what way?"

"Well..." she gestured around the place. "It's no' exactly fancy here. What would Miss Adair say?"

I looked at them both. "Floss would say it's a marvellous idea, and I think so too."

THE DEVIL'S DRAPER

TUESDAY 31ST AUGUST 1920
JOHNNIE

Johnnie knocked on the door of the war room and went in. Meg was surrounded by pieces of paper and was busy adding up long strings of numbers on a pad in front of her. She held up her hand and finished the column she was working on and then smiled up at Johnnie, waving her to a seat.

"Evvy still isn't back." Johnnie had told Meg what had happened at Arrol's, but Meg hadn't seemed concerned, and Johnnie wondered at her lack of care, once again.

Meg shrugged. "She'll be back. She probably just got fed up of watching you an' slipped out without you seein' her. You know what these young ones are like."

Johnnie was only a couple of years older than Evvy and she wouldn't have done that. "It doesn't seem like her."

"How do you know? She's only been here a wee while."

Johnnie tried again, just to see what Meg would say. "Like Ruby."

Meg looked annoyed. "Aye, like Ruby. Some girls work out, some don't. You know that."

"But Evvy just disappeared, right in the middle of what we were doing. I don't think—"

"Look, Johnnie, I've been doin' this for years, since I was their age, an' I've seen loads of lassies just like them come and go. It's why we don't tell any of yous too much until you've been here a year or so. They come, they go, but they don't know too much, so it disnae matter. Evvy disnae have too many of our secrets to take with her, so you don't need to worry."

Johnnie raised her voice, unable to stop herself. "But it's not *that* I'm worried about. I'm worried about what's happened to them. That's two young lassies from the Avengers disappeared in as many weeks. An' one of them's now dead."

Meg put her hands on her hips and stared at Johnnie. "Aye, an' she killed herself, that's aw. Lassies who join us don't do so because they've got stable lives and pots of money. For some, we're their only hope, you know that. Ruby's not the first one we've lost to suicide, an' Evvy won't be the first one to run away, if that's what she's done. It's no' an easy life, not for any of us. Not out there, an' not in here, either."

Johnnie knew that. It had been the same for her. A da that beat her, an uncle that did worse. It had been Big Annie who'd found her one day, after she'd run away from what was left of her so-called family and was scavenging for food at the back of a restaurant up one of the lanes in the Merchant City. In the St Thenue's Avengers she'd found a community. As long as you worked hard and were loyal, you were accepted and respected. It was a hard life for the girls and women who chose to do it and prison was still a frequent occurrence, but at least when you came out, you would have a home to go to.

There was something approaching love here, too. If you proved yourself, they cared. You had everything you needed, and sometimes it felt as though you might even have a future. You weren't expected to be always brave, but you *were* expected to do as you were told; Meg was big on discipline and rightly so. You were given another chance if you messed up, but only one. After that, you were out. Meg was a businesswoman. Some of the lassies found that hard to take. Perhaps Evvy *had* simply got fed up, but Johnnie didn't think so. However, it was clear that Meg had made up her mind.

Johnnie sighed. "Maybe you're right. I hope you are."

Meg righted the papers in front of her and slammed shut the big ledger. "Now, I'm glad you're here, Johnnie. We have a big job on tomorrow, something different. An' I want you in on it."

WEDNESDAY 1ST SEPTEMBER 1920
MABEL

Beatrice was pacing my office – a feat in itself, since she could only take four steps in one direction and three in the other. I was fearful for the safety of the mop and bucket. "Beatrice, sit down, do." I pushed the mug of steaming tea over to the other side of my desk and she reluctantly pulled out the rickety chair and sat down.

"He has to be stopped. He assaulted that young lady in the stock room. Simply followed her in, locked the door and then attacked her. Just because he owns the place, it doesn't mean he owns these women, too, you know."

I held up my hands in a placatory gesture to try and calm her. "I know that, Beatrice. It's dreadful."

"And I was there. In that very building; possibly that very department, while it was going on. I feel sick and ashamed. I should have been able to stop it."

"How? How could you have stopped it? You didn't know it was happening."

She slammed her hands down onto her knees. "Not at that very moment, I didn't, no. But I know what he does to them. I've spoken to some of the other girls, remember. And Elsie…"

Elsie was the girl who had put her head in the oven, I knew, so I said gently, "Yes, but you can't just sit about in the stock room all day, waiting."

She looked up at me and I could see the frustration and pain in her eyes. "Well, what *can* I do, then?"

Sadly, I knew that there wasn't much. "Has anyone else seen it happen?"

She shook her head. "No. All of the girls that it's happened to told me that no-one else was about at the time."

THE DEVIL'S DRAPER

We'd talked about this all before. Corroborative evidence was needed. Even if exactly the same thing had happened to two girls, twenty girls, two hundred girls, somebody else needed to corroborate what they said. Gently, I said, "I've seen this before in so many other cases, too. I've taken statements from women who were assaulted. They were so brave to walk through the doors into this place to tell their stories, only for me to say that although *I* believed every word they'd told me, that a court wouldn't care about their experience unless someone else had seen it."

"But surely the fact that there are now six young women who can tell exactly the same story, that he lured them into the stock room, raped them, hit them…my God, he said exactly the same words to at least four of them while he was assaulting them, not just similar, *exactly* the same, and they can all testify to that. Surely that must count for something?"

She placed her cup down on the desk and I reached out and briefly touched her hand. "I wish it did. You'd think it would, but it doesn't." There was so much that was unfair about the law, especially when it came to the treatment of women and children. "Somebody else needs to have seen it."

She thought for a moment. "Well, maybe they did."

"They did? But I thought you said there were no witnesses to any of the assaults?"

She gazed at me defiantly. "Maybe I was wrong."

I looked at her, puzzled. She'd told me several times that no one else saw. "You mean, you think some of the potential witnesses weren't telling the truth? That they're scared to speak out?"

"That too, possibly. But what if *I'm* the witness?"

"You? But you said…" Light suddenly dawned. "Oh no, Beatrice; you can't do that. You'd have to go into court and lie."

"So?"

She would do it, I knew, but I couldn't let her.

THE DEVIL'S DRAPER

THURSDAY 2ND SEPTEMBER 1920
JOHNNIE

Johnnie was waiting nervously in the shadows. She knew that Meg, Big Annie and Gracie were nearby, and she guessed that they, too, might be feeling the same way, with the possible exception of Meg, who never showed nerves. That Meg was there at all was also unusual; she never usually came on jobs with them. This was a new venture.

Johnnie heard a low whistle. She checked her watch, half past one. Meg had been watching the fur warehouse on the Broomielaw herself every night for the past fortnight. In all that time, there had been no police activity around the area between one and three in the morning. The warehouse was secured by a high fence with wire on top and the gate was padlocked. When Meg had been watching, she'd seen no overnight security coming and going, but she'd impressed on them that that didn't mean to say that there wasn't anyone inside the warehouse and they needed to be careful.

Johnnie came out of her hiding place and joined Meg and Big Annie at the gates. Meg had already sawn through the padlock, which she now took off, and they slipped inside the gates. She replaced the now destroyed padlock with one of her own, locking the gate behind them, until they could be sure that no-one was on the premises.

They tried two of the doors leading into the building, but both were locked. The third, however, was unlocked and Meg opened it slowly and carefully. A dim light inside revealed a man seated on a hard chair, a newspaper in his hand, but his head lolling onto his chest.

Big Annie crept up behind him and swiftly circled an arm around his throat, putting a hand over his mouth and, with her other hand, pressing the blade of her razor against his cheek.

THE DEVIL'S DRAPER

Meg slipped on the mask she had brought with her and knelt down in front of the man. He was awake now and looked at her, eyes wide and fearful. "Anyone else here?" He shook his head and mumbled something incomprehensible against Annie's hand. Meg signalled to Annie to let him speak and she moved her hand away from his mouth, but kept her arm around his neck.

He gasped in a much-needed breath, before saying, "Don't kill me. Ah've a family."

Meg patted him on the knee. "We'll no' kill ye. But if you're lyin' tae us about anyone else bein' here, we will." Her voice was a whisper, but her message was clear.

"Ah'm no lyin', ah promise. It's just me. The owner's a miserable bastard an' won't pay for more than one man. Take whit yis want. Ah'll no' complain."

Meg nodded at Johnnie, who opened the bottle of chloroform she held and took a rag out of one of her pockets, tipping the liquid onto the cloth. She held the rag under the man's nose. He struggled for a brief moment, gave a low moan, but was then still, his eyes fluttering closed once again. Annie lowered him to the floor.

Johnnie was concerned. "He'll be alright, won't he?"

Meg laughed. "Aye, he'll be fine. A wee nap, maybe a bit of a sore head when he wakes up, but that's all. Let's get him tied up, just in case he wakes a wee bit too early. Johnnie, here's the key for the padlock; go and let Gracie in."

Johnnie took the key and ran back to the gate, undoing the padlock and pulling the gates wide open. They swung back silently. Meg had oiled them on her last two visits. A dark shape approached the gates and Gracie drove the lorry slowly through them, headlights off. As Johnnie closed and locked the gates once more, Gracie pulled the lorry around the corner of the warehouse, where even if there *were* police patrols before they'd finished, the vehicle wouldn't be noticed.

Johnnie took a last look through the gates, before she and Gracie entered the warehouse once again. Everything was as dark,

THE DEVIL'S DRAPER

still and silent as it had been before they arrived.

The place was huge, but they were only concerned with this floor, in accordance with Meg's instructions, gleaned from a source inside the factory, who had been easily bribed with a bottle of hard liquor. The top floor was the offices and the floor underneath was the finished furs. Meg had told them not to take any of those — they could easily be traced. Instead, they were to concentrate on the ground floor, where the unfinished skins were. They were completely untraceable and easy to fence if you knew where to go, and Meg did. She'd been in contact with a furrier in Liverpool, who would take them off their hands.

The warehouse had a unique smell, musky and pungent, a combination of smoked leather, stale fat, dust, and damp hair. It wasn't exactly unpleasant, but Johnnie wouldn't want to spend too long there. For those who worked there, it must linger in their nostrils when they left to go home. Perhaps they got used to it.

She could recognise some of the skins and walked around the room, stretching a hand out to touch the different types of furs as she passed - the glossy, luxurious sheen of the minks, looking almost wet; the softness of the sable and its rich dark brown and golden tones, the silky blue-grey fur of the chinchilla. She lingered on the soft richness of the beaver fur, stroking the dense pile back and forth. Meg had told them about the different properties of each fur and Johnnie had rolled the names around in her mouth: musquash, louterine, nutria, coney, blue wolf, black seal and opossum, as she tried to remember each one. Meg had given them strict instructions as to what to take and what to leave and she looked for the silver fox, which, she knew, was one of the most valuable of the furs here, with the fineness of its fur and the beautiful colourings that ranged from a pure silver-white to a deep, rich black.

The four of them worked silently, passing each other innumerable times as they went in and out of the warehouse, piling the furs into the back of the lorry. When it was almost full, they

THE DEVIL'S DRAPER

finished the load off with hundreds of fox and squirrel tails and closed the back of the lorry.

Johnnie glanced at her watch. They had been here for two hours. Meg went to open the gates and Gracie drove the lorry out, waving to them as she set out on her long trek down to Liverpool to meet up with the fence. Johnnie went back inside to check on the security guard. He was still snoring away and Johnnie tucked one of the cheaper furs they had left behind under his head and covered him up with a couple more of the larger ones. She went back outside. Big Annie had gone and Meg was waiting impatiently outside the gates. Johnnie slipped through the narrow gap and Meg locked the padlock once more, pocketing her key. It would still be several hours before anyone came to unlock for the day, and a little while longer before they would be able to make their way into the warehouse, through a padlock they wouldn't be able to open. By that time, Gracie would be well on her way to meet the fence and Meg, Annie and Johnnie would be tucked up in bed.

Thursday 2nd September 1920
Mabel

This was the third day in a row that I had noticed the elderly man as I stepped out of the house. He was wearing a well-made, but old-fashioned suit and his sparse grey hair was rather long and straggly. I didn't recognise him and didn't recall ever having seen him before. I hadn't yet mentioned him to Floss and Jo, as I wasn't sure if I was just imagining things. I'd turned round a couple of times as I walked to work and hadn't spotted him following me, so assumed that he, too, lived on Blythswood Square and was simply taking the air.

I turned around when I reached Argyle Street and he was nowhere to be seen, so I continued on my way to St Andrew's Square and the police station. This was my last day at work for the week. I'd taken the next day off – much to Superintendent Orr's disgust – in order to accompany my grandmother down to the public lavatory to spend the day with Winnie. As I'd expected, Floss had been delighted with this development and had sorted my grandmother out with a new pair of comfortable shoes. One of the chairs from the house, which had become my grandmother's favourite, had already been delivered to the lavatory and placed next to Winnie's. It made the already cramped space almost impossible to move in, but Winnie pronounced it cosy and just the thing. I think she was looking forward to the company even more than she was the additional help. We had decided amongst us that my grandmother would spend Friday and Saturday with Winnie, but only for a few hours each day. Winnie worked from seven in the morning until ten at night and that would be far too much for my grandmother. It was really far too much for Winnie, but she wouldn't dream of giving up her job. I didn't think that she needed the money, but she enjoyed the many chats she had throughout the

THE DEVIL'S DRAPER

day with the variety of women who came through the doors. And she liked to help those in need; the young women who worked and lived on the streets. She plied them with food and let them use the facilities for free, providing comfort, succour and words of motherly advice.

I left them there, happily rearranging the furniture and continued to St Andrew's Square. I arrived at the station to find the whole place in an uproar. Constable Ferguson raised his eyebrows at me. "Orr's on the warpath."

"For me?" I had no idea what I might have done this time, but it always seemed as though I were to blame for something.

Ferguson grinned at me, "Naw, lassie, you're not to blame this time. There was a major theft last night. One of the fur warehouses on the Broomielaw. They practically cleaned the place out overnight, stealing thousands of pounds' worth of furs. It looked as though they knew what to take, too. Very disciplined by all accounts."

"Do we know who did it?"

Ferguson shook his head. "Naw, the security guard said he was overpowered by several armed men, who threatened to kill him and then drugged him and tied him up. Seems like he's lucky to be alive by the sound of it."

"Oh, that's dreadful."

"Aye. Orr's beelin' about this gang havin' the audacity, as he called it, to do this on his patch. He's got practically the whole station on the case."

I sighed. "Except me, of course."

Ferguson laughed. "Aye, lassie, except you. Anyway, I'd better get off before he starts coming after me." He turned before leaving the building. "I've left ye a wee slice of ginger parkin on your desk. Hopefully that'll make up a wee bit for bein' excluded from all the fun."

"Aw, thanks, Archie. It will, I'm sure."

THE DEVIL'S DRAPER

I spent the next few hours typing up statements in my broom cupboard, trying not to feel jealous at the hive of activity going on around me. Archie Ferguson had been wrong about the wee slice of ginger parkin, it was more like half a cake and I had been tucking into it all morning.

Around lunchtime, there was a knock at my door and Detective Inspector Lorrimer poked his head in. I waved him in. "James, do come in and tell me about all the excitement. I take it you've been part of enquiries?"

"I have indeed. I've been interviewing the security guard, but it's been rather a pointless exercise."

I waved him to a seat. "Why?"

James adjusted his pinned sleeve with his good arm and sat down. "Well, the number of his assailants has increased in direct proportion to his bravery. First of all, there were three – all of them huge fellows, of course – and by the end of my questioning there were at least ten. He made sure that I knew – several times – that he fought back with courage, taking a terrible beating, but giving as good as he got."

"Oh dear, the poor man."

Lorrimer laughed. "That poor man didn't have a scratch on him." He was silent for a few moments and his brow furrowed. "Something he said made me wonder..."

He was pensive and I had to tap my pen on the desk to rouse him from his reverie. "What? What did you wonder?"

"Well, this gang of ours..."

It took me a moment to grasp his meaning. "Ours as in the ones who paid for all our dinners at Chez Antoine? St Thenue's Avengers?"

Lorrimer nodded. "Mmmm. Something Mackey, the security guard, let slip. Said '*she*' at one point, when referring to the robber who tied him up. 'She knows a knot', he said, and then corrected himself to 'he'."

THE DEVIL'S DRAPER

I was shocked at the thought. "You think it might have been them who carried out this robbery?"

He shrugged. "Why not?"

I thought about Johnnie. She had trusted me when she came in to tell me about her friend and there was something about her that made me want to protect her, but she *was* an Avenger. I hadn't told Lorrimer about her when we were doing our surveillance at Chez Antoine, because we hadn't been sure if they were involved in that business. As it turned out, they hadn't been, so I was glad at the time that I hadn't told him about Johnnie coming to see me. However, I couldn't – and wouldn't – protect her if the Avengers were involved with this fur warehouse business. He would be angry with me, I was sure. "Do you remember the young girl – the suicide?"

"In the Clyde? The one you thought could have been murder; Ruby something?" I nodded. "I meant to mention that business to you earlier, actually, Mabel."

I licked my finger and dabbed at the last couple of crumbs of ginger parkin on my desk. "Did you talk to Orr about it after all?"

"No, not yet, what with this warehouse robbery. But it looks as though you could have been right."

"About it being murder, you mean?" I hadn't expected this.

"Yes. They fished another body out of the Clyde this morning. Another young girl, about the same age as the first one. They're still trying to identify her."

I felt sick at the thought of it. "Are they linking the two girls, then?"

Lorrimer's face was pained. "Aye. She went in at the same place, according to Geddes from the Humane Society, off the Jamaica Street Bridge, and she had the same type of head injuries, as well as marks around her neck. Geddes fishes a lot of dead bodies from the Clyde and he was struck by the similarities."

"James, we can't let Orr palm this one off as a suicide, just because he's got bigger fish to fry." I knew that he would try to.

The death of another young girl he would consider dispensable would mean nothing to him. But it did mean something to me and I wasn't going to let it be ignored.

"Don't worry, we won't."

FRIDAY 3RD SEPTEMBER 1920
JOHNNIE

"You're to go and see someone called Winnie." Jane was a woman of few words and, as soon as she'd delivered her message, she had turned round and was off again.

Johnnie opened her door wider. "Did she say why?"

"Naw. I didnae speak tae her; ah'm just the messenger." Jane didn't even turn around, simply carried on stomping down the stairs as though she was annoyed at having to walk up them in the first place, which she probably was. Johnnie wasn't fond of Jane and seldom spoke to her. As far as she was concerned, the woman was lazy and untrustworthy.

Johnnie picked up a light shawl and ran down the stairs. She wondered if Winnie wanted to see her about Evvy. The pit of her stomach churned. There had been no news of Evvy since she'd disappeared in Arrol's and Johnnie seemed to be the only one who was concerned.

She practically ran to Wilson Street and by the time she got there, she was breathing heavily. Inside the public lavatory, Winnie was sitting with another woman. She was small and slender, with long, wispy, grey hair, piled into a loose bun. She gazed at Johnnie with the most piercing blue eyes she had ever seen.

Johnnie hesitated. "You wanted to see me, Winnie?"

"Aye, hen." Winnie's face and voice were sober and the knot in Johnnie's stomach grew bigger and started to claw at her. Winnie saw how she was looking at the woman with her and said, "This is Miss Gilfillan. Don't worry about her, she's a friend."

"Lillias," said the woman in a quiet, musical voice. "Do call me Lillias."

Johnnie nodded briefly and then turned back to Winnie,

probably rudely, but she didn't care. "Is it Evvy? Have you heard something about her?"

Winnie rested a hand on her arm. "Ah'm no' sure, hen. Another young lass was taken out of the Clyde in the early hours of yesterday morning."

"Evvy?"

"They don't know, hen. Nobody's claimed her an' she had nothin' to say who she might be. But the description I heard matches what you told me. Does she have a family?"

Johnnie shook her head. "No, just us."

Winnie took one of Johnnie's hands in hers. "She's at the polis' station, where they took Ruby."

"I'll go down now."

FRIDAY 3RD SEPTEMBER 1920
MABEL

I was on my way to interview an elderly woman in her home in Cowcaddens. She had been knocked down and robbed just outside the door of the close and was now afraid to leave her flat. A neighbour had come down to the station to let us know and Detective Inspector Channing had asked me to go and see her and take her statement about the attack.

I paused outside the police station doors, shrugged into my raincoat and pulled my hat down more firmly on my head.

"Miss Adair."

"Johnnie? What are you doing here? Are you here about Ruby?"

"No...Aye."

She looked distressed and I glanced at my watch. "Come inside." We went back into my office and I took off my coat and hat again and hung them up. Johnnie shook her head when I asked her if she wanted to take her shawl off. She seemed close to tears and it was all I could do to get her to sit down.

"Now, what is it? Have you found something out about her death?"

"Her roommate..."

"The one you mentioned before?"

"Aye. Evvy. She disappeared a few days ago. In Arrol's. We were...in Arrol's. An' she just disappeared. An' now...She might be here."

"Here? At the station?" She nodded. "You mean in the cells? She's been arrested?"

"Naw. Her... body."

Of course, the young woman who had drowned in the Clyde. "I'll come with you." She looked stricken and I didn't want her to have to go through that on her own. "What's her full name?"

"Evelina Brodie."

"Does she have any family?" She shook her head. "Say she's your cousin if they ask. Otherwise they might not let you see her." I didn't add that they might not let *me* in either. I wasn't allowed to accompany any of the women I interviewed – whether as criminals, victims or witnesses – when they appeared in court upstairs, in the very same building as I worked, because Orr said it wasn't seemly. I was kept away from crime scenes for the same reason, and, I had no doubt, in case I should faint. According to Orr, that was something that was likely to happen to a woman at any time, triggered by a dead body, the sight of blood, an exposed male body part, or an overheard oath. But Orr didn't have to know I'd been down to see the body and, by the time he did, it would be too late.

I knew where the body of the young woman would be and we hurried through the corridors. As we got to the door of the outer room, I put out a hand to stop her. "Have you ever seen a body before?"

She laughed humourlessly. "Aye, of course I have." Her look was scornful. "Have you?"

"Yes, I have actually."

I turned the door handle and we entered the room. A policeman guarding the inner door looked up from his newspaper briefly and nodded at me. I nodded back and acted as if I were here officially. "This young woman has come to identify the body of the girl found in the Clyde." He shrugged and went back to his newspaper and I opened the door of the small inner room.

The body was lying on a table, covered by a sheet. I took the top of the sheet in my hands and glanced at Johnnie. She nodded once and I pulled the sheet down, so that she could see the face of the girl.

"Aye, that's Evvy." Her voice was steady and matter-of-fact, but her fingers trembled, as she reached out and touched the forehead of the dead girl, as if she were a priest giving a blessing. Then she took the sheet out of my hands and gently covered Evvy's face once more, before turning away and walking out of the room.

I had to almost run to catch her up and we walked in silence back up the corridor. Before we reached the outside door of the station, I placed a hand on her arm to stop her. "Come to my office."

She rounded on me, angrily. "Why? What are you gonnae do? You told me Ruby had killed herself and you'll probably say the same about Evvy."

"I didn't say that Ruby had killed herself."

"Aye, ye did."

"I didn't. I said that her death had been recorded as a suicide. As it happens, I agree with *you*. I think Ruby's death was murder and I think Evvy was murdered too. And you need to help me." Her gaze was still angry and I ploughed on. "I need you to tell me the truth, so that we can find out what happened to them." One of the sergeants walked past us on his way out of the building, eyeing us curiously. "Come on, let's go to my office."

I turned away, leading the way, hoping that she would follow and was relieved when she did. I hadn't expected her to and wouldn't have blamed her if she hadn't. I'd come across too many women who'd been let down, neglected and downright mistreated by the system. I felt like that myself, and I was part of that system.

I pulled a seat out for her and went to make her a cup of tea for her shock. I made sure the tea was strong and sweet, without any reason to believe that it did any good, but it was what I always did. But when I got back to my office with a cup for each of us, Johnnie had gone.

FRIDAY 3RD SEPTEMBER 1920
BEATRICE

The fluttering feeling Beatrice had in her chest was getting worse and she rubbed at the familiar spot just below her collarbone. She knew what it was, that mixture of anxiety, worry and the sense of everything being out of control. It was something she'd felt before, first when her son had died and then again when her husband had followed him. Back then, she was helpless against it. This time, though, she had the opportunity to do something about it. She was not going to let Hector Arrol get away with abuse.

Thefts from Arrol's had reduced since she had come to work there and she had proved her worth. She wasn't going to be able to keep it up much longer, though – she was exhausted with her job at Arrol's and keeping on top of Price's Employment Agency, and she knew she would need to get help in. For now, though, she didn't have time to think about that.

She continued on her rounds of the store, but their nature had changed. Previously, she had spent equal amounts of time on every floor, at least half an hour on each, speaking to the Arrol sons and daughter, chatting with all the staff, watching the customers and, occasionally, catching the odd shoplifter. In the last day or so, however, she had initiated a new strategy: a quick tour of the lower floors, just to show her face, and no chitchat. The rest of the time she spent in the drapery department, carefully watching Hector Arrol and how he conducted himself with the young women in his employ. So far, she had noticed nothing untoward, but the two women working in the department over the last couple of days were both older women. That was something Beatrice could use in the future when sending new employees to work at Arrol's, but it wasn't a strategy she could rely on. Hector Arrol was the boss. He could move employees around at will. For now, though, she was satisfied that her presence up here wasn't required and she could concentrate on her actual job. Beatrice walked down the sweeping staircase in the centre of the store. She would start in the basement and make her way up.

Gilbert was overseeing the changing of a display of lamps. "I say, Mrs P, how are you, today? Haven't seen you about so much recently. Father keeping you busy up in the giddy heights, is he?"

Beatrice laughed. "Something like that, Gilbert, yes."

"Splendid, splendid. I say, what do you think of these new standard lamps? Delightful, are they not?"

"Very modern." Beatrice knew that the word would please him, and it did.

"Oh, modern, yes, absolutely. All the rage in London, these."

Beatrice took one more tour of the basement and then headed back up the stairs. Roderick Arrol was nowhere to be seen, for which Beatrice was grateful. She found his constant self-aggrandisement tedious in the extreme and he was always saying to her that she should tell his father how wonderfully she thought he, Roderick, was doing. Beatrice never did, of course.

As she strolled around the department, she saw a young woman standing by the display of dressing table items. She was picking them up one by one, but putting them down again without even looking at them. She seemed more intent on watching the people around her, just as Beatrice was.

Beatrice had a good memory for faces and she felt that she had seen her before on occasion, once or twice by herself, and once with a girl a couple of years younger. The young woman looked distressed and Beatrice watched her for a few minutes. She was rooted to the spot and continued to pick up and put down items without, apparently, even looking at them at all.

Beatrice walked over to her and tapped her on the shoulder. "Are you feeling alright, my dear?"

The young woman looked at her without really seeing her, put down the silver box she was holding and walked out of Arrol's.

FRIDAY 3RD SEPTEMBER 1920
MABEL

I set off from the station annoyed and frustrated in equal measure. Inspector Channing had torn me off a strip for not going to interview Mrs Allen, the elderly woman he had asked me to go and see in Cowcaddens, and I was annoyed at myself because of that, too. I promised Channing I would go and see her the very next day. The poor woman had been attacked and injured and she was rightly expecting someone to care about that fact. I did care, but how was she to know that?

By the time I had accompanied Johnnie to see Evvy's body and then rushed outside to try to find her after she had disappeared, there was no time to go and interview Mrs Allen. Cowcaddens, though nearby, might as well have been on the moon. My shift had ended, but duty called elsewhere – Grandmother awaited, her day with Winnie drawing to a close.

Questions about Ruby and Evvy gnawed at me, their connection to Arrol's a tantalizing thread I longed to unravel. Johnnie's knowing look haunted me, but the memory of that shadowy place I'd followed her to held me back. I needed to speak to her, but I didn't want to put her at risk.

My boots struck the pavement with unnecessary force, as I made my way to the public toilets. As I pushed open the heavy door, a wave of warmth and savoury aromas enveloped me. The tension in my shoulders began to ebb.

They both came to greet me, accompanied by the delicious smell of Winnie's steak and kidney pudding, one of my favourites.

My eyes searched my grandmother's face, seeking signs of fatigue or strain. Instead, I found a sparkle that had been absent since she came to Glasgow. She stood straighter, more at ease in her new surroundings.

THE DEVIL'S DRAPER

I had known that she and Winnie would get on – who wouldn't get on with Winnie, after all? She positively exuded kindness and generosity of spirit, but I had been concerned about my grandmother's strength and ability to sustain a day at work.

I kissed her lightly on her papery, lavender-scented cheek, and gave Winnie one on her own, more robust one. In her turn, she smelled of beeswax and cloves. "I hope she hasn't been overworking you, grandmother."

She beamed at me. "I've had a lovely day. We polished the brass, did some sewing and chatted to all the lovely customers. And Winnie showed me how to make her steak and kidney pudding – would you like some?"

"I'd better not," I said reluctantly. "Mrs Dugan is cooking a special meal to celebrate your new job, and she would never forgive me if I didn't do it justice. Winnie, you're invited by the way."

Winnie beamed. "Aw, that's lovely, hen. Ah'd be delighted to accept your kind invitation. But you can have a wee mouthful of my pudding, that won't do you any harm. You need feedin' up, doesn't she, Lil?"

It took me a few moments to realise she was referring to my grandmother, who giggled delightedly. It was a sound I hadn't heard before and it made me smile, although I pretended to be angry. "Well, I'm very happy you two have had such fun today. My day was awful."

Winnie came over, carrying a bowl of steak and kidney pudding that was about twenty times the size of 'a wee mouthful'. "What's wrong, hen?"

There was no-one else there, so we sat down in Winnie's cosy cubicle and I told them all about my day. "So I have no idea how I can get in touch with this Johnnie without alerting this gang of hers, assuming that's where they are."

"Oh dear," said Winnie. "That sounds like an insurmountable problem, eh, Lil?"

THE DEVIL'S DRAPER

My grandmother giggled once again. "Indeed it does, Winnie. Shame someone can't solve it for her, isn't it?"

I looked from one to the other in turn. What on earth was wrong with them?

Winnie saw my confusion and put me out of my misery. "Well, I can get hold of Johnnie for you, hen. After all, it was me as told her she should come and see you in the first place, wasn't it?"

I hit myself on the forehead with the palm of my hand in jest. "Of course you did. I'm sorry. I must be a bit slow today."

She patted my hand. "I knew you'd look after her. She's a wee bit flinty, but she has a good heart, I think, and she cares about her pals. She's jist cautious is all, what with her profession bein' what it is, an' yours bein' what yours is." She glanced up at the clock. "Now, you two had best be gettin' off. My daughter's comin' to take over in an hour or so, so I'll be up to Blythswood Square then. Tell your maw thanks for the invitation."

Grandmother and I set off to walk slowly up the hill towards Blythswood Square, my grandmother chattering happily about her day and all the people she had met. As we turned off West George Street onto Blythswood Street, I spotted the elderly man with the straggly hair again, watching us intently from the other side of the road. I took my grandmother's elbow to steer her away from him and we walked along the pavement in the opposite direction.

The man kept pace with us on the other side of the road. Was he about to ask us for money? I felt in my pocket for a few coins to give him, as he crossed the street towards us. I felt suddenly uncomfortable and held on to my grandmother's arm more tightly. I felt her stiffen as the man stepped in front of us. "Please move out of our way, sir." He ignored me, his gaze fixed intently on my grandmother, who started to tremble. "Sir, you're scaring this lady, I'll thank you to let us pass."

"Scaring the lady?" His voice was hoarse, as though he didn't use it much. "How can I scare her? She's my wife, and I'll thank *you* to let me speak to her."

THE DEVIL'S DRAPER

"What do you mean, your——"

He ignored me and addressed my grandmother. "Lillias, it's me, Arthur, your husband."

My grandmother straightened and a look I hadn't seen on her before crossed her face. The trembling had stopped and she seemed straighter and taller and, despite the pallor of her cheeks, her head was held high with a quiet dignity. Her voice when she spoke was firm and determined. "You no longer have the right to call yourself my husband, Arthur. You lost that privilege long ago. Now, as my granddaughter has asked, step aside and let us pass." It was a good thing that *she* was able to speak; I had lost the ability to do so. "And I never want to see you again, Arthur, so you can slink back to where you've come from. I'm not the weak, young woman, whose life you destroyed all those years ago."

He stayed where he was, as we walked around the side of the Square to the safety of home, but he called out after us. "You're still my wife, Lillias Strang, and we both know that that gives me rights."

She turned around and glared at him. "I no longer recognise that evil name. I'm Lillias Gilfillan. The only thing you want from me is money and you took all that years ago. I have nothing left."

He took a few steps towards us and I stepped in front of my grandmother to shield her, stretching out an arm to ward him off. "*You* might not have anything, Lillias." He looked me up and down, his lip curling. "But this fancy granddaughter of yours does, and so does this rich woman who took her in and has now taken *you* in. I'm sure *she* has plenty to spare."

Saturday 4th September 1920
Johnnie

"Johnnie, you listenin'?"

Meg's voice was sharp and Johnnie was pulled away from her thoughts of Ruby and Evvy. "Sorry, Meg. I was…"

"Aye, I know what you were about, but you need to snap out of it. They're just two wee lassies. We have plenty of wee lassies here who come and go. I don't see you getting' upset about them."

Johnnie had tried to explain it over and over. "I know, but Ruby and Evvy…they were killed by someone."

"You dinnae ken that for sure." The frustration was evident in Meg's voice.

"No, but there's too much of a connection—"

Meg snorted. "There's no connection. You're makin' up wee stories where they don't exist." She was rubbing away at the blackboard, as if she were trying to rub the very surface off it.

Johnnie refused to take the hint. "It's Arrol's, I know it is."

Meg threw the cloth she was using down onto the floor. A puff of chalk rose into the air. "Jeez-o, Johnnie. Will ye pipe down about it? They're gone, they didnae know anything about the Avengers that could lead anyone to us and we cannae dae anythin' about their deaths, or it'll put the whole lot of us at risk."

"But if the St Thenue's Avengers can't look out for our own, can't look after the women who are with us, then—"

Meg stormed over to Johnnie and brought her face close. "Don't you dare say that to me! To *me*." She poked a finger in Johnnie's chest and Johnnie rocked back on her heels. "You know I dae everything for ma lassies. I feed yis, clothe yis, look after yis when yis are sent tae prison. Ah'm lookin' out for the rest of yis. How dare you say I don't care!"

"I'm…I'm sorry, Meg, I didn't mean—"

THE DEVIL'S DRAPER

"All I ask is loyalty." She looked at Johnnie questioningly. "An' right now, ah'm no' sure I have yours."

Johnnie could feel tears pricking at her eyelids and she blinked them away. "I'm sorry Meg; of course you have my loyalty. I wouldnae be alive if it wasn't for you."

Meg stared at her, unblinking, then nodded her head once and turned away. Johnnie knew Meg was right. There was nothing she could do that wouldn't put the rest of them in danger, and she didn't want to do that – the Avengers were the only people she could call family and this was the only home she knew. But Meg didn't seem to understand that the rest of them might already *be* in danger. If Johnnie was right, and there was a connection between the deaths of Ruby and Evvy, then someone already had the Avengers in their sights. Meg had poured scorn on that suggestion, but Johnnie wasn't convinced. And, besides that, somebody needed to pay for murdering the two girls and nothing Meg could say would convince Johnnie otherwise.

Johnnie rubbed her eyes. There was no-one she could turn to. Talking to anyone else in the Avengers was completely out of the question; she couldn't go back to the Adair woman – the police wouldn't be on her side and she could get the whole lot of them in real bother if she did that; and she couldn't simply lurk around Arrol's or she would get into trouble herself.

She would go and speak to Winnie. She, at least, was someone Johnnie felt she could trust, someone who wouldn't judge her, and someone who would offer wise counsel.

Saturday 4th September 1920
Mabel

My grandmother had taken to her bed after the encounter with her husband and had been there ever since. Even Mrs Dugan's food had been unable to tempt her out. The quiet strength she had shown when faced with Arthur Strang had deserted her as soon as she reached home, where she collapsed, trembling and sobbing.

Floss, Jo and I were downstairs, discussing events in hushed tones. Floss had spoken to her lawyer to see what could be done.

"Armitage says that divorce is only possible where there's been adultery. And it's particularly unfair for women."

"Of course it is," said Jo, drily. "It always is."

Floss nodded. "Indeed. A wife has to meet a higher standard. Not only does she have to prove that the husband has committed adultery, but it has to be aggravated by some other conduct, such as cruelty or desertion."

"Well, I think we've got him on that one," I said. "He was unutterably cruel to her. He committed her to an asylum for absolutely no reason, left her there for nearly fifty years and stole all her money. Not to mention that he may have had her aunt murdered." We'd had the whole story from Lillias in bits and pieces, since she'd come to live with us, each revelation causing her pain as she told us. "And God only knows what else." I started to cry.

Floss rested her hand on my arm. "Oh, there's no doubt that she could prove cruelty and desertion, if we wanted to put her through such an ordeal in court; but she's never said anything about adultery, and that has to be a factor for her to be able to divorce him."

Jo came over with a handkerchief and a kiss for the top of my head. "It's terribly cruel."

THE DEVIL'S DRAPER

Floss stood and poured each of us a whisky. "It's utterly ridiculous. Armitage says that the only desire of the courts is to preserve the institution of marriage and the purity of the home, as he put it."

"Purity of the home? Good grief." I took a big swig of the drink she handed me and coughed.

Floss sighed. "Yes, I'm afraid the Christian ideal of purity has a lot to answer for." She and Jo exchanged a smile.

Jo stretched out her legs and rested them on a footstool. "So, what's to be done about this horrible little man?"

Floss sighed. "According to Armitage, there's not much that *can* be done. He suggests that we pay Strang off."

I slammed my glass down on the side table. "Pay him off? That's exactly what he wants! And what good would that do anyway? He'd just come back for more and more. We need to get rid of him permanently, so that he can never bother grandmother again."

Floss came over and refilled my glass. "And what are you suggesting, Mabel? That we organise some sort of unfortunate accident for him? No, I think Armitage is right. He suggests that we can get him to sign a contract."

"And how can we be sure he'll abide by the terms of this contract?"

"Well, we'll just have to make sure that both the reward for complying and the risk for not doing so is sufficiently great, won't we? I suggest that we see exactly what we can find out about him."

"How are we going to do that?"

Jo laughed. "You forget, dear Mabel, that Flossie's friends in high places are not just in Glasgow."

THE DEVIL'S DRAPER

Saturday 4th September 1920
Johnnie

Johnnie was ensconced in one of Winnie's comfortable armchairs, her hands curled around a mug of strong tea. Winnie had listened wordlessly to Johnnie's story, breaking off only when anyone came in to use the lavatories. Johnnie had watched as she had dished out bowls of delicious-smelling, thick soup that would stick to your ribs, pennies for the doors to those women who didn't have coins of their own, wise advice offered when asked for and kind words when not. She knew from watching Winnie dispense all of these with care, sympathy and cheerfulness, that she had been right to come to her. Johnnie didn't hold anything back. The very act of setting it all out for Winnie clarified things in her own mind.

Now Winnie sat back in the other chair, humming to herself as she thought about what Johnnie had told her. She had shown no shock and given no judgement, simply reacted with looks of concern and the occasional pat of Johnnie's hand. Finally, she spoke. "An' what dae *you* think you should dae, hen?"

Johnnie sighed. "Should do for *who*? That's the problem. For the St Thenue's Avengers, I should stay quiet; for Ruby and Evvy... well, I need to speak up."

Winnie was silent for a few seconds and then smoothed back a lock of Johnnie's hair, her clear eyes focussed on the girl's. "An' whit about for you? Whit dae ye need to dae for *you*?"

Johnnie only needed a moment to answer this one. "I need to speak for Ruby and Evvy, because they cannae speak for themselves."

"An' how are you gonnae dae that?"

Johnnie shrugged helplessly. "That's what I don't know." Her voice was almost a whisper.

THE DEVIL'S DRAPER

Winnie leaned forwards and took both Johnnie's hands in hers, squeezing them almost until they hurt. The room was silent, other than the sound of the pot of soup bubbling reassuringly on the stove. "Dae ye want my advice, hen?" Johnnie nodded and Winnie pursed her lips. "Ye might no' like it."

"Give me it anyway."

"Speak tae Mabel; tae Miss Adair. She's polis, aye, but she's good an' she's fair an' she'll dae her level best tae get justice for they young lassies. Speak tae her."

Johnnie sighed. "I knew you were gonnae say that."

THE DEVIL'S DRAPER

Sunday 5th September 1920
Mabel

Winnie had sent a boy up to the house with a message, asking me to come down and see her, so early on Sunday morning I left Floss and Jo talking over the problem of Arthur Strang. I looked carefully around as I left, but he wasn't in the Square. Perhaps now he'd got his message across, he felt that he didn't need to haunt the pavements outside our home. I was relieved not to see him, but still glanced back over my shoulder several times as I made my way down to Wilson Street. The streets were quiet and I was more or less on my own. Even if he *was* following me, at least the public lavatory was somewhere I would be free from his ominous and unwanted presence.

I pushed open the heavy door and entered the cheerful space. "It's me, Winnie."

"Come away in, hen," was her bright response. "Want some porridge?"

I could smell the nutty, slightly sweet smell and my stomach rumbled. I'd left the house without having any breakfast that morning. "Yes, please, Winnie, that would be—" I stopped short as I turned the corner. Sitting comfortably on one of Winnie's chairs was Johnnie. She grinned nervously when she saw me.

Winnie bustled over with a plate of porridge and a spoon. I read the look she gave me as a warning to go easy on the young woman, who looked utterly miserable.

I said nothing at all, simply sat down and dipped my spoon into the bowl of steaming porridge. Johnnie launched into her story, some of which, of course, I already knew, but this time she told me everything, colouring slightly when she mentioned St Thenue's Avengers and criminal activities. I noticed, however, that other than Ruby and Evvy, she didn't mention any names. By the time

THE DEVIL'S DRAPER

I had finished my second bowl of porridge, she had gone through everything, but there was one thing I didn't quite understand. "And why do you think there's a link with Arrol's?"

She pursed her lips before speaking. "It's more of a feeling, really, but Ruby had the box which she stole from there and Evvy said that Ruby had talked about a man and being scared."

"But she didn't say that it was a man actually inside Arrol's?"

"No, I suppose it could have been later, out on the street, but... An' then we were in Arrol's and Evvy just disappeared. Just as I tell't you, she saw someone when we were on the staircase – a man – and I went back to see if I could see who she meant, and when I turned back round, she'd disappeared. I thought she'd meant someone on the floor below, so that's where I was looking, but maybe she meant the floor we were on..."

I was dubious. "It's not much, is it?" She shook her head, looking disconsolate. "But it's all we've got, so we'll simply have to start there, won't we?"

She looked at me. "So you believe me then?"

"Of course I do."

"An' you'll help me to find out what happened to them?"

I scraped the last bit of porridge up and popped the spoon into my mouth, savouring the final mouthful. "I'll do my best."

"An' you won't tell the polis? The rest of them, I mean."

This I couldn't entirely promise, but I didn't want to scare her off. "Not unless I have to."

She looked at me suspiciously. "An' what does that mean? I cannae put the Avengers at risk. That would be like betraying my family."

I stood up and poured some of the hot water from the kettle that was always on the stove into an enamel dish. I cleaned out my bowl and spoon, before I spoke. "I'm in the police force, Johnnie; it's my job to uphold the law." She opened her mouth to speak and I held up a hand. "But I promise you that I won't say anything about what you've told me, unless someone's in danger."

THE DEVIL'S DRAPER

She nodded reluctantly. "Aye, well, alright then, that'll have to do."

I let out the breath I'd been holding. "Shoplifting's one thing but for goodness' sake, don't tell me anything about jewellery heists or robberies from fur warehouses, because I definitely can't promise to keep those quiet."

She covered her mouth, but I could see the grin that formed on her lips behind her hand. "I don't know what you mean, Miss Adair."

"Oh, I'm sure you don't. And if I'm going to be some sort of partner in crime, you'd better call me Mabel."

Winnie had been sitting quietly, knitting, but now she jumped up to refill the kettle. "Aw, this is lovely, ain't it? I'll make us some tea."

Johnnie sat back, more relaxed now. "So what do we do now?"

I was wondering the very same thing, but the inklings of an idea were starting to come to me.

Sunday 5th September 1920
Beatrice

Unable to sleep, Beatrice had been at her desk since the early hours of the morning. The streets of Glasgow were starting to come alive, slightly later on a Sunday morning, and Beatrice relished the relative quiet and calm as she walked to her office.

She had already opened a big heap of mail and sorted it into neat piles on her desk, when the telephone rang, startling her. The switchboard operator put the call through and she answered it with curiosity as to who could be calling her on a Sunday morning. "Hello, this is Beatrice Price."

"Beatrice! I was hoping you'd be there. I thought you would be."

It took Beatrice a few moments to place the voice. "Mabel?"

There was a laugh at the other end of the line. "Oh, yes, sorry, I should have said. Can we meet?"

"Meet? Yes, of course. What's it about?" Beatrice picked up her pen and pulled a scrap of paper over to her. She had no idea why Mabel Adair would call like this, but she liked the young woman and was intrigued.

"I'd rather tell you when I see you, if you don't mind. I thought you'd be at your office. Are you free now?"

"Well, I'm just catching up on some work but…yes, I don't see why not. Do you want to come here, or do you want me to come to you? Where are you?"

Mabel's voice when it came was slightly guarded, as if she was trying not to be overheard. "I'm at the police station right now, but I only came in to use the phone. No, not here and not your office. Do you know the public lavatories in Wilson Street?"

Beatrice was confused. "The…no, I don't."

"They're at the corner of Wilson Street and Glassford Street. Can you meet me there as soon as possible?"

Beatrice wasn't quite sure she had heard correctly. "You want me to meet you outside a public convenience?"

The musical laugh came once more. "No, inside, but don't worry; you won't need to spend a penny."

SUNDAY 5TH SEPTEMBER 1920
MABEL

It was a good job that Sunday was a quiet day for Winnie. Her little office-cum-kitchen-cum-store room was too small for the four of us to all sit in comfortably and we had spilled out into the main part of the space. Beatrice and Winnie were in the armchairs, Johnnie was sitting on a stool and I was sitting on a low footstool at Winnie's feet, leaning against her legs.

Winnie had made a big pot of tea so strong you could stand your spoon up in it and Johnnie had just told her story for the third time that morning. As she lapsed into silence, Winnie stood up and went over to the stove, where a big pan of butter beans had been boiling away merrily for the last half hour. She drained them off and added beef and onions. Almost immediately, the contents of the pan started to sizzle and the glorious smell of onions frying permeated the room. It was the scent of home, wherever that was. I had always loved to sit in the kitchen with Mrs Dugan when I was a child, watching her as she worked and the scent and sizzle took me back to that moment of my childhood. After a few minutes, Winnie added back in some of the butter bean liquor to make a gravy, stirred the pan and put the lid on top once more, before sitting back down again with a groan.

This seemed to be the signal for us to rouse ourselves from our onion-scented stupor. "So you think this man Ruby saw is from Arrol's?" said Beatrice.

Johnnie pushed her hair back from her face. "Or was in there at the time, aye. But since Evvy disappeared from there too..."

She drifted off and Beatrice considered the implications. "It does seem rather a coincidence that the same man would be in there both times, if he doesn't work there."

I rubbed my nose, which was itching from the pepper Winnie

had just shaken generously into the pot. "But maybe it wasn't the same man."

Beatrice looked doubtful. "Still rather a coincidence, don't you think?"

"An' there's how they both died, too," Johnnie added. "Both drowned, both fished out of the river in the same place, both with wounds to their heads that were alike."

Beatrice nodded slowly. "Yes. It does seem quite plausible that there's a link."

"So, are you gonnae help us?" Johnnie's question was almost accusatory in tone. I had sensed a certain wariness from both her and Beatrice. Each of them had recognised the other from a previous meeting in Arrol's.

Beatrice's response was almost as sharp. "How, exactly, do you suggest that I do that? And why would I even want to try?"

Johnnie lifted her chin defiantly. "To help a thief, you mean?"

Beatrice shrugged. "Well, that's what you are, isn't it?"

The two women were glaring at each other and I tried to smooth the situation. "She doesn't mean that, do you, Beatrice?"

"Well, actually, I do, as a matter of fact. My job is to hinder thieves who want to steal from Arrol's."

I stood up and went over to her chair, putting a hand on her shoulder. "But that's *not* actually your job, is it, Beatrice? You went in there with the intention of helping young women who were being assaulted."

"Yes, you're right. Young women who are my responsibility, who *I'd* placed there."

"And Johnnie wants to help the young women who *she* feels responsible for."

We were all silent for a minute or so and then Beatrice nodded and looked at Johnnie as if considering, her face softening. "Well, perhaps I *can* help you. But you'll have to help *me* in return."

Johnnie frowned. "Aye? How's that then?"

THE DEVIL'S DRAPER

Beatrice's smile was a very satisfied one. "Well, Johnnie, I can get you into Arrol's so that you can follow up this theory of yours and, at the same time, you can help me with my plans."

"An' how are you gonnae get me in there exactly?"

"Easily. Price's Employment Agency for Ladies is going to put you forward for a job in the drapery and haberdashery department, with one Mr Hector Arrol."

Sunday 5th September 1920
Mabel

While I'd been out meeting Beatrice and Johnnie, Floss and Jo had been busy visiting and making phone calls to various friends and acquaintances in Glasgow and beyond. Some of them had helped get my grandmother out of the asylum.

We had kept Lillias out of the conversations up to now, until we had investigated things further and considered the various options. She was still mostly keeping to her bed and was too scared to leave the house, in case she should bump into Arthur Strang. Despite her bravery when faced with him, the encounter had really knocked her, but we were all determined that she should be part of the decisions. She'd spent nearly all her life having no choices and not being part of any decisions that involved her; we were determined that that situation would continue no longer.

Floss was summarising the various discussions she'd had and the information that she'd unearthed. "So, this McAllister seemingly has an influence over Strang, and Strang owes him a substantial sum of money."

My grandmother shuddered. "I recall him very well. He's an awful man, very manipulative and cruel. Arthur was a good man until he met him, I know he was."

My eyes met Floss' over the top of Lillias' head and she put a finger on her lips, warning me not to say anything to the contrary. "My contact in Stirling tells me that McAllister threatened Strang and that the latter immediately left town. Presumably, that's when he came here and started lurking around outside. Goodness knows how he discovered she was here. I would imagine he contacted the asylum, to see if there was a last few pounds he could squeeze out of Lillias." She put a reassuring hand on my grandmother's shoulder. "Anyway, this chap says that Strang is so afraid of McAllister that he'll do anything to get him off his back. We can use that to our advantage."

"Who's this contact of yours, anyway? He seems to know a lot." Floss was never usually quite so cagey.

Floss and Jo exchanged glances. "I'd rather not say; it's someone from our militant days. He also told me something else, you see, something which would send Strang and McAllister to prison for the rest of their lives, but which could also put *him* in a rather awkward position."

"Oh yes?"

"Yes. And I'm going to get my lawyer to draw up a contract, which states that we'll give Arthur sufficient money to get McAllister off his back, but that if he ever contacts Lillias again, this…something else… will be revealed, and that it will not go well for Strang if it is."

Tuesday 7th September 1920
Johnnie

There was no way that Johnnie could tell Meg what she was up to. She would be thrown out of the Avengers, possibly worse, if any of them ever found out that she had spoken to an outsider – let alone the police – about their business. Meg was very understanding about them not working all the time, so that wasn't a problem, but she couldn't just *not* tell her anything either. What if Johnnie should be on duty behind the haberdashery counter at Arrol's, and one of the gang was allocated the store to steal items? No, that didn't bear thinking about. She needed to come up with a good reason.

Big Annie had told her that Meg was in the war office. She was busy with some papers, but smiled at Johnnie and patted the sofa next to her. Johnnie went over and sat down.

She might as well just come right out with it. "A girl I know has put me in the way of what might be a good opportunity."

"Aye? Whit's that then?" Meg stacked the papers she was working on and put them to one side, giving Johnnie all of her attention.

"She's working at Arrol's, but is just about to hand in her notice as she's got a better paid job in the ladies' fashion department at Treron's." Meg nodded, so Johnnie continued. "Anyway, we were chatting about wages an' that an' she was telling me about how they do it at Arrol's."

Meg narrowed her eyes. "An' why would she do that? Does she know you're with the Avengers?"

"Naw, naw. Nothing like that. She thinks I work at the tobacco warehouse in the Gorbals." It was a story Johnnie used often, and Meg nodded, reassured. "It was just something she said in passing, about seeing the clerk heading off to the bank and how she wouldn't like to be the one that goes to pick up the wages every week; that she'd be scared of getting robbed. It just got me thinking, is all, that it might be a good score for us."

Meg waved a hand dismissively. "They wouldnae just let the clerk roam about the streets with a big bag of cash. It wouldnae be just him and he'd be in a car. It's too much o' a risk for us. Besides, that's something we'd need guns for and that's no' oor style. You know that."

"I didnae mean that. This girl says the clerk goes to get the money from the bank on a Thursday afternoon, an' they don't pay the wages until a Friday. It's just lying there overnight."

Meg shrugged dismissively. "Aye, in a safe."

This was where Johnnie had to be convincing. "That's the thing. No safe. They lock it in a cupboard overnight in the boss' office."

"An' how does she know that?" Johnnie could tell that this had got Meg's interest, but she was still wary.

"She's winching one of the clerk's assistants. He was boasting about stuffing the cupboard with this big bag of money every Thursday to impress her one day."

Meg put her feet on the table in front of her and crossed her arms. She sat back on the sofa and rested her chin on one of her hands, pondering what Johnnie had told her. "So are you sayin' we should break in one Thursday night? Do we know where this office is? Whether there's any security on overnight?"

"Aye, well, that's the thing. When she tell't me she were leaving, I asked her if she could put a good word in for me with the manager, so she has." She paused for a moment to consider her next words and Meg gestured to her to continue. "I thought I could check things out, see if I can answer those questions, an' any others you can think of. I can work out the best way to get in. But more than that, I can hide in there when the place closes on a Thursday evening."

THE DEVIL'S DRAPER

Meg gave a short laugh. "Just let us in the back way, you mean?"

"With any luck. Who knows; maybe it *will* be as easy as that. Worth a try though, eh?"

"Aye, mibbe so." She stood and went over to a cupboard, where there were a few bottles and glasses. She pulled out a bottle of gin and a glass and poured herself a short measure. "Aye, hen...well done. An' even if this disnae work out, then mibbe you'll spot some other opportunities there. At any rate, we've got nothin' tae lose from havin' you in Arrol's for a couple of weeks, an' possibly tons tae gain."

Johnnie gave a silent sigh of relief. "At thirty shillings a week, maybe I should just stay and work there full time."

Tuesday 7th September 1920
Beatrice

It was a week now since Anna Nicholls had been at work. When she came back from seeing Anna at her home in Battlefield, Beatrice had made good on the promise that she had made to the girl – to find her a new job where she wouldn't need to worry about the boss. She'd given Anna two weeks' wages and found her employment with a seamstress on the South Side, a middle-aged woman, who had two other young women working for her. The wages weren't quite as good as they were at Arrol's, but Anna was happy that she didn't have to travel right into the city centre each day, and that she would be working with three other women.

Hector's secretary waved her into the outer office and she knocked on Hector's door and turned the handle at his cheery, "Come away in."

"Hector, I've heard from Anna." He looked none the wiser. "Anna Nicholls, who's been working for you in the drapery department. She went off sick a week or so ago and I've just heard from her to say she won't be returning." She watched Hector's face for any signs of guilt or embarrassment, or anything at all, but there was nothing there. It took all her will to continue to smile at him, when what she really wanted to do was to punch him on the chin. "You're quite unfortunate with staff in the drapery department. None of them seem to stay very long."

"Ah, well." Hector leaned back in his chair and stretched. "These young girls today don't seem to care for working. Too spoiled during the War, earning men's wages."

Beatrice gritted her teeth. "Well, don't worry. I've found you someone to replace her."

"Already? Beatrice, you're worth your weight in gold!"

"I'm glad you think so, Hector. She'll be starting tomorrow."

"A pleasant girl?"

"Very." That was probably a lie, but one Beatrice was prepared to tell under the circumstances. She and Johnnie had not exactly hit it off, but Beatrice thought that they understood each other well enough, and it would be good to have a young woman in the department who could, Beatrice guessed, put Hector Arrol firmly in his place, should the occasion arise.

"Her name?"

They had discussed this. "Johanna Smith." The first part was true, the second wasn't.

"And her age?"

"Sixteen." Johnnie could pass for sixteen but no younger; she'd lived too much life.

Hector Arrol frowned slightly. "I do prefer a girl of fourteen or fifteen. They're easier to train."

Beatrice had no doubt of that. "I think you'll find her extremely biddable, Hector." She'd told Johnnie exactly how to behave.

Arrol beamed happily. "Excellent, excellent."

Tuesday 7th September 1920
Mabel

When I arrived for work, Lorrimer was lurking in the corridor outside my office.

"Ah, Mabel, I was waiting for you."

"You should have gone in and had a seat."

He raised an eyebrow. "Quite frankly, I prefer to stand in this dingy corridor than spend more time than I need to in your so-called office."

My response was heartfelt. "I know exactly how you feel, James, believe me. I've often thought of bringing my desk out into the corridor. Do you want to stand out here and talk then?"

He smiled. "You're here now, that makes your tiny cupboard bearable." It was my turn to raise my eyebrows at him and he laughed again, this time with a little embarrassment. "Only slightly more bearable, mind you, for five minutes, anyway."

"Oh, thank you, you certainly know how to flatter a girl."

We went inside. Lorrimer wrinkled his nose. "What the hell is that smell?" As usual, the cleaner, Mrs Wilson, hadn't emptied the water out of her mop bucket the night before and the room smelled of a mixture of disinfectant and stagnant pond. I tried to keep my door open during the day, but when I arrived and the room had been shut up all night, the smell was generally overpowering.

"It's Mrs Wilson's spare mop bucket."

"I thought she had a room in the basement for all her supplies now?"

"She does, but 'I can't be bothered lugging the bucket up all those stairs, dearie'." I was quite pleased with my impression of Mrs Wilson and Lorrimer gratified me by laughing, a sound that came so infrequently that I hadn't yet got used to it. Neither, I think, had he, because he always looked slightly shocked afterwards. "And as

THE DEVIL'S DRAPER

she is a fortunate woman to be in possession of *two* mop buckets, she leaves one of them up here. Now, what can I do for you?"

"Yes, well, you recall the jewellery raid in the Argyll Arcade that we believe was the work of the St Thenue's gang?" I nodded. "Well, we've caught a young woman from the gang and she's in one of the cells. I don't know if she was involved - she was caught shoplifting in Sauchiehall Street - but I'd like you to interview her and see if you can get anything out of her."

I pulled over a notepad and pen, to try and give myself some more time. What if it was Johnnie? I prayed that it wasn't Johnnie. "What's her name?" I tried to sound as casual as I could.

"May Renton."

Thank goodness for that. I hoped that May wasn't just going to cave at the sound of my voice and give up the whole gang. Not for the first time, I considered the tightrope I was walking. There was something about Johnnie that I had warmed to, but she *was* a criminal. I wanted to help her find out what had happened to her friends, Ruby and Evvy. If they *had* been murdered – and I agreed with Johnnie that they had – then they deserved justice, and justice was in short supply if you were a woman, especially a working-class woman. However, my desire to bring their killers to justice couldn't take away from the fact that I was a police officer, no matter what Superintendent Orr thought, and I had a duty to uphold the law. That all sounded very grand and very pompous, even to myself, but it was important to me.

Lorrimer looked relieved to be leaving my office and I went downstairs to the cells, promising to let him know what I found out from May Renton. The turnkey, a woman known to all as Mrs M – I still hadn't worked out what the M stood for - was a stout, red-faced woman and the widow of a policeman who had been killed in the War. With two children to feed, she'd been given a job at the police station in an unusual act of kindness by Superintendent Orr, who'd been a friend of her husband. As a result, Mrs M, too, was not fond of me. Her face, although perpetually cheerful-looking on

THE DEVIL'S DRAPER

the outside, was belied by her sharp tongue. In recent months, she had taken to calling me 'Your Ladyship', and I was certain that this was how Orr referred to me when I wasn't around.

"Your Ladyship'll be here tae see that skinny wee minx in cell two ah'm guessin'?"

"If that's May Renton, then yes."

Mrs M nodded slowly. "Well, you'll want tae watch out for her; she bites." She rubbed at her arm.

I made my way down the white-tiled hallway to cell two and stood aside to let Mrs M unlock the door for me, with the huge ring of keys attached to her waist. As usual, she shoved me in with a "Bang the door when ye want oot" and locked the door behind me once more.

It took a few moments for my eyes to grow accustomed to the gloom. The corridor outside was dull, lit as it was by permanently flickering lights, but the cells were even darker, with one pathetic bulb, scarcely brighter than a glow worm. A young woman was sitting on the bare mattress covering the slatted pallet that formed the hard bed. Her legs were drawn up to her chest and she was hugging her knees to her. It was chill and damp down here and she was wearing only a thin cotton dress.

I went back to the door and banged on it. Mrs M's face appeared at the opening. "That was quick; did she bite you?" She said this with some relish, I noted.

"Could you please bring a blanket."

"A blanket?"

"Yes, please."

She tutted and stomped back off up the corridor, mumbling something about The Savoy, but returned quickly and opened the door, shoving a rough grey blanket into my hand.

I walked over to the girl and draped the blanket over her shoulders and she clasped it at her neck with one hand, looking up at me. "She's lyin'. I didnae bite her."

THE DEVIL'S DRAPER

I smiled and sat down next to her on the bed, since there wasn't any other option in the small cell. "Hello, May. I'm Miss Adair. I'm a policewoman here."

Her eyes widened. "A woman polis?"

I got that reaction a lot. "Yes, there are two of us here at this station." In the whole of Glasgow, actually – quite possibly in the whole of Scotland, but I kept that to myself.

Her eyes narrowed. "I thought you were a do-gooder. Ah'm no' speaking to the polis."

I got that reaction a lot, too. "That's fine if you don't want to talk to me, but if you did, it might help."

She snorted, but continued looking at me curiously. Her eyes were clear and brown and her hair was a shiny waterfall of cinnamon brown curls. She looked to be about sixteen.

"How old are you, May?"

She considered the question a moment, before deciding it was a harmless one. "Nineteen."

"And where do you live?" This time, she didn't answer. "I understand you were arrested as you left Copland & Lye with some articles that you hadn't paid for." Again, no response. I opened my notebook. "I believe you were wearing three extra petticoats that you'd stolen and that you had two corselets wrapped in a newspaper, four pairs of stockings, some silk handkerchiefs and a fur collar. Is that right?"

She shrugged. "Whit you askin' me for if you've got it all there written down in that wee book?"

We went on like this for some time. If she was a St Thenue's Avenger, the rest of the gang would have been very proud of her. She gave absolutely nothing away, denied all knowledge of any other robberies and, according to her, she knew absolutely no-one in Glasgow, or at all, in fact. She stopped short of saying that she didn't even know where Glasgow was, but she might just as well have done. Eventually, I closed my notebook with a sigh and stood up. "Well, it's been lovely chatting to you, May."

A brief smile flickered across her lips. "How long do ye think ah'll get?"

I looked down at her. "Probably a month or two."

"Wi' hard labour?"

"I should say so, yes."

She grunted and then tucked herself back into a ball, her arms around her knees. "Aye, well, it'll not be the first time." I lingered for a moment longer and then banged on the door to be let out.

"Ta for the blanket, Miss."

I nodded and left the cell, leaving Mrs M to slam the door behind me once again.

THE DEVIL'S DRAPER

WEDNESDAY 8TH SEPTEMBER 1920
JOHNNIE

Johnnie had dressed very carefully for her first day of work. Beatrice had given her strict instructions on how to dress and how to act, neither of which had pleased her. She had gone out yesterday to shoplift a suitable outfit – not from Arrol's of course. It wasn't what she would normally have chosen – either for herself or to steal for the Avengers – it was too cheap, too plain and too unfashionable: a navy skirt that was longer than the current fashion, a high-collared white blouse and a pair of plain black shoes. She'd done her hair neatly and plainly. She looked at herself in the mirror and didn't like what she saw. She liked to look older than her years, not younger and she much preferred wearing men's clothes. She had to admit, however, that looking unobtrusive and forgettable might be useful in the future, so it was an outfit that could stand her in good stead.

Beatrice had told her that she needed to act meek, pliable and obedient, three things which she definitely wasn't. She'd practised walking around the room in a way that was as far as possible from her usual confident stride and it felt very strange to her. Beatrice had also told her that she needed to be feminine, willing and pleasant, another three things which she wasn't. Johnnie sighed. This might be more of a challenge than she'd thought.

Johnnie put on a straw hat and bounded down the stairs. Outside in the street, however, she practised her new persona. Where she would normally have marched along with her head up, making way for nobody, she now pitter-pattered along, taking tiny steps and looking down at the pavement, avoiding eye contact with everyone and making sure she didn't get in anyone's way. By the time she reached Arrol's, she had entered fully in to the persona of Johanna Smith and was hating every minute of it.

WEDNESDAY 8TH SEPTEMBER 1920
MABEL

When I left to go to work, a familiar figure was hovering around outside, like a malevolent scarecrow. I'd been expecting him to turn up sooner or later, of course, but it was still an unpleasant sight and put a tight knot in the pit of my stomach.

"Well?"

"Well, what?" I kept walking and, indeed, quickened my pace.

"Have you thought any more about my offer?"

"Your *offer*? Your demand, you mean. My grandmother doesn't owe you anything."

His voice was almost a whine. "She's my wife, and that entitles me to—"

"You're not entitled to anything. You deserted her."

"The Court wouldn't see it that way." He was puffing slightly, trying to keep up with me and I started walking faster. I wanted him away from the house; his presence there sullied the air around it.

"Slow down." His voice had an obnoxious mewling sound.

"I can't. I'll be late for work." I walked even faster, so much so that I was now puffing too.

He snorted. "Work? Is that where you're off to? Surely you don't need to work. Or does that fine Miss Adair of yours make you toil for her?" His face was twisted into an ugly sneer.

He didn't know everything then. "Yes, I'm in the police force." For the first time, I saw the arrogant, misplaced confidence leave his face and something approaching fear flashed across it.

"What are you? A typist?"

"A police officer."

He laughed, a wheezing laugh that sounded awkward and uncomfortable and not something that often came from him. "A

THE DEVIL'S DRAPER

police officer? That's funny."

I stopped in my tracks and he almost fell over. I whirled round to face him. "Yes, a police officer. Last year, I solved the murder of my birth mother. Your daughter."

For the first time, I saw something in his face that wasn't wholly nasty, a brief look of regret and pain. This man was my grandfather and at one time my grandmother had loved him. She'd insisted that he'd loved her at one point, too, but I was finding that hard to believe. "Murdered? I knew that she was dead, but..."

"Yes," I put my hands on my hips and glared at him. "Ultimately because of you. You and your friend, McAllister." At the name, he winced, but I was so angry now that I ploughed on. "You had her committed to that place—"

He shrank away from me, the pathetic whine now back in his voice. "She was ill, she—"

"She wasn't ill. She was young, and naïve, and you took advantage of her. You took all of her money and you left her there for fifty years."

His eyes narrowed. "She was—"

"And you didn't visit her. Not once. You didn't visit your own daughter, either." I found this impossible to understand. "You never saw your own daughter. Not once."

"I—"

"And her aunt. Was that you, too? Or McAllister?" I was fishing, here. My grandmother's aunt had died in a supposed accident, on her way up to see my grandmother in the asylum. Lillias hadn't blamed Arthur Strang for her death, hadn't even raised it as a suspicion, but Floss and I had discussed the possibility.

Strang's face closed down and he shook his head. "I...I just need money, that's all. Give me money and I'll go. And I won't come back, if that's what you're thinking. This will be the end of it." The confident look was back on his face and this annoyed me even further.

THE DEVIL'S DRAPER

"You took all her money. Over the years, you bled her dry. Not all at once, because of the way her aunt's will was written, you couldn't – that must have annoyed you. But you took as much as you could, when you could, and when it was all gone, you still left my grandmother there, to be treated as a pauper. And all that time – *all* that time, you could have got her out."

I didn't understand this aspect. He'd kept her in the asylum, her inheritance paying for her board there. If he'd had her released to his care, not only would he have avoided paying the fees of the asylum, but my grandmother would have been back under his influence. Although some of the scales had fallen from her eyes when she was in the asylum and she'd grown stronger and more independent, she was still trusting and naïve. He could have coaxed her round, and then he would have had full access to her inheritance.

He was shaking his head. Back and forth, back and forth. "I couldn't...I couldn't. McAllister would..." He went back to just shaking his head.

We were still standing stock still in the middle of the pavement on Renfield Street, outside Cranston's Picture House; passers-by were looking at us curiously. I surveyed him silently for a few moments and then it dawned on me what he was *not* saying. "McAllister would have..." But I, too, stopped short of finishing the sentence that had formed in my mind; the idea horrified me.

He stopped shaking his head and looked at me. "I loved her, you know; I was a weak man and I didn't know how to...but he would have..." He snapped back into whining mode. "I need money. I owe money."

"To him." It wasn't a question; I already knew the answer. I made sure not to show it, but his reply had shocked me. Perhaps he did have a small shred of compassion for my grandmother, perhaps he *had* loved her. Leaving her in the asylum might have saved her life.

He shrugged. "Amongst others."

THE DEVIL'S DRAPER

I was calmer now, sickened and numb. I just wanted it all over with. "How much do you want?"

He looked at me for a moment, assessing me. "Ten thousand."

It was a lot of money, but about what we'd expected he would ask. We knew what he owed McAllister; Floss had found that out. I shook my head and carried on walking. "It's too much."

"Oh, I'm sure your Miss Adair can afford it. In fact, I know she can. I did my homework before I came to see you, you know."

"You mean McAllister did." He shrugged, but didn't deny it. "Well, we did *our* homework too." A look of what might have been fear flashed across his face. I put my hands on my hips. "Five thousand."

He gave a hoarse and humourless bark of laughter. "Don't insult me. I could insist on your grandmother coming home with me, you know."

That this man was my grandfather made me feel sick to my stomach. We didn't exactly know if he could do what he threatened, but to put my grandmother through something like that would be simply cruel and we weren't prepared to do it. I turned away from him again and started walking.

His voice was firm. "Nine thousand."

I stopped walking again and turned to him, my face close to his. I could smell his sour breath, stale beer and bad hygiene. "Seven thousand." He opened his mouth to speak and I held up my hand to stop him. "I haven't finished. You can tell McAllister we're prepared to pay seven thousand and that's it, but we'll pay an additional thousand pounds into a separate account, which you can set up. Up to you if you tell McAllister about it or not." A sly look appeared on his face. I had him. "But you have to sign a legally binding contract, that you won't ever contact my grandmother or us ever again. And it will set out some things that you and this McAllister wouldn't want to come out; I think you know exactly what I mean. Do you understand?"

THE DEVIL'S DRAPER

He hesitated, clearly considering what we might know and then nodded, as I knew he would. "When will I get the money?"

"My mother will meet you at her lawyer's office on Friday morning, first thing." I handed him a piece of paper with the address on it.

He looked down at the address and then back up at me. "Doesn't want me to set foot in her fancy house, is that it?"

Bargaining for my grandmother's life had left a sour taste in my mouth and I wanted to be as far away from him as I possibly could. "Exactly." I turned on my heel and almost ran the rest of the way to St Andrew's Square. I wanted the familiarity of my dingy little office, the comfort of a piece of Sergeant Ferguson's wife's cake, the monotony of a day typing up statements. Even a dressing down from Superintendent Orr at his most wrath-filled would be a thousand times better than another second in that hideous man's company.

Thursday 9th September 1920
Beatrice

In order to allow Johnnie to have some freedom to roam the store, at least for a few days, and the chance of speaking to any member of staff that she wished to, including the Arrol offspring, Beatrice had come up with a new policy for Arrol's. She was rather pleased with this policy, and with herself. For some reason, Hector Arrol had taken a shine to her and listened to her ideas with a willingness she hadn't really expected. She had worked out how to flatter him and make it seem as if the things she was suggesting had been his ideas in the first place.

The weekly Thursday morning meeting before the store opened gave her the opportunity to see how her latest suggestion went down with the management staff. The three-line whip for these management meetings meant that they were all there.

Hector Arrol and his children, with the exception of Gilbert, who was lounging casually against the door frame, all sat at the highly-polished boardroom table, along with the most senior management staff. The more junior managers stood uncomfortably along one wall. Beatrice, as the only woman there, other than Eliza Arrol, was also granted a seat at the table.

The usual meeting agenda about new stock, promotions and sales having come to its tedious end, Hector Arrol cleared his throat. "We are introducing a policy for new staff or, at least, those who will be speaking to customers." He paused and looked around the room. "All such staff will be visiting each department in their first week or so of employment, in order to become familiar with every aspect of Arrol's business. They will speak to all managers and any other staff, where they feel it would be useful to do so. This, I believe, is a policy which will set us apart from our competitors and will mean that our staff are fully prepared and feel comfortable

THE DEVIL'S DRAPER

about recommending goods in other departments, hmmmm?"

"A splendid idea, Father." Roderick, of course, was the first to weigh in on the subject. "For my part, I think this is an excellent innovation. My own department will—"

"Thank you, Roddy, but it's Mrs Price you should be praising." Hector Arrol bowed his head towards Beatrice with a smile. "It's entirely her idea. But I'm glad it meets with such fulsome approval." His voice was sarcastic, but Roderick beamed and sat back in his chair, looking at those around him with a self-satisfied smile.

"Well, I'm sorry, but I just don't have the time to speak to every little shop girl we employ." Alfred's tone was sharp. "Eliza can do it. She knows the clothing departments just as well as I."

"More so, I would say, Alfred. They'll be far better off speaking to Eliza anyway. Can't have new staff bored to death in their first week." Gilbert's drawl was a mocking one and Alfred turned round towards him, his face reddening.

Hector Arrol broke in, before Alfred could start blustering. "Do stand up straight, Gilbert. You're always leaning all over everything."

Gilbert straightened. "I say, sorry, Father. And I approve wholeheartedly of Mrs Price's idea, if anyone wants my opinion. A jolly good idea it is; I'll be happy to speak to all the new little shop girls, even if Alfred won't."

"Of course you will," Alfred snapped. "Any excuse not to do any actual work. Perhaps you can invite them all for tea and cake, just as you did with Miss Adair, when she was here."

"Yes, Gilbert. That was poor form indeed. I'm sure Father would agree." Roddy looked to his father for approval, but Hector ignored his comment.

"As I say, I expect *all* of you to comply with this new policy, which will start immediately. It's a few minutes out of your day when we have a new member of staff, that's all. Apart from anything else, you should all become familiar with all our new staff members in any case." He looked over at Gilbert. "Not so familiar that you invite all of them to take tea in the café, Gilbert – that does have an impact on our profits, after all. Talking of profits, we will, of course, be monitoring the effect on sales." Hector looked over at the bespectacled accounts clerk, who was busy scribbling away, but looked up to nod his agreement. "I have tasked Mrs Price with checking that the new procedure is followed and we will put this item on the agenda for a month's time to see how everything is going. Are we all quite clear, hmmmm?"

They were. Even Alfred had nothing further to say. Beatrice was delighted with herself.

FRIDAY 10TH SEPTEMBER 1920
JOHNNIE

Johnnie had managed to catch Beatrice in her office. "You don't need to keep following me around like that. I'm not going to steal anything." She'd had enough of seeing Beatrice's face everywhere she went. "I'm a professional."

"Exactly." Beatrice folded her arms. "That's what I'm worried about."

"I mean I'm here to do a job and I'll be professional about it. I'm not going to spoil everything by taking something." She lifted her chin defiantly. "I could come back any time I liked and do that."

Beatrice shook her head, firmly. "Oh no you can't. After all this is over, Arrol's is out for you and your gang, as long as I'm here."

"Fine." Johnnie knew that Beatrice wasn't intending to stay for long. She was only here in the first place to protect the young women she'd sent here. Although she and Beatrice had not got off to a good start, and she wasn't particularly fond of the woman, Johnnie had to admire her for that, at least. "I promise."

Beatrice sniffed. "I'll take that with a pinch of salt."

Johnnie sighed. The woman was as stubborn as *she* was. "Look, I'm only here to find out what happened to Ruby and Evvy."

Beatrice pointed an accusatory finger at her. "And to get some evidence about what Hector Arrol has been up to, that was our bargain."

"Aye, that too, an' as I say, I'm not going to put any of that at risk for a wee bit of fur or a couple of handkerchiefs. If I get the fancy for anythin', I promise you I'll nip out to Treron's or Copland & Lye on my lunchbreak. That alright with you?"

Beatrice's lips twitched. "You'd better not."

Johnnie laughed. "I willnae. I mean it. I promise."

Beatrice stood up and went over to one of the windows. "And I promise I won't follow you around the place watching you like a hawk. Is that a deal?"

"Aye, that's a deal."

Beatrice leaned against the window sill and crossed one ankle over the other. "Good. Any progress so far on either front?"

Johnnie shook her head. "No' much. I tell you, I don't know how anybody stands to do this job as a permanent thing. I've only been here a few days an' I'm already out of my mind with boredom. It's been 'yes, Mr Arrol; no, Mr Arrol; three bags full Mr Arrol' an' listening to him droning on about coating serge and worsted weight and two-inch elastic and striped blousings and French flannel…oh, I'm boring myself to death here."

"Well, I trust that you've outwardly at least been meek and amenable and hung on his every word?"

"Aye, well, he hasnae spotted my eyes glazing over yet. I've been so meek you wouldn't believe it. He says he wants to teach me all about it, that he can tell I'm a good student an' a good girl an' that I have a future with Arrol's. God forbid."

Beatrice sat back down again and opened one of her drawers. She took out a poke of Pontefract cakes and one of glacier mints, passing both bags across to Johnnie, who took one of each sweet. "And the other matter?"

Johnnie raised her eyes towards the ceiling and bit viciously into the soft Pontefract cake, releasing a burst of liquorice flavour that was both slightly sweet and slightly bitter. She chewed for a moment and then said, "I've spoken to Alfred, or Mr Arrol Junior as he insisted I call him. He's as bad as his father. Are they all like that?"

Beatrice laughed. "Thankfully, no, although all are probably equally annoying in their own ways. He spoke to you then, Alfred?"

"Aye, but not for long. He was keen as mustard to pass me over to his sister an' I have to say I was quite relieved. I liked her; she seems like a nice lassie."

THE DEVIL'S DRAPER

Beatrice took a glacier mint. "She is. Quiet, but friendly. And kind to the staff. Long-suffering."

"Aye, well, she would have to be with a brother like Alfred." Johnnie stood up from her chair with a sigh. "I suppose I'd better go and speak to the other two. An' then I'll work my way round the rest of the staff."

"Good luck."

"I think I'll need it." Johnnie made her way slowly down the two flights of circular stairs, looking about her and trying to see again what Evvy might have seen before she disappeared. They'd been on the clothing floor at the time. It was a huge place, split into several sections by fancy screens and fake walls. The ladies' department alone had separate sections for hats, coats, lingerie and furs. There were several changing rooms and a couple of offices, plus another staircase over towards the rear of the shop where the lift was, too. She would need to speak to the lift operator.

As she walked slowly down the staircase to the ground floor, she could see Roderick Arrol speaking to one of his sales assistants. Whereas the drapery department was mostly staffed by women, other than Hector Arrol, and the men's and women's clothing floor was equally split between male and female staff, the ground floor appeared to be mostly male assistants, other than the toiletries section, which was primarily young girls in the charge of a woman who looked to be in her fifties. She would need to speak to as many of them as possible; it seemed an almost impossible task – she hadn't realised quite so many people worked here.

Johnnie went over to where Roderick Arrol was talking to his assistant and hovered, trying to look nervous and demure.

Eventually, he spotted her and came over. "Can I help you, Miss...?"

"Smith, said Johnnie, "Johanna Smith. I'm new, up in the drapery department."

"Ah, of course. And you're here thanks to my father's innovative new protocol, eh? Very clever man, my father, eh?"

THE DEVIL'S DRAPER

"Oh, indeed, sir."

"You can call me Mr Roddy, Miss Smith. Unlike my brother Alfred, I don't stand on ceremony." He looked at her properly for the first time. "I say, have we met before?"

Johnnie's heart leapt. She had thought she'd done a good job of trying to make herself look different, but maybe she hadn't been as careful as she'd thought. "Well, I've been here for a few days, Mr Roddy."

"No, no, it's not that. I've definitely seen you before." He surveyed her with cool grey eyes. "Ah, I have it. Are you a member of the Queens Park Bowling and Tennis Club?"

"No, sir...Mr Roddy."

"Do you play tennis at all?"

"No, I don't, I'm afraid."

"I see." He thought for a moment and then his face cleared. "Ah well, never mind. Now, what would you like to know, Miss Smith?"

Johnnie's sole aim in her meetings with staff members was to get a feel for who they were. She didn't want to raise suspicions by asking questions about where they were when Evvy disappeared, or anything specifically related to Ruby or Evvy, but given that Ruby had stolen a box from Roderick Arrol's department, she'd wanted to specifically ask him about shoplifting. However, since he'd thought he might have recognised her, she stuck to more innocent questions about where he sourced his items, and what was new or popular.

Johnnie was glad when she could take her leave and head to the basement to speak to Gilbert. Based on what both Miss Adair and Mrs Price had told her, she had expected to find Gilbert Arrol not quite as annoying as his brothers but that wasn't the case. His first words to her were, "So, Miss Smith, what do you have to say for yourself?"

Johnnie hadn't come here to talk about herself and the lazy drawl with which he asked the question immediately put her off.

She struggled to stay in the timid persona of Johanna Smith and not react with sarcasm. "Oh, I don't have much to say for myself, Mr Gilbert. I just wanted to ask you some questions about your stock is all."

Gilbert Arrol seemed disappointed and looked past her shoulder, as if he were at a party where he was trying to find someone more interesting to talk to. "How very dull. I was expecting more sport. Oh well then, ask away, ask away."

Admittedly, he was polite and answered her questions with less pomposity than his two brothers, but she was glad to flee back upstairs, looking forward to the day when she need never speak to any of the Arrol men ever again.

Friday 10th September 1920
Mabel

I hadn't been able to concentrate all morning, thinking of Floss at the lawyers, dealing with the obnoxious Arthur Strang. Thus, I was glad of the interruption of a knock at my office door. I looked at my watch and it was about Archie's usual time for a chat and a cuppa, so I called out, "Come in, and you'd better be bringing cake." I was surprised when the door opened and it was Lorrimer.

"Sorry, Mabel, no cake. I didn't realise that was the price of entry these days. Am I interrupting you? It isn't work I've come to see you about, I'm afraid."

I waved him in. "Oh, don't worry, I'm delighted to be interrupted. I thought you were Archie...Constable Ferguson, with some of his wife's delicious baking. You're nowhere near as welcome, but you'll do."

"Why, thank you for that vote of confidence." He came in and sat down, waving the newspaper he was carrying. "I thought you might be interested in this. One of your friends."

"One of my friends?" I had no idea what he meant.

"Yes." Rather awkwardly, because of only being able to use his one good arm, he folded the newspaper over and scanned it. "Here it is. An art exhibition at a gallery owned by your friend, Gilbert Arrol."

"Really? I had no idea. Gilbert? I can't imagine he owns an art gallery — it would be too much bother."

"Mmmm. Apparently a newish venture, according to this piece. And his first show is that rather extravagant woman we met at Chez Antoine."

"Countess Coco?"

"The very same. I found out about it, because the show is reviewed in the newspaper here. The critic...well, let's say he

THE DEVIL'S DRAPER

doesn't appear to think very highly of the show."

I laughed. "Oh, do tell me what he says."

Lorrimer lifted the paper with a flourish. "Prepare yourself, Mabel. The title of the piece is *What's Wrong With Modern Art?*"

I sat back. "Excellent. I can't wait for him to tell us."

What was wrong with modern art, apparently, was absolutely everything. The drawings were distorted, the perspectives faulty, the colours crude and the painting execrable. Lorrimer was enjoying reading it to me, I could tell. "You'll like this bit. '*In general, these examples of modernist art are degenerate, entirely pathological and part of Bolshevik propaganda*'. How about that?"

"Oh my! Bolshevik propaganda, indeed. He really doesn't care for modernism, does he?"

"Oh, he hasn't finished yet: '*these new forms of so-called art are merely a symptom of a general movement throughout the world for breaking down law and order, the revolutionary destruction of our social system and identical in aspect to the visual derangement of the drawings of insane people in asylums.*'"

I winced. "Ouch. That's rather savage."

"In respect of Coco herself, he says: '*The works of the Countess Colette von der Weid are not fit to be called art. The pieces exhibited here are childish in the extreme, as well as bewildering and grotesque. Her paintings represent the flinging of a pot of paint in the face of the public; her designs appear to be made out of any old items she has found, including blotting paper, train tickets, curtain rings and pen nibs; and the thing she is most proud of, something she terms photo-montage, could very well be the result of the frenzied tantrum of a five-year old. If this is representative of Dada, then I want my Mama.*'" Lorrimer looked up. "I sense he was particularly proud of that little bon mot." He looked back down at the paper again. "Wait until you hear his parting shot: '*I left the gallery feeling as though I had just escaped a nightmare of vast proportions. This is the most illogical craze that has come under my observation during my fifty years' association with art and artists.*'"

"Oh dear, I hope poor Coco doesn't read this."

THE DEVIL'S DRAPER

Lorrimer tapped the newspaper on his knee. "Oh, I don't know. From the impression I got of her at Chez Antoine, I think she'd rather relish this."

"You may be right."

"Your friend Gilbert doesn't get off lightly either: '*The gallery is owned by one of the scions of the Arrol family of department store fame. By all accounts, he is a foppish gadabout and this gallery is the latest in a string of foolish endeavours. It is to be hoped that Arrol père is taking nothing to do with this nonsense. It would be a shame if the ladies of Glasgow were forced to buy vases that look as though someone has welded together a football, a handful of cough lozenges and a vacuum cleaner.*'"

I gasped at the vitriol in this passage. "That's rather cruel; Gilbert's a tad silly, but he's harmless, and he's great fun. I do hope this doesn't upset him. Where is this gallery?"

"An old warehouse on Tobago Street. In the East End."

"A warehouse?"

Lorrimer shook his head. "Mabel, nothing about this is normal. I'm sure a warehouse is the perfect aesthetic for a Dadaist artist's exhibition. It's just along the road from the police office there."

"Goodness, I'd like to see the exhibition."

"Well, that's what I was coming to say. According to this," he waved the newspaper once more, "the final day of the exhibition is tomorrow and Countess Coco will be putting on some sort of performance art event. Do you want to come?"

"With you, you mean?"

"Yes, of course. I'm intrigued by the whole thing too. Besides, thanks to you I'm personally acquainted with the artist. I think that means I *have* to go, don't I?"

SATURDAY 11TH SEPTEMBER 1920
JOHNNIE

One of the other young women in the drapery department had been given leave to go home due to illness, so Johnnie had been busier than usual, measuring and cutting lengths of cretonne and cambric, chiffon and charmeuse; matching and counting buttons and beads; and advising on the best width of waxed ribbon for trimming a cloche or a leghorn or a Breton sailor hat. Despite herself, she had enjoyed the day, although her feet were aching in the unaccustomed high heel of her Box Gibson shoes. Her more usual footwear, the battered men's Oxfords that were comfortably worn-in and familiar, would have been frowned upon here. They would probably be an immediate sacking offence.

She glanced at her watch. The last customer had left the floor and the store would soon be closing. Mr Arrol was over at the other side of the department with the remaining sales assistant, Isa, a quiet woman in her forties. As Johnnie watched, Hector Arrol shooed Isa away and she – rather reluctantly, it seemed to Johnnie – headed off towards the stairs. As she went, she glanced over at Johnnie, a frown creasing her forehead. She hesitated for a moment on the top step and then made her way downstairs, disappearing from view, as she rounded the bend in the staircase.

Johnnie started to fold the bolt of tweed suiting material on the counter, which she had been cutting for the last of her customers for the day. She longed to put her feet in a bowl of Reudel bath salts.

"You may leave that, Johanna, hmmmm?"

Johnnie started. She hadn't heard Hector Arrol's approach. "Oh, I'm sorry, Mr Arrol, I didn't see you there."

He laughed easily. "I'll finish doing that and put it away."

"Thank you, sir. That's most kind." Johnnie came out from

THE DEVIL'S DRAPER

behind the desk and headed over to the staircase. "I'll see you on Monday, Mr Arrol. I hope you enjoy the rest of the weekend."

He caught her arm as she passed. "One moment, Johanna."

She looked down at the hand on her arm and then up at his face, questioningly. Staying in character she said, "Yes, sir? I hope I've done nothing wrong, sir."

"Not at all, not at all." He was still holding on to her arm and his hand was unpleasantly moist, but Johnnie couldn't pull her arm away without giving offence. "Before you go, I'd like you to help me out with something, that's all."

"Yes, sir? Of course, sir."

"Good, good. We'll just go into the stock room, shall we, hmmmm?"

SATURDAY 11TH SEPTEMBER 1920
MABEL

I had arranged to meet Lorrimer at Ferguson and Forrester's in Buchanan Street after work. Floss and Jo had taken my grandmother on the afternoon sailing to Dunoon and Rothesay and they wouldn't be back until about ten, and I didn't feel like eating dinner on my own at home. By unspoken agreement, Lorrimer and I decided not to leave the station together; there was already plenty of gossip about our work-related dinners at Chez Antoine. Goodness only knows what people would have thought if we'd told them we were off to dinner and an art exhibition *not* paid for by Superintendent Orr.

Ferguson and Forrester's was one of my favourite restaurants. Not only was the food excellent, but it had the best-dressed and most elegant waiters in the whole of Glasgow. After a rather splendid fillet of beef and a delightful mandarin sorbet, we sat relaxing over a cup of coffee. The exhibition didn't open for another hour.

"Were you a policeman before the War, James?"

He added a spoonful of sugar to his cup. "Yes. I was one of the lucky ones, since it meant I was able to come straight back into a job. Well," he gestured to his empty sleeve, "almost straight away, anyway. A lot of the men I served with didn't have that luxury. After giving up their youth, and often their lives, to serve their country, those who survived were given twenty-six shillings a week for six months and then…nothing."

I nodded. "It's dreadful to see so many men in Glasgow out of work. And very few of the homes fit for heroes they were promised."

"It's just as bad in the rural areas. My family came from a village in Fife and I served with many men from there." He looked at the ceiling, but, I imagined, without seeing its gilt and carvings.

THE DEVIL'S DRAPER

"When I think of that village now, I see nothing but ghosts."

To be quite honest, I didn't know what to say, but James was well-practiced in changing the focus away from himself. "And what about you, Mabel? I think you were on factory patrol during the War. Is that right?"

"Yes. Here in Glasgow and at various munitions factories throughout Scotland."

"And how did you find it?"

I laughed. "It was...an experience, shall I say. Nobody really liked us. The Ministry of Munitions didn't know how to deal with the huge influx of women into their factories – you know, 'the trouble with women' as they kept saying – and they didn't really want either them, or the patrols, there. We had to buy our own uniforms, and they gave us very little guidance. And the women workers objected to us spying on them, as they termed it. We might all have been women, but the factory patrols were generally upper and middle class and the munitions workers resented us for it. Probably quite rightly."

Lorrimer looked at me curiously. "Why d'you say that?"

"Well, let's just say that some of my colleagues were a bit heavy-handed. These young women worked twelve-hour days, seven days a week, in dangerous conditions, what with the ether in the cordite and the TNT turning their skin yellow, not to mention the explosions."

"We sometimes got letters from them, you know." Lorrimer had a faint smile on his face.

"From who?"

"The women who worked in the munitions' factories. Sometimes they tucked a letter into the box of munitions. Some of them even put their names and addresses. All the lads would pounce if they saw them; it made their day. One of the men in my battalion – well, a boy, really – started up a correspondence with one of the young ladies who wrote."

I thought this was delightful. "Did they ever meet?"

THE DEVIL'S DRAPER

He shrugged. "I don't know. I was invalided out. I hope so."

I didn't want to push, by asking more questions – he didn't talk about his past very often – but I felt as though our conversation had given me a better understanding of him. I hoped it had done the same for him. I debated telling him about Johnnie, but thought better of it. Our tentative friendship wasn't quite on firm enough ground for that just yet. We sat in companionable silence, as Lorrimer finished his cigarette and I took a sip of my now cold coffee. "Well, James, it's time for us to be fashionably late to this event. I have to confess I'm rather looking forward to it."

We paid the bill and walked out into the evening. We could have got the train the couple of stops from Central to Glasgow Green Station, but we decided to walk along Argyle Street and the Trongate, both heaving with people heading for restaurants or music halls or clubs, or simply out for a stroll and from there into the relative quiet of London Street. I don't think either of us was in much of a mood for chatting, but it wasn't an unpleasant silence.

The gallery was at the end of Tobago Street. It certainly didn't look like a gallery, more like the warehouse that it had originally been. There was also no sign proclaiming it as a gallery, simply a stark black and white plaque announcing the place as *Fluxus*. We might have walked past it, but for the elegant man standing outside, in a heavily and beautifully embroidered evening jacket, smoking.

He turned a studiedly bored glance on us and we nodded at him and pushed the door open. We walked into a vast space, with high ceilings and exposed metal pillars and rafters. I wondered if the place had once been a slaughterhouse, as huge metal hooks on thick chains hung from the rafters, swinging as people passed them. The walls were crumbling brick and large windows set high in them let in the moonlight from outside. Inside, lighting was provided by a mish mash of lamps and lights including car and bicycle lamps, exposed bulbs on long wires and extravagant looking chandeliers.

The place was a riot of noise and colour, with a large crowd gathered. Everyone was sipping from glasses of champagne and chatting in small groups in the large, empty central space. Very few of the attendees were looking at the art works themselves, which gave Lorrimer and I the opportunity to see them unimpeded by other people.

The first thing that struck me was the huge canvases on one of the walls, similar in style to the artworks that had been in Gilbert's office, but much larger. They were bold, abstract designs in scarlets and blues and greens and golds, distorted versions of reality. Crooked and collapsing buildings mixed with crooked and collapsing faces, in a stark display of something that was at the same time rich and austere. I particularly loved one that was entitled *Self* and which was painted entirely in shades of red and black, except for the angular, harsh face with a slash of green across it. It didn't much look like Coco, but it was utterly compelling.

Lorrimer and I walked around the room, looking at everything in turn. A second wall had only two canvases, entitled *The Dear Departed* and *Collecting the Prisoners*. From a distance, they looked like simple landscapes, but on closer inspection, they were collages of photographs and newspaper cuttings and scraps of fabric mixed with paint. The newspaper cuttings were death notices, those awful lists that had become longer and longer as the War progressed. The newspapers were international; I recognised French, German, Russian and Italian, as well as English, and the images were cut from photographs of battles and the desolate stretches of no-man's land that were so familiar.

Lorrimer turned quickly away from those and I followed him, touching his arm briefly. The third wall was a mixture of poetry and more sculptural pieces made from textiles and buttons, keys, twisted pieces of wire, springs, glass and the curtain rings mentioned by the scathing art critic in the newspaper.

I moved back to the colourful paintings that had attracted me as soon as we walked into the gallery. "Delicious, aren't they? Coco calls it her 'colour scream'." I turned round to find Gilbert standing behind me. "How are you, Mabel? 'Tis delightful to see you."

THE DEVIL'S DRAPER

"This is amazing, Gilbert. Very powerful. She's extremely talented."

He beamed at me. "I'm delighted you get it, Mabel." He sighed. "So many people don't." I guessed he had seen the newspaper article after all. He gestured towards the painting nearest to us. "It's her way of showing an intensified sensation of reality that I find so very moving. Giving us the very essence of the thing she's depicting. This one, for example, *Forestspring*, don't you just love how she portrays the essential qualities of the forest, I don't know...the very *treeness* of the trees?"

Before I could answer, Lorrimer came over. Gilbert greeted him as though they were best friends. "Ah, James, delightful, delightful. Now, what do you both think of my new venture? I've always wanted to have an art gallery."

"It's a very impressive space." Lorrimer peered upwards. Is there another floor above?"

"No, just the basements below. A couple of offices and secure rooms, where we can store artworks before and after exhibitions."

"It must be a big responsibility," I said. "Do you have help then? You said 'we'."

Gilbert grinned. "Ah, you've caught me out, Mabel. I do indeed have a partner in this venture, although you'd never guess who: Roddy."

"Your brother?" I was rather surprised. Roderick didn't strike me as being a fan of art, particularly of the modern kind.

Gilbert put a finger to his lips. "Whatever you do, don't tell my father. He would never approve and Roddy would never forgive me; you know how he sucks up to father. No, Roddy is quite the admirer of modern art, just as I am, but he doesn't like to shout about it. A gallery was something we've been discussing for some time, though, and then Roddy found this place and we thought it'd be perfect."

"Oh, it is, absolutely perfect." A sudden clanging and scraping noise stopped me from saying anything else.

THE DEVIL'S DRAPER

Gilbert turned towards the sound. "Ah, it looks as though Coco is about to start her performance. I'll have to go and help her onto the stage." He gestured to a waiter carrying a tray. "But do get yourselves a glass of champagne. I do hope you can hang around afterwards, several of us are going for supper." And with that, he was off.

The crowd had surged forwards towards a small stage that had been built at the far end of the room and Lorrimer and I followed them, just in time to see Coco appear from behind a folding screen and present herself with a flourish. Her costume was a diaphanous, scarlet silk robe over which she wore a bullfighter's bolero jacket, trimmed with gold braid and items that looked as though she had found them in the street – tin cans, train tickets, pins, pages from books, an old shoe and small pieces of metal from who knew where. She was a living, breathing artwork. This evening she wore a monocle and her hair had been cut into a very severe shape and dyed jet black. Kohl rimmed her eyes as when we had met her at Chez Antoine's and her lips were a bright red. She had also, it seemed, smeared the same lipstick across her eyelids and postage stamps were stuck to her cheeks and chin. Lorrimer glanced at me and raised his eyebrows.

Gilbert held a hand out to her and with that as her only support, she sprang onto the stage. Her feet were bare and she swayed and strutted and danced on the stage, moving her body in movements which were, by turn, fluid and jerking. She would flow across the stage with the grace and beauty of a ballet dancer and then suddenly halt and stand on one leg, with the other bent into the air, elbows sticking out and fingers spread. As she moved, the cans and pieces of metal adorning her body clanked and rattled and scraped against each other.

Finally, she collapsed in a heap at the front of the stage, remaining there for a long minute, immobile. The room remained in complete silence – it seemed that those gathered knew there was more to come. And, indeed there was. Eventually, she rose in one swift movement and bent forward from the waist, swaying as she looked at the audience, in the same way we had looked at her. Just as I was beginning to feel uncomfortable under her scrutiny, she started to speak. She recited something which she called a sonic poem. It was made up of unintelligible words, which she recited at an ever-increasing level of sound until, by the end, she was bellowing the noises at us. And we were all spellbound. This time when silence fell again, the crowd, including Lorrimer and I, burst into rapturous applause.

THE DEVIL'S DRAPER

Sunday 12th September 1920
Beatrice

Beatrice rubbed at puffy eyes. She was working more than twelve hours a day, seven days a week. Mondays to Saturdays she would work at Arrol's and then go to her employment agency. On Sundays, she would spend from seven in the morning until nine at night at the agency, trying to keep up. She couldn't let the agency fail; it had been her lifeline since her husband's death. And she couldn't stay at Arrol's forever; she enjoyed the work there and she felt she had a knack for it, but her main aim had been to keep the young women safe from abuse, and she had seen nothing, heard nothing. She believed the young women, of course, but what could she do to change things? And if they weren't being abused at Arrol's, then they would be abused elsewhere. And she was so tired. She'd had to leave Arrol's early the previous afternoon, as her head was spinning and she'd fallen asleep as soon as she got home and woken up at three in the morning, sitting in her armchair and fully dressed, with a crick in her neck.

She opened mail, wrote letters, made phone calls, filled out her records, filed away correspondence and put other correspondence to one side to deal with later. And then she put her head down on her desk, just for a few minutes, to rest her eyes.

A sharp rapping at the door woke Beatrice up. She looked at the clock on the wall. Just after ten. She'd been asleep for a whole hour. She patted her cheeks to wake herself up and got up to unlock the door, which she always locked behind herself on a Sunday, as there was no-one else in the building that day.

Johnnie stood outside, glowering. She pushed past Beatrice and threw herself into the visitor's chair. "Well, he did it."

Beatrice, still groggy and half-asleep, was confused. "Who? Did what?"

THE DEVIL'S DRAPER

"That wee creep, Hector Arrol."

Beatrice sat on the edge of the desk, concerned. "Are you alright? Did he...?"

Johnnie snorted. "Naw, of course not, but not for want of tryin'. He wanted me to go in the stock room with him, after everyone else had gone home."

Beatrice clutched the edge of the desk. "Oh my goodness. You didn't, did you?"

"Aye, of course I went. You wanted me to get some proof, didn't you?"

A wave of nausea overtook Beatrice. "Well, yes, but...I didn't want you to put yourself in danger. You're just there to...to watch."

Johnnie's eyes narrowed. "You wanted me to be like the other wee lassies he's gone for, quiet an' timid an' who wouldnae say boo to a goose. You must have known he would try something wi' me."

Beatrice was horrified. Johnnie was right, of course. She'd put the girl there as bait, pure and simple. "I'm...I'm so sorry. I shouldn't have put you in that position."

Johnnie shook her head. "Don't be. I can deal wi' the likes of him; after all, I've dealt with worse."

"Did he hurt you?"

Johnnie shook her head. "Naw. Quite the gentleman he was, at least at first. But there's something under that charm that isnae nice." She shuddered. "I'd rather not talk about it. Slimy wee toad."

Beatrice rubbed at her eyes, which were cloudy with tears. "How did you get away?"

"Told him I was on my monthlies. He couldn't back off fast enough. But he'll try again, I'm sure of that, an' that excuse will only hold him off for so long."

Beatrice slapped the desk. "Well, that's it. You can't go back there. I'll not have you being put through that again."

Johnnie shook her head. "Naw. I have to go back. I still need to find out what happened to Ruby and Evvy. Don't worry. I've got the measure of him now an' I'll make sure I'm not alone with him.

THE DEVIL'S DRAPER

If it looks like it's going that way an' he wants me to stay late or something, I'll be prepared." She took out a mother of pearl and silver pocketknife and expertly flicked out the two blades, button hook and scissors.

"Well, I'll make sure I'm always around when you're working and I'll keep an eye out. He *will* try again; just like you said, I'm sure of that. But at some point, if he doesn't get what he wants, you'll be for the off, dismissed, you know that?"

Johnnie nodded. "Aye. I know. But there's someone else you might want to talk to. Isa Graham. In the drapery department."

"Isa?"

"Aye. She knows somethin', I'm sure. She was the last one to leave an' she looked at me as though she wanted to say something before she left. He got rid of her sharpish."

TUESDAY 14TH SEPTEMBER 1920
MABEL

I had arranged to meet Beatrice and Johnnie after work at what I'd come to refer to as 'Winnie's Place'. That way, I could walk home with my grandmother afterwards. This was the first day she'd been out since Floss had paid off Arthur Strang. None of us had seen hide nor hair of him since that day, so we were hoping we'd seen the last of him, and my grandmother had finally felt confident enough to face the world once more. The contract that Floss' lawyer had had Arthur Strang sign had been very specific: if he came back, then steps would be taken and investigations made that would cause him difficulties. Floss hadn't elaborated, but she'd seemed pretty sure that Strang had understood the consequences. Luckily, his greed had been greater than his sense of self-preservation and by all accounts, he'd signed with alacrity. But who knew what would happen when the money ran out?

Beatrice, Johnnie and I were gathered in Winnie's tiny office, with Johnnie sitting on the floor and me perched on a rickety stool. My grandmother was sitting quietly knitting and Winnie was out in the main part of the room, cleaning and polishing and chatting to any customers who came in. Johnnie had been telling us about her horrible experience with Hector Arrol and had reluctantly agreed with Beatrice and I that she wasn't to stay there for much longer, even if she hadn't managed to find anything out about what had happened to Evvy and Ruby. She'd begun to think that the connection both girls had with Arrol's was purely a coincidence anyway. She'd now spoken to most of the staff, and no-one had shed any light on things, and Johnnie had neither seen nor heard anything untoward, other than Hector Arrol's abominable behaviour.

THE DEVIL'S DRAPER

"And what about you, Beatrice?" I asked. "What about this business with Hector Arrol?"

Beatrice had been mostly silent since we'd been here and now she sighed. "Well, sadly, it's once again his word against a young woman's, and we all know who everyone is going to believe. He's very good at making sure that there's no-one else around when he assaults them. Johnnie suggested I speak to one of the members of staff in his department, Isa Graham, but she's so far been really evasive. Says that she's seen nothing and heard nothing and even if she did, she'd say nothing." Beatrice sniffed. "She's quite the three wise monkeys. But I'll keep trying on that front."

Johnnie sighed. "There's no point. What's gonnae happen anyway? He's got money, influence and power, an' me, all those lassies he's assaulted, Isa Graham an' even you, Beatrice, don't have *any* of those." She turned her gaze on me. "An' you an' your polis cannae do anything either so, aye, there's no point – he'll just carry on doing it." Her voice was defeated and her face pinched. I wanted to reach out and hug her, but I knew she wouldn't want that.

Beatrice tipped her head to one side and then the other, as if trying to work out a knot in her neck. "To be frank," she said, "I don't know how much longer I'll be able to keep going anyway."

I leaned forward, concerned. "What do you mean, Beatrice? Is something wrong?"

She waved a hand in dismissal. "Oh, I'm perfectly fine, simply tired is all. I've been trying to keep up with two jobs and I'm exhausted. I've been concentrating on Arrol's and feel that I'm letting the women down who come to Price's Employment Agency looking for jobs. I've piles of correspondence that's gone unanswered, my books to keep and employers to chase up. At some point soon, I need to get back to that."

"I'm sorry, Beatrice," I said. "I know you've been working long hours, but I didn't realise things were so bad. Is there anything we can do to make things easier for you in the meantime?"

THE DEVIL'S DRAPER

"I'll do it." We all turned to my grandmother, who had been quiet up until now. "I'll do it," she repeated. "I used to help my aunt out with keeping the household's books, when she took me in after my parents died." She laughed. "It was a long time ago, but I think I can still count. And we didn't have any typewriters in the asylum, of course, but I'm sure I can soon pick it up."

Thursday 16th September 1920
Johnnie

Johnnie had spent the last three days avoiding Hector Arrol. Luckily, he wasn't always on the shop floor and whenever she saw him come out of the offices, if she wasn't busy serving a customer, she would avoid him by heading down to the other floors, with the excuse of speaking to members of staff. If she hadn't wanted to avoid Arrol, she would have given up on that tack by now – she felt that the chances of her investigations leading to any clues about the deaths of Ruby and Evvy were slim to nil and she was, by now, convinced that there was no link with Arrol's. She might never find out what had happened to the two girls and she would have to accept it.

Today, she wanted to speak to the three security guards who patrolled the building on a regular basis. She strolled around the second floor, enjoying the calm elegance of the men's and women's fashion departments. It was only ten o'clock in the morning and the fancy ladies of Glasgow didn't, generally, come out to shop until the afternoon. As a result, all the big stores were heaving between two and five every afternoon and staff were standing around with little to do in the mornings. For the Avengers, too, therefore, the afternoons were better for shoplifting, as they could lose themselves more easily in the crowds of shoppers. Just after the War, however, Hector Arrol had brought in 'forenoon shopping' and advertised it in all the newspapers. On Mondays, Wednesdays and Fridays, an ever-changing array of special goods were set aside and available only to those who arrived before midday. This enticed the women of Glasgow to come out early, with the result that on those days, as soon as Arrol's opened, women from all across the city streamed in to get the special bargains.

THE DEVIL'S DRAPER

This morning, being a Thursday, there were very few shoppers around: a man trying on hats in a very desultory fashion – Johnnie thought he was early for an appointment somewhere and had come in simply to pass the time – and a woman with a pram, who was browsing in the children's wear section. Johnnie walked through each of the departments, her eye caught from time to time by a jade silk blouse, a men's tweed suit, an evening gown in violet satin.

None of the security guards were to be seen up here, so Johnnie made her way to the back staircase, which was the nearest to her. It wasn't as fancy as the central circular staircase and it was mostly used by staff, rather than customers. Nobody was on it, as she ran down the stairs. On the ground floor, the staircase opened immediately onto a new display of gloves and scarves, ready for the autumn and winter season. Chamois, suede, lisle and woollen gloves, and scarves of every hue and pattern. Johnnie had heard from other members of staff that Roderick was always the first to update for the new season.

She stopped and admired a beautiful display of heavily fringed scarves in black, bronze, mauve, rose, cream, primrose, mint green, sky blue, navy, dove grey and putty. Each scarf seemed to flow into the next and each colour sat beautifully next to its neighbour, forming an autumnal rainbow of pleasing shades and tones.

"Delightful, is it not, Miss...Smith?"

Johnnie started; she hadn't heard him approaching. "It is indeed, Mr Roderick. Very lovely."

"I do hope that it doesn't give you ideas, Miss ...Smith."

Once again, he had hesitated when he said her name. "I'm sorry, Mr Roddy; what do you mean?"

He smiled at her and gently took her arm, leading her back towards the rear staircase. "I mean that I've remembered where I saw you. Now, I think you and I should have a little talk."

THE DEVIL'S DRAPER

SATURDAY 18TH SEPTEMBER 1920
MABEL

Ellen had called me to the phone. Beatrice didn't even say hello. "Johnnie's disappeared." She sounded on edge.

"What do you mean, disappeared?"

"Exactly what it sounds like. I'm here in my office at Arrol's. She was here on Thursday morning, going about her duties as normal. I popped out of my office at various times to check on her, to make sure Hector Arrol wasn't up to his nonsense, and I didn't see her after about ten. I went through the whole store, thinking she might have been speaking to staff members, but she was nowhere to be found."

I pulled over a chair close to the table the telephone was on. "It's a big place. Perhaps she was on one staircase while you were on the other or something and you just missed each other."

"No, I went around the whole store three or four times. There was no sign of hide nor hair of her. Besides, she was supposed to be coming to my office in the afternoon to update me and she didn't turn up." There was a muffled noise on the other end of the phone and I heard her say, "I'll be with you in a minute."

Ellen brought me a cup of tea and I mouthed a thank you to her. "Maybe she just got fed up with the straight and narrow. Remember, she said she was coming round to the fact that she wasn't going to find anything out about her friends. Maybe she simply gave it up as a bad job."

Beatrice's voice when she spoke sounded exasperated with me. "She wouldn't do that. And she wasn't in yesterday either. Nor today. I think something's happened to her."

"Well, she's hardly likely to have disappeared from Arrol's in broad daylight, is she?" I took a huge gulp of my tea.

"Why not?" Beatrice snapped. "Evvy did."

THE DEVIL'S DRAPER

She was right, that's exactly what Johnnie had said had happened to Evvy. I thought for a moment. "I'll go and see if she's at home."

"Home? You know where she lives?"

"I think so." I wasn't sure if the close I had seen her going into *was* her home, but it would be a good place to start.

"You *think* so?" Beatrice now sounded even more worried than she had been before. "You can't just go into somewhere you *think* is where she lives. What if it's the St Thenue's Avengers headquarters? They might be women, but they're still a gang. And dangerous. They won't want a police officer meddling in their business."

She was right, of course, but now she'd made *me* worry about Johnnie. "It'll be alright. I know she hasn't told them about me, and, let's face it, nobody ever believes me when I say I'm a police officer anyway. If that is the gang's headquarters and anyone else is there, I'll just tell them I'm one of her friends."

She was clearly dubious. "Well, be careful."

"It's an address in Merchant Lane. Number 8. If I don't phone you back in an hour, call the station and ask for either Detective Inspector Lorrimer or Sergeant Ferguson."

I told Floss and Jo the same as I'd told Beatrice. Jo offered to drive me down and wait for me, but I didn't think a Hispano-Suiza turning up outside what might be a gang's headquarters would be a very good idea, so I decided to walk.

On the way, I deliberated what I would say when I got there, if I couldn't find Johnnie. I was almost sure that she would be there and that Beatrice's fears were unfounded.

On the ground floor of the close that Johnnie had gone into was a rope manufacturer. It was shut today, so I went into the close and walked up the first flight of stairs. The close itself was plain and simple, with none of the fancy tiles of some of Glasgow's finer examples. The stoops weren't as sparkling as some I had seen, and the windows halfway between each floor were dirty with the soot that characterised many of Glasgow's buildings, but the stairs were swept and each flat had solid-looking storm doors, which were

THE DEVIL'S DRAPER

all carefully painted the same deep, reddish brown. The staircase smelled of fish and I could imagine that in the heat of the summer the smell might be unbearable.

I didn't know which flat Johnnie might have gone into, of course, so I decided to start at the bottom and work my way up. I knocked on the first door and waited for a few moments. There was no answer and I couldn't hear any movement behind the door, so I moved on to the middle one. It was pulled open by a woman who looked to be in her mid-thirties, about ten years older than me.

"Aye?" She looked at me suspiciously.

"I'm looking for Johnnie."

"Aye?"

I nodded. "I wasn't sure which flat was hers."

"Naw?"

I could feel myself starting to sweat under this woman's distrustful gaze. "Do you know if she's in?"

"Naw."

I wasn't sure if she meant Johnnie wasn't in, or whether she simply didn't know whether she was or not. I was almost out of questions. Clearly, I hadn't thought enough about this on the walk down. "Have you seen her recently?"

All of a sudden she stepped out, shutting the door firmly behind her, and pushed past me. "You jist wait here, missy." She disappeared down the stairs. I peered over the banister and saw her disappearing out of a door at the back of the close, which I assumed led into the back court. When she wasn't back in a few minutes, I wondered if I had misheard her and whether I should just continue knocking on doors, or, more likely, leave. As I dithered, someone opened the door at the back of the close again and I heard two sets of footsteps on the stone steps.

I looked down as they came into view. The glowering woman, who had opened the door to me, was preceded by a tall, substantial woman in her early fifties. She took the stairs two at a time and

THE DEVIL'S DRAPER

came to stand in front of me, her hands on her hips, staring me coolly in the eyes. We stood for a moment like that, taking the measure of each other, before she quietly said, "Aye?"

I hoped she wasn't going to be as monosyllabic as her friend. "I was looking for Johnnie and wasn't sure exactly which flat was hers."

"An' who might you be?"

"I'm a friend of hers. My name's Mabel."

"She's never mentioned you."

To be honest, I didn't think she would have, but just settled for a brief, "No?" Two could play at that game.

"Naw."

Clearly, it was some sort of stand-off, and I was the first to cave. "I'm a bit worried about her."

"An' why might that be, then?"

I had decided to keep it vague, in the hope that it would be more believable that way and that I wouldn't be caught out. "I was supposed to be meeting her on Thursday and she didn't turn up and I haven't heard from her since."

"Naw?"

"Have you seen her recently?"

This time she didn't answer at all, simply continuing to gaze at me. I, too, kept my mouth shut. Finally, she broke the silence. "I dinnae ken who you are, or what ye want, but when I see Johnnie, ah'll be askin' her about ye."

I took from that answer both that she hadn't seen Johnnie recently and that I had outstayed my welcome, such as it had been.

"Well, when you do see her, please let her know I've been looking for her." I made to walk past them both, but she grabbed my arm.

"What sort of a friend are you?"

I turned to face her, trying not to look as though her grip was hurting me. "I'm sorry?"

"How d'ye know her?"

THE DEVIL'S DRAPER

I'd thought about this question, too. "Oh, I see. Well, I haven't known her long. I work at Arrol's, in the ladies' shoe department and we got chatting one day."

"An' you were supposed to be meeting on Thursday?"

"Yes, we spoke on Thursday morning. She said she needed a new pair of shoes and I said I'd see her right, if she came and saw me at the end of the day."

"New shoes?"

"Yes, we had a few pairs in her size in the store room. Old stock. I said I'd sort her out a pair at a good discount."

"New shoes?" She said it again, this time even more dubiously. "That disnae sound like our Johnnie, does it Chrissie?"

"Naw."

"Oh, well," I said breezily. "Never mind. Hopefully, I'll see her soon at Arrol's." And, with that, I pulled my arm away from her grasp, pushed past them both and ran down the stairs.

As I reached the bottom, I heard the voice of the older woman behind me. "Here, how did ye know where tae come?"

I fled out of the close and up the lane towards the Briggait. I didn't have an answer for that one.

Sunday 19th September 1920
Johnnie

"We'll try again, shall we, Johanna?" She still hadn't told him her real name, hadn't told him anything at all, in fact. "I want to be part of this little enterprise you and these so-called Avengers have going."

Johnnie raised her head. "I have no idea what you mean."

"Oh, don't give me that." He kicked the leg of the chair she was tied to and it wobbled dangerously. She leaned the top part of her body over, to counterbalance the wobble. It was bad enough being sat in one position like this; she didn't want to be sent crashing to the damp, cold floor. The ropes against her stomach and ribs pulled her back into the chair, but it remained upright. "Your friends told me all about this gang of yours and the lucrative business you have going on. I've heard about these jewellery heists and raids on fur warehouses."

"Aye? Well, if they told you so much, why are you askin' me?"

He slapped her face, his own a mask of cold rage. "A gang of women," he scoffed. "What nonsense!"

"Then why are you so bothered, if it's just nonsense?" She tried to make her voice firm and strong, but she could feel the tremor of fear in her chest.

"Because it could be more. I could make it more. It was your little friend Ruby that gave me the idea. I caught her shoplifting one day and she boasted about your gang. She said she'd tell me about where I could find a safe stuffed full of money, if I didn't turn her in to the police."

Poor, silly little Ruby. She didn't know anything about a safe full of money. There wasn't any safe full of money. Meg put all the proceeds of the jobs they did into the bank. "So why did you kill her?"

THE DEVIL'S DRAPER

He sighed. "A mistake."

"And Evvy?"

"Is that the name of the other girl?"

The other girl. He didn't even know her name. "Aye."

He shrugged. "I saw you both on the stairs and I was watching you. And I saw the way her face changed when she saw me. She looked just like the other girl, scrawny and pale, so I grabbed her when you weren't looking and brought her here."

Here was the small, dark, empty space Johnnie had been in for the last few days – exactly how long she wasn't quite sure. He'd given her chloroform to knock her out on a couple of occasions and had mostly left the blindfold on. Her arms were tied around the back of the chair and, as far as she could tell, had been that way ever since she'd been brought here. Her shoulders were burning with tension and pain. In turn, the chair was chained tightly to a metal pipe that ran straight up the wall. The room had dirt floors and stone walls, with a couple of small barred windows set high up. She assumed they were in a basement. She'd been blindfolded when he brought her there, but she could tell that they had come down stairs into what felt like a larger space and then through two doors into this room.

On one occasion, she'd heard the faint noises of someone moving something around and had pushed her chair backwards and forwards as much as she could, so that the chain rattled against the pipe, in the hope that someone would hear and come and free her. She was blindfolded and gagged and it was the only thing she could do to make a noise. He'd immediately come in and hit her, sending her head backwards, cracking it hard against the wall. The chloroformed rag had once again been put under her nose and when she woke up, her arms were tied even tighter and the chains around the chair were more firmly tied. She couldn't move it at all now.

It was only when he was here that the blindfold and gag came off. "I need it," he said now.

THE DEVIL'S DRAPER

"What?"

"Money, of course. I want to be in charge."

Despite the circumstances, Johnnie held back a smile. Meg would never let that happen. Others had tried and failed, stronger, more powerful men than this soft-handed weakling.

However, this soft-handed weakling had her locked up here and she could easily end up like Ruby and Evvy and there was absolutely no reason she wouldn't. Nobody knew she was here.

THE DEVIL'S DRAPER

Monday 20th September 1920
Mabel

I'd phoned in sick. Since I'd joined the police force, over eighteen months before, I hadn't taken a day off sick; I'd hardly had a day's holiday, because Superintendent Orr rostered me for all the public holidays out of spite. The only days I had off were Sundays, to allow me - as Orr said - to go to church.

Beatrice and I had discussed it. I didn't think it was worth asking Orr for a couple of days to spend at Arrol's. Beatrice was going to tell Arrol that the Glasgow police force was concerned about an influx of shoplifting gangs into Glasgow city centre and so they were sending me back to be stationed there for a couple of days. So my secondment was totally unsanctioned by any form of authority but, hopefully, by the time anyone ever found out, it would be too late to do anything about it.

Beatrice had done a good job planting the seeds. As I made my way to her office to discuss tactics, a beaming Hector Arrol stopped me on the main staircase and grabbed my hand, shaking it enthusiastically. "Miss Adair, how lovely to have you back. How is your dear mother? Well, I hope? I dare say she'll be gearing up towards the festive season and hosting some of her autumn and winter soirees very soon." I could tell he was angling for an invitation.

"We were just talking about you the other day, Mr Arrol." I didn't tell him we were discussing how sleazy his behaviour was and what a little toad he was.

"Oh, splendid, splendid." He beamed and patted my hand, which he was still holding between his own unpleasantly warm ones. "Well, I'd better let you get on with keeping us safe from miscreants and ne'er-do-wells. I do think it's very reassuring that the police are treating a threat such as this with all the seriousness

THE DEVIL'S DRAPER

that it merits. I was shocked when Mrs Price told me about these new gangs. Dreadful business, dreadful business. I shall pass my gratitude on to Chief Constable James Stevenson when I next see him. We're members of the same Club, you know, hmmmm."

I didn't know, but it didn't surprise me. I was sure that the Chief Constable would be very puzzled by both the thanks, and the knowledge that marauding shoplifters were targeting the fine department stores of Glasgow but, once again, once the whole subterfuge had been traced back to Beatrice and I, hopefully it would be too late by then.

After I finally managed to get away from Hector Arrol and his disagreeable hands, I continued up the stairs to find Beatrice. She led me into her office and shut the door.

"Have you heard from her?" I asked. I'd told her the day before about my visit to try and find Johnnie and we were both worried now. We'd concluded that Johnnie had been right about a connection with Arrol's since the last place – or nearly the last place – Ruby, Evvy and now Johnnie had been seen was at Arrol's. Hence today's subterfuge.

She shook her head. "Not a thing. So, what do you think we should do?"

"I want to speak to the Arrol sons and some of the other staff, the security guards in particular – they're the people who are most likely to notice anything happening, even if they don't realise it."

Beatrice nodded. "I'm going to speak to Isa again."

"Do you think this has anything to do with Hector Arrol?

She shrugged. "Somehow, I doubt it. It's possible, but I don't see how he would have had any contact with Ruby and Evvy. And he seems oblivious to the harm he's done to the others: Agnes Black, Nell Donald, Anna Nicholls, poor, poor Elsie McNiven, the ones who wouldn't or couldn't speak to me, and the countless others over the years, no doubt." She drifted off into thought. "I'm sure Isa Graham knows something. Maybe not about what happened to Johnnie, but I'm sure she knows something about Hector Arrol's behaviour. She's spent a good long time working in his department, after all."

I stood up and brushed my skirt down. "I'll ease myself in gently with a visit to Gilbert. I'm not sure I'm ready for Alfred or Roddy yet."

The store was still fairly quiet. As I ran down the stairs, I spotted Alfred in the menswear department, talking to one of his minions and pointing towards a rack of ties with a fervour which ties simply didn't warrant. I put my head down and hurried on down the stairs. When I reached the ground floor, Roddy was nowhere to be seen, for which I was grateful. In the basement, Gilbert appeared to be waiting for me.

"Mabel! How delicious. They said you were here. Come and have some tea, dear girl."

I agreed with alacrity and we went into the café, which was quiet at this time of day. It really was a lovely place, all peacock blue and apple green, with shining gilt fixtures and fittings and potted palms everywhere. We went to sit at what was my favourite table, from where I could look over the whole place. I ordered a cup of tea and a scone and we settled in.

"How's Coco?" I asked.

"Ah, I shall miss her. She headed off yesterday on a ship to New York. Expect tales of wild parties and even wilder exhibitions."

I piled clotted cream and jam onto my scone. "Did she sail with all her artworks then?"

Gilbert laughed. "Oh no, Coco has a whole new exhibition planned for New York. We've taken all her pieces down and stored them at the gallery and will send them on to her next destination in due course. Well, I say 'we', but Roddy insisted he'd do all that."

"I have to say that I didn't have Roddy down as an art lover." My voice was slightly muffled by the delicious bite of scone I'd just taken.

"Oh, me neither. I was rather surprised when he said he'd take charge of the de-install. He was quite insistent, said I'd done all the hard work so far and that I must be shattered. He's told me to stay away from the gallery and that he'll deal with everything. He's never been solicitous about my welfare before, but what is it they say about never looking a gift horse in the mouth?"

I licked the remaining cream and jam off my fingers. "I didn't see him upstairs earlier, is he here?"

Gilbert shrugged. "I don't believe so. Who knows where he is? Ayr? Hamilton? He's got a bit of a gambling habit my brother and he's been spending rather a lot of time at the races recently. Father's not best pleased. I've tried to cover for him, but..."

"Roddy?" I was quite shocked to learn this. Roderick didn't seem the type – either to gamble or to go against his father.

"Oh yes, father's had to bail him out many times. Says he's not going to do it anymore, though." A look of horror suddenly crossed Gilbert's face. "Oh, I say...you don't think he only offered to deal with Coco's works so that he could sell them, do you? Perhaps I'd better get over there and check."

"I'm sure that's not the case," I reassured him. But I was beginning to wonder if there was another reason that Roddy wanted to keep Gilbert away from the gallery. I picked up my handbag and hat. "Thanks for the tea, Gilbert. I need to get back up to see Beatrice."

THE DEVIL'S DRAPER

MONDAY 20TH SEPTEMBER 1920
MABEL

Beatrice insisted on coming with me and, quite honestly, I wasn't going to turn her down. We debated going to the police station and letting them deal with it, but I knew that the only person who would possibly take any notice of me was Lorrimer, and it was his day off. I did, however, ring Floss, and ask her to get Jo to pick us up. It was the quickest way to get to Tobago Street. I had to tell her a little of what was happening and why we needed Jo so quickly, so I wasn't surprised when the Hispano-Suiza came to a screeching halt outside Arrol's and not only was Jo in the driver's seat, but Floss was sitting in the passenger seat next to her.

"What are *you* doing here?"

Floss wafted an exasperated hand at me. "No time, no time, just get in."

Beatrice and I climbed in and Jo sped off, wending her way expertly through the streets out to the East End. On the way down, I explained briefly what was happening.

"Stop at the end of Tobago Street!" I didn't want Roderick Arrol to be alerted by a car pulling up outside the gallery. I gave them strict instructions not to follow us on foot, but to keep an eye out and, if they spotted anything untoward, or we shouted for them, they had to immediately go to the police station at the other end of the street.

It was the middle of the day, but the street was almost deserted here. This was both good and bad. Four well-dressed women and a Hispano-Suiza weren't usual sights around here and we didn't want to draw attention to ourselves. On the other hand, if we got into trouble, then we definitely *did* want to draw attention to ourselves.

There were no windows in the lower part of the building, just a large archway that housed the heavy wooden doors. The building

THE DEVIL'S DRAPER

was an old factory of some sort and the double door was the solid type that was definitely meant to keep unwanted visitors out. One side had a round metal handle above a keyhole. It was shiny with wear, and I grasped it. The door remained firmly shut.

I looked around. "This isn't going to open. There's an alleyway just up there. Maybe there'll be a window round the side or somewhere round the back we can get in," I whispered. I could feel Beatrice's breath on my neck.

"Let me try the lock." I jumped and turned to face Floss, who was standing to the side of me.

"I told you to stay in the – oh, never mind."

She pushed me aside and pulled two hairgrips from her head. I'd seen her do this before. She bent down and carefully inserted one of the hairpins into the lock. Less than a minute later and there was a click. Floss stood up and gently pushed on the door, which opened, luckily almost soundlessly. She nodded me in and I shoo-ed her back to the car, waiting for her to do as I told her for a change.

I tentatively entered the space and Beatrice followed. Light poured in from the large windows at the top of the walls. The room looked entirely different without Coco's artworks and the metal hooks on the thick chains hanging from the ceiling looked much more sinister, without the crowds of gay people and glasses of champagne that had been here previously.

The floors were stone, and I tiptoed as I moved over to a door on the right. I cursed myself for not taking more notice when I was last here. The door had a small glass panel at the top and I peered carefully in. It looked to be some sort of office, very small and dark and there was clearly no-one inside.

At the other end of the space was a further door. I nodded at Beatrice and we made our way over to it. I put my ear to the door and could hear nothing on the other side, so I slowly turned the handle and pulled it open.

THE DEVIL'S DRAPER

There was a slight *creak* as I did so and I paused, my knuckles white as I gripped the door to stop it moving. Cold, stale air rose up to greet me and I guessed that the door must lead downwards into a basement of some sort. There was no sound, so I pushed it open wider.

Stone steps led into darkness, and I took a couple of tentative steps down. I could make out a small, square landing halfway down and then nothing. I came back up the stairs. I whispered up to Beatrice: "Look for something we could use as a weapon."

There was still some debris from the exhibition lying around and I cast about for something useful. Over in one corner, I saw an L-shaped metal bracket and I picked it up, hefting it in my hand. It was solid; the long leg was about eighteen inches in length, the other about a foot long. Beatrice had found herself a piece of heavy chain that looked as though it had come from one of the hooks in the ceiling. She coiled it around her arm so that it wouldn't make a noise when she moved.

We went back over to the door and made our way slowly down the stairs into the darkness. The steps were wide and even, but by the time we reached the small landing and the stairs curved down out of sight, we trod more carefully. It was impossible to see our feet and I put a hand out to the wall to steady me. The bricks were rough and cold under my fingers. With each step, I felt for the stair below, making sure it was solidly under my foot before I took my next. Every few steps, I gently reached out behind me and placed a warning hand on Beatrice and we stopped to listen. There was still no sound and I was beginning to wonder if I had made a mistake.

Eventually, there were no more stairs and I reached a foot forwards, taking tiny steps and using my arms to feel for what was around me. It was colder down here, and musty and the floor beneath my feet felt different. It wasn't stone any longer, but hard earth, rougher and not as even as the stairs had been.

I inched forwards, Beatrice close behind me, holding on to my arm. It wasn't long before the quality of the air changed and my

THE DEVIL'S DRAPER

outstretched hand touched a wall. I felt along it, until I came to what seemed to be a door. I put my ear to it. I could hear something very faintly, as though it was still some way in the distance. I felt around the door for the handle and, very gently, twisted it, holding my breath for a creak, but this one turned smoothly and quietly.

Holding my breath, I opened the door a few inches and looked around the edge of it. The room the door opened onto wasn't quite as dark as the staircase we had just come down; there was a faint light coming from somewhere and I could just make out the wall nearest to me. As I turned my head, I started back in shock. A shrouded figure loomed out of the murky shadows. I bit back a scream and retreated behind the door, clutching Beatrice's arm. She gave a tiny squeal.

We stood for a second, unmoving, as the silence wrapped itself around us. Finally, I took the chance to poke my head around the door once more. The shrouded figure was still there in exactly the same place, but this time I recognised it for what it was, a dust sheet covering a strange shape. A few smaller shapes surrounded it. One of them wasn't covered in a sheet and I recognised it as one of Coco's wire and glass sculptures. I took a step into the room. Rectangular shapes of different sizes were propped against the walls, most of them covered with sheets, or wrapped in brown paper; Coco's paintings and collages, I assumed.

The source of the faint light in the room was a small door at the far end. Beatrice and I picked our way carefully through the paintings and sculptures towards the door. Once again, we stood listening. The noise that I'd heard before began again. Now I could make out the laboured grunts of someone moving or dragging something heavy. But it still wasn't close. I held a hand up to stop Beatrice and crept up to the door. Crouching down as near to floor level as possible, I looked quickly through the narrow opening, without touching the door. The room beyond was smaller than the one we were in, but totally empty, a narrow ante-room with yet another door in the far wall. That one was half open and the noises were coming from there, louder now.

I could hear low, rhythmic grunting that accompanied the dragging noises but now I discerned something else: a soft whimper. The dragging noise stopped, but then came a muttered, "God damn it!" This was followed by a scuffling and more whimpers. I ran over to the door, this time not bothering to try and hide myself, as I looked around it.

Roderick Arrol was crouched over Johnnie. In the light from the lamp, Arrol's shadow loomed huge and black on the opposite wall, like a scene from a horror film. He had his hands around her neck and was shaking her violently. Her hands clutched weakly at his arms and her feet jerked.

I rushed forward, holding the metal bracket outstretched and swung it at Roderick Arrol's back. Pain shot through my arm as it connected. Roderick's screech was louder than mine. He collapsed on top of Johnnie and I used my foot to kick him off her.

She lay unmoving, bruised and bloodied. I froze, staring at the red marks around her neck, where he had strangled her. Arrol dragged himself up to standing and stood in front of me, slightly swaying.

I lifted the metal bracket over my head once more, but he launched himself at me with a cry. The bracket flew from my hand, landing on the hard dirt floor with a dull clunk.

Arrol pushed me to the floor, pinning me down with his knees. His hands seized my neck and I felt the pressure for just a few seconds, before something caught him on the side of the head. Beatrice. The chain. He fell back, releasing my neck and clutching at his ear. Beatrice swung the chain once more, this time catching him across the brow. He groaned and lay unmoving.

Over in one corner of the room was an overturned chair and around it lay ropes and chains, which had apparently been used to attach the chair – presumably with Johnnie in it – to the sturdy pipe on the wall behind it.

THE DEVIL'S DRAPER

I staggered upright and fetched the rope, tying it around Arrol's wrists and ankles. His breath was laboured and rasping, but I didn't trust that he would remain that way for long, so I moved quickly, trussing him up as tightly as I could.

I glanced over to where Beatrice was cradling Johnnie's head on her lap, quietly sobbing.

FRIDAY 8TH OCTOBER 1920
MABEL

Beatrice, Johnnie and I were crammed into my tiny office. If Superintendent Orr asked, I was taking their statements; in actual fact, we were drinking tea and eating clootie dumpling. I had persuaded Archie to give us the whole lot he had brought in today and we were tucking into it with relish, as we went over the events of the last few weeks.

Roderick Arrol was now sitting in a jail cell at Duke Street prison, awaiting trial. Johnnie, other than numerous cuts and bruises from where she had been beaten and kicked, that were now yellowing and healing, and a broken arm that would take slightly longer to do so, was quieter and more thoughtful than she normally was. It was painful for her to speak and her neck still bore the red marks from where Roderick Arrol had tried to strangle her. We had spent quite a lot of time together since we'd rescued her from the basement. Floss had given her a room at home and my grandmother and I had nursed her wounds and injuries over the last couple of weeks, with frequent visits from Beatrice. There had been no visits, however, from the St Thenue's Avengers. I'd been down there to tell the woman, Meg, what had happened, at Johnnie's insistence. She had remained stony-faced while I told her. Johnnie hadn't said anything, but I got the impression that she was disappointed that Meg hadn't been to see her or even to enquire about her.

Beatrice was now back full time at Price's Employment Agency for Ladies. Hector Arrol, once he found out the role she had played in having Roderick arrested, had promptly told her to leave Arrol's. He'd tried to do the same with me, of course, but I'd told him that since I wasn't employed at Arrol's, all he could do would be to stop me from shopping there in the future. He'd ended up blustering

THE DEVIL'S DRAPER

that he would let the Chief Constable know how unprofessionally I had behaved. I had told him he was welcome to and let slip that the Chief Constable was Floss' cousin. He'd soon piped down.

I was sorry about Beatrice, though, but she was philosophical about the whole thing. "It was all too much, anyway. I was neglecting the employment agency. I can now concentrate on that. Although..."

I could tell there was something on her mind. "Although what, Beatrice?"

She grinned, slightly. "Well, I did enjoy all the store detective side of it. And I think I did rather a good job."

Johnnie laughed. "Aye, you did. Too good of a job. The Avengers have more or less crossed Arrol's off our list of places to hoist from. I can now tell Meg that you're no longer there. She'll be delighted."

"So you're going back, then?" I asked.

"Back? To the Avengers? Aye, why wouldn't I?"

For a moment, I couldn't work out why I felt disappointed, but then I realised. "No reason. It's just...I won't get to see you, is all."

She thought for a moment. "Aye, I suppose it wouldnae do for a policewoman an' a thief to be pals, would it?"

Beatrice cleared her throat. "Well, as it happens, I have a little idea." We both looked at her. "The office next to mine has just become vacant. I was thinking about setting up Price's Private Detective Agency."

I laughed. "Beatrice! You've just told us that you've been neglecting the employment agency! How would you cope with that, too?"

"Well, Mabel, I have to say that your grandmother is doing a splendid job of looking after things on a day-to-day basis and, well, I was rather hoping that Johnnie here would join me in the detective agency?"

Johnnie looked flabbergasted. "Me?"

THE DEVIL'S DRAPER

"Yes, why not? Your disguise skills would come in very handy. Not to mention the way you can...well, let's just say...sneak about." Johnnie snorted. "What do you say?"

Johnnie screwed her nose up and considered for a moment. "I'll think about it."

"Excellent."

"I haven't said aye."

Beatrice waved a hand. "Thinking about it is good enough for me."

We sat silently for a few minutes, each of us in our own heads. Finally, Beatrice sighed. "I do have one regret about not being at Arrol's, though."

I knew exactly what she meant. "I know, Beatrice. But even if you could get any of those young women to speak—"

"Surely if I could get two or three of them to say what he did to them, then that would be enough for the Court?"

"I'll tell them what he did to me," Johnnie said. "I'd love to."

We'd discussed this before. "Even if you found fifty young women he'd assaulted and got them *all* to give evidence against him, there's nothing and no-one to corroborate that evidence."

"But they'd all be telling the same story. Don't they corroborate each other?" I knew Beatrice was frustrated, and I was too.

"Unfortunately not. Every single case would need a second piece of evidence, or a witness."

Beatrice slammed her mug down on the desk and tea slopped over the sides. "So he's just going to get away with it? What he did to Johnnie and Agnes, Nell, Anna. And Elsie. What about Elsie? She took her own life because of him. Isn't that as good as murder?"

There was nothing I could say and we lapsed into silence.

The knock at the door came as a welcome relief. The desk sergeant poked his head around the door. "There's a Miss Graham to see you." Without waiting for an answer, he ushered her in. Isa Graham, from the drapery department of Arrol's. She was clutching her handbag in front of her, like a shield.

THE DEVIL'S DRAPER

She took a look around at the three of us crammed into that tiny space: me, Johnnie and Beatrice. Her words came out tremulously, one on top of the other. "I've come to tell you what I saw, what I saw him do to some of those lassies. I saw him. I was there."

Acknowledgements and Thanks

There are so many people who I want to thank, starting with everyone who read, reviewed, commented on, blogged about and engaged with The Unpicking; and all those who came along to book launches and events, said kind words about the book and asked for more. I didn't intend to write a follow-up to The Unpicking, but that support meant the world to me, and spurred me on to write The Devil's Draper, so thank you all.

Sincere thanks and big love to everyone at Glasgow Women's Library. Going into work and seeing my book on the shelves of a place that's so special to me, does my heart good. And special thanks to Wendy Kirk – GWL's lovely librarian – and to the wonderful women who attend Story Café for their interest, support and encouragement.

I owe a huge debt of gratitude to Isabelle Kenyon and Fly on the Wall Press, a truly inspirational woman and fabulous publisher, for believing in both books and for making the whole process so utterly joyful.

I couldn't have written this without the support of my partner, Ewan, who is king of tea-making and titles. And I am forever grateful to my Mum and Dad, Joyce and Patrick Moore for giving me a love of stories.

The Devil's Draper is set a decade before the Moorov doctrine, which has helped victims of sexual assault in the decades since. I hope that the book might in some way stand as a testament to the real women throughout history who have suffered abuse, injustice and discrimination within patriarchal systems. Sadly, that abuse, injustice and discrimination still continues today.

About the Author

Donna Moore is the author of crime fiction and historical fiction. Her first novel, a Private Eye spoof called 'Go To Helena Handbasket' won the Lefty Award for most humorous crime fiction novel and her second novel 'Old Dogs', was shortlisted for both the Lefty and Last Laugh Awards. 'The Devil's Draper' is the follow up to her 2023 novel, 'The Unpicking'.
www.donnamooreauthor.com

Book Club Questions

1. How have societal views on women in policing evolved, and in what ways might they still mirror the challenges Mabel faces in the story?

2. What does Johnnie's aversion to traditional femininity reveal about her personality and character?

3. Why do you think the women's restroom becomes so significant as a gathering space in the story?

4. How do Mabel, Beatrice, and Johnnie develop as characters throughout the book? Do their journeys reflect a shared transformation?

5. How do Ruby and Evvy's deaths impact you as the reader?

6. How would you describe the dynamic and importance of Lorrimer and Mabel's relationship?

7. Is Meg's indifference towards the missing girls symbolic of something deeper? Why do you think she appears apathetic?

8. What are your thoughts on Isa coming forward about witnessing the attacks on the young girls at the end? Why do you think she ultimately chose to speak up?

About Fly on the Wall Press

A publisher with a conscience.
Political, Sustainable, Ethical.
Publishing politically-engaged, international fiction, poetry and cross-genre anthologies on pressing issues. Founded in 2018 by founding editor, Isabelle Kenyon.

Some other publications:

The Sound of the Earth Singing to Herself by Ricky Ray

We Saw It All Happen by Julian Bishop

Imperfect Beginnings by Viv Fogel

These Mothers of Gods by Rachel Bower

Sin Is Due To Open In A Room Above Kitty's by Morag Anderson

The Process of Poetry edited by Rosanna McGlone

Demos Rising edited by Isabelle Kenyon

The Wager and the Bear by John Ironmonger

Your Sons and Your Daughters are Beyond by Rosie Garland

The State of Us by Charlie Hill

The Unpicking by Donna Moore

The Sleepless by Liam Bell

Lying Perfectly Still by Laura Fish

Social Media:

@fly_press (X) @flyonthewallpress (Instagram)

@flyonthewallpress (Facebook, Bluesky and TikTok)

www.flyonthewallpress.co.uk